Places Untamed

Book 6 of the *Moving Mountains* series

ISBN: 978-1-9991282-9-6

One

TORONTO, ONTARIO

If there was one thing Kyleigh hated more than shopping for groceries, it was carrying multiple bags of food up seven flights of stairs. The elevator had been broken for years, and despite ongoing complaints from the tenants, nothing was ever done to fix it. Same went for the lights in the third-floor stairwell, which barely illuminated the wobbly handrail and chipped floor tiles. Last winter, an elderly lady had slipped on the icy sidewalk outside the building, sustaining a laceration on her face that required a trip to the hospital. After the landlord had found himself in hot water, he'd promised to finally tackle the other safety issues he'd been ignoring for months—only to disappear under the radar and leave his son, a self-proclaimed "handyman," in charge of the repairs.

At least once a week, Kyleigh debated packing everything up and leaving. But the apartment was close to her boyfriend, Derek's, job, and within walking distance of their favourite Vietnamese restaurant. Besides, if she really focused, she could see the bright side of virtually every single complaint. Not having an elevator meant never being trapped between floors if the power suddenly went out; climbing seven flights of stairs meant she could skip going to the gym. And while the bad lighting made it easier for burglars to sneak around, who would ever want to rob a building that was visibly falling apart? It wasn't an ideal situation, but in a city as expensive as Toronto, few people could afford to be picky.

Kyleigh hauled open the door marked 7, her posse of cloth bags bumping against her knees and shins as she stumbled into the hallway on the other side. A series of black doors with crooked, stick-on numbers lined the carpeted corridor on either side of her. For all the problems this building had, at least their neighbours were decent. There was Mrs. Stevenson, the old widow who always brought them a fruitcake at

Christmastime, and Marcia, the York University student studying to be an immigration lawyer. Then there was the O'Dell family in 708, whose kids were always fighting over whose turn it was to use the Xbox. One time, Derek had gone over to ask them to keep the noise down and ended up playing three rounds of NBA with the two youngest boys instead. But Derek had always been good with kids: it was one of the qualities Kyleigh had been drawn to when they'd first started dating. People who were good with kids were people she could trust, and trust was the foundation of every lasting relationship.

She slipped her key into the lock on door 712, adjusted her grip on the bags, and turned the knob to enter the two-bedroom unit. The kitchen lay ahead on her right: she despised the tacky white cupboards, but the appliances were still going strong—and best of all, she seldom had to use them, since Derek did most of the cooking. Adjacent to the kitchen was the living room, which featured a large window overlooking a mall parking lot, a flatscreen TV, and two couches they'd purchased on Facebook Marketplace for fifty dollars each.

"Derek?" Kyleigh called out. She ferried the grocery bags into the kitchen and set them on the floor. Reaching into the first bag, she pulled out a pack of ground beef and laid it on the counter, imagining all the things he could make with it—meatloaf, enchiladas, chili, shepherd's pie.

Kyleigh went on, "My boss gave us an early day, so I decided to do a little shopping." When there was still no reply, she put down the bag of apples and turned to look behind her. "Derek?"

He's probably on a call, she thought as she made her way down the hall. At the end of it was their bedroom, which doubled as Derek's office on the days he worked from home.

Kyleigh turned the knob. As the door swung open, Derek emerged from the sea of pillows covering the bed, his eyes wide as they settled on her.

"What are you doing?" Kyleigh asked.

There was a soft rustle from the opposite side of the mattress. Moments later, a woman with a blonde pixie cut sat up as well, clutching the grey covers to her chest.

2

"Kyle," Derek said, shattering the silence that had fallen over the room. "I wasn't expecting you to be home so early."

She shook her head, her ears ringing as she spun away from the room. He wasn't expecting her to be home so early? What the hell kind of excuse was *that*?

Derek scrambled forward, grabbing at the covers to throw them aside. "Kyle, wait," he said, struggling to pull on his jeans as he stumbled after her. "I can explain."

Kyleigh snatched her purse off the kitchen counter and beelined for the front door.

"What's there to explain? What possible justification could you have for sleeping with someone else?" She whipped around to face him. "Who *is* she?"

"Her name's Leanne. We work together." As Kyleigh continued to stare at him, Derek said, "I never meant for things to go this far. We got put on the same project and one thing led to another…"

"Oh, save it." Kyleigh twisted the knob to let herself out of the apartment. Derek trailed her into the hall, apparently forgetting he was only half-dressed.

"Kyle, come on." Derek wrapped his hand around her arm, pulling her to a stop.

"Don't touch me." Kyleigh yanked herself free. If she had a superpower, it would be the ability to summon a hive of angry bees to attack anybody on command. It was childish, of course, but so were the tears streaming down her face, leaving their scalding tracks on her skin.

"How could you do this?" she asked. As painful as it was to look at him, Kyleigh forced herself to meet Derek's gaze. He'd always looked young for his age, but that didn't mean he was innocent. "I trusted you. I gave five years of my life to you—and this is how you treat me?"

Derek's voice softened, his eyes pleading for a second chance. "I know I did a horrible, unforgiveable thing. I have no excuse for hurting you like this."

"Actually, you do. Your excuse is that you were counting on me never finding out." Kyleigh waited for him to counter this, to defend his actions with some rambling list of grievances about their relationship. Was this the first time he'd cheated, or simply the first time he'd been caught in the act?

She glimpsed the door to their apartment—only now it was just Derek's apartment, because there was no way in hell she was sleeping in that bed ever again.

"I hope you and Leanne will be very happy together," Kyleigh said. Turning away, she walked toward the stairwell door and threw it open. Everything in this building was slowly falling apart, from the crumbling walls to the faulty wiring. She'd never expected to find her relationship on that list too.

*

"This wasn't your fault, you know. No one forced Derek to be a lying, cheating piece of shit."

"I know. I'm not upset because I feel guilty. I'm upset because I didn't see the signs sooner. He even used the whole 'working late' excuse. Jesus Christ, could he not have been a bit more creative?"

Anvi topped up her wine glass. When Kyleigh had told her about Derek's transgression, Anvi had cleared out her guest bedroom and demanded Kyleigh move in immediately, before she had a chance to change her mind about the breakup.

"Listen, I hear what you're saying, but it still sounds like you're blaming yourself," Anvi said, taking a sip. "You did the right thing by walking away."

"From a five-year relationship. I mean, we were talking about getting married." Kyleigh clutched the orange-and-pink silk throw pillow a little tighter and shook her head emphatically. "I just feel like I should've known, you know? And I suspected nothing. *Nothing.*"

Kyleigh glanced down at her phone, lying on the couch cushion between them. It was Derek, again. He'd been calling non-stop for days, bombarding her with text messages, and generally acting obnoxious online, since they followed each other on practically every social media platform in existence. Anvi had a strict rule about not having access to technology during a breakup, but she had made an exception for today seeing as Kyleigh's parents were on their way home from Thailand. Like her, Samantha and Terry had fallen under Derek's spell, opening their hearts to him from day one. And now, Kyleigh would have to let them in on his dirty little secret.

They watched the phone ring. As soon as it stopped, Anvi said, "It'll get easier to ignore him. You're still detoxing."

"I'm not detoxing from anything." Which was a lie. On her first night in Anvi's apartment, Kyleigh had locked herself in the guest room and fallen asleep on top of the covers gasping for air between sobs. The following morning, she'd woken up to a pounding headache and the overwhelming urge to call Derek. Thankfully, Anvi had confiscated her devices the previous evening and stowed them in a safe in her office, promising they would be returned once the initial wave of grief had passed and Kyleigh was no longer at risk of having a "relationship relapse."

"Yes, you are," Anvi insisted. "The good news is, once this is all over, you won't make the mistake of dating men like Derek again."

"No, I won't make the mistake of dating men again, period. Too much bullshit for such a small farm."

Anvi stood up and crossed to the kitchen, decorated from floor to ceiling in shades of saffron and grapefruit. The counter was home to a cherry-red Kitchenaid stand mixer, an espresso machine, and numerous other appliances that Anvi seemed to have little use for, as someone who spent most of her time at the hospital where she worked. Then again, what business did Kyleigh have questioning her best friend's home life when hers had proven to be an elaborate charade?

"You know, they say women make love better than men do," she said as she walked back into the room carrying a plate of olives.

"And they probably don't cheat nearly as often."

Anvi offered her the kalamatas. "It gets easier," she said again. "Trust me. I'm a doctor, after all."

Just like that, Kyleigh felt the next wave of grief rise up and wash over her. Anvi took the pillow from her and placed it in her lap, then coaxed Kyleigh to rest her head on top of it as her body spasmed with grief. Derek's incoming call, like all the others, went straight to voicemail.

Two

It was funny sometimes, the things Kyleigh recalled from her childhood.

For instance, she remembered her fourth birthday party in almost perfect detail. The condo where she'd grown up didn't allow farm animals inside, so her parents had reserved a whole afternoon at the local petting zoo, complete with googly-eyed goats and a fleet of fat, docile ponies being led around a pen by women in cargo shorts, petting zoo t-shirts, and bucket hats. The cake had been mermaid-themed, with little white starfish sprinkles and metallic blue-green icing piped around the edges in the shape of ocean waves. When the presents were brought out, Kyleigh had ripped into the biggest one first and discovered a camping playset that included a fake firepit, mini binoculars, and a single-person tent, which she outgrew within two years.

After that, her memories became a little spotty. She remembered her first day of school, walking home with Terry and stopping for a Happy Meal at McDonald's. She remembered waking up the morning after losing her first tooth and finding nothing under her pillow, then crying because the tooth fairy had clearly lost their address, or maybe he didn't stop at condos because he didn't know how to use the elevator. But when she'd walked into the kitchen, she'd found a five-dollar bill on her plate along with a note signed by the tooth fairy that said *Thanks for the tooth! Don't forget to eat your vegetables tonight!*

As the years passed, the magic of childhood seemed to fade away, although her parents still tried to make certain occasions special. But when, at nine-years-old, Kyleigh had walked in on Samantha crying, she'd wondered if adults remembered happy moments differently. If she'd done something to cause her mom so much pain.

It took three days for Kyleigh to get her phone and laptop back, after arguing that the latter was necessary to keep her job. Before leaving for work this morning, Anvi had proposed having lunch together at the hospital cafeteria, which Kyleigh had declined. The truth was, as much as she was grateful for Anvi's support, she needed to be alone in order to figure out her next steps. Even when the silence of the empty apartment threatened to drive her insane, there was some comfort to be found in her solitude too, with no one around to witness her unchoreographed dance moves or the fictitious conversations she had—out loud—with her ex-boyfriend.

"I don't understand why you won't just come and live with us," Samantha said the day after Kyleigh had told her parents about the breakup through WhatsApp.

"Because, mom, you and dad were in Thailand when all of this happened. Besides, Anvi's being very generous about letting me stay here and I don't want to be rude." Kyleigh went on slicing the shallots as Samantha stared at her through the phone screen. She didn't know what she was making, exactly, only that she was bored and lonely in this minute and needed a distraction.

Suddenly, Samantha asked, "Do you want us to talk to Derek's parents?"

"*Please* do not call Derek's parents. Derek and I are adults, and we're going to handle this like adults. No parental mediation required."

"I know, I just hate seeing you like this. And your dad and I are so close to Jenny and Paul—"

"Mom. Please, do not interfere. I beg of you."

Samantha sighed. "All right."

"Say you won't call them."

"I won't call them."

"Thank you."

Kyleigh stopped cutting the shallot and set down the knife. She'd never been much of a chef, but she'd loved watching Derek whip up a lemon tart or a hearty bowl of goulash on chilly winter nights. Food was an expression of his love for people, and his ability to combine the right ingredients in the right quantities had seemed like magic to her, having come from a household where TV dinners and takeout were common.

"Honey, you're crying into your onions," Samantha said with palpable concern.

"They're *shallots*," Kyleigh corrected her, picking up the knife again. "And I'm fine."

"I wish I could come and give you a big hug. It's going to be okay. Once you and Derek talk this out—"

"There's nothing to talk about. He cheated on me, mom. How can I possibly trust him after that?"

Terry edged into view. He'd caught a cold while abroad and his nose was still red and stuffy. Seeing him, Kyleigh was reminded of another memory: sitting at the front of a two-person sled with her dad's legs bracketed around her, his one hand holding her and the other clinging to the rope as they careened down a hill that seemed to go on forever. He'd come down with the flu two days before, but she'd begged him to take her sledding at the local park, saying that if they didn't hurry all the snow would melt and they'd miss their chance. So, Terry had dragged himself out of bed, wrapped them both in layers of warm clothing, and braved the hordes of beet-faced, screaming kids, all so she could gloat about how her sled, while old and clunky, was the fastest sled in the city. It was embarrassing, the things she believed back then. Just like how she believed Derek truly loved her and wasn't looking for anyone else.

"Hi, dad," Kyleigh said. Before he could ask, she added, "I'm fine. My shallots are fine. Everything is fine."

"Well, I think that's up for debate, but please know that if you need anything, we're only a phone call away."

"Thanks."

"Of course. How's Anvi?"

"She's all right. Working too much, as always."

"Tell her we miss her, and that we should all grab dinner sometime when she's free."

9

Kyleigh smiled. "I will."

With that, Terry disappeared from view, eager to sleep off the jetlag and the dregs of whatever virus had followed them home. Samantha looked wearier than usual too, with more wrinkles around her eyes than Kyleigh could recall from recent memory. Of course, she knew her parents were getting older: they were in their sixties now, visibly worn down from the rigors of parenting but still spry enough to travel the globe and fret about her imploding love life. It was an odd feeling to suddenly be in their position, worrying about their health and safety the way they'd worried about her for the past twenty-five years.

Samantha said, "I'm glad you have Anvi. It's important to have friends in difficult times."

"I know." Kyleigh cleared her throat. "Anyway, I should probably go back to making dinner. I'll call you again in a few days."

"I love you, honey."

"I love you, too."

As Samantha ended the call, Kyleigh felt the tension drain out of her body. This time, when the grief rose up, it wasn't strictly because of Derek, and it wasn't purely sadness either. She wrapped her hand around the knife's handle and continued chopping the shallots into tiny pieces, imagining these were the remnants of her old life getting smaller and smaller. When she eventually scraped the slush into the pan of hot oil, she felt an odd sense of satisfaction in watching the pieces go from brown to black, burnt beyond all recognition.

She was still swirling the contents around the pan when Anvi walked through the door and wrinkled her nose. "What's that smell?"

"I'm cooking," Kyleigh announced, trying to sound optimistic. "Want some?"

Anvi set down her work bag and cautiously approached the stove to find the bottom of the pan covered in a layer of char.

"What were you trying to make? Besides my fire alarm go off," Anvi added wryly.

Kyleigh bit her lip and moved the blackened pan to the back burner. "Goulash?"

"Goulash doesn't call for nine shallots."

"Then I guess I'm the only person in the city of Toronto who doesn't know how to make goulash."

Anvi snorted and hooked her arm through Kyleigh's to lead her out of the kitchen.

"We're going out for dinner," she said, cracking open the door to her balcony to air out the apartment. "How do you feel about pancakes?"

Three

Josh Hammond's life seemed like a bad joke. At twenty-eight, he was still sleeping in the same room he'd grown up in, contorting his adult body to fit the lumpy old twin bed he'd wrecked by jumping into it too many times when he was a kid. Shoved into the corner of the room were his old PlayStation console and collection of video games, organized alphabetically on the shelf beneath the octagon window. In high school, most of his friends had been on one sports team or another: their weekends consisted of basketball practice or hockey tryouts, and when it became clear that Josh didn't have a single athletic bone in his body, they'd stopped inviting him to hang out after class.

His social life hadn't improved much after graduation. At eighteen, he'd moved out of his parents' house to study game development at Virginia Tech, which translated into spending even more time alone in his dorm room. In the video game world, life made a lot more sense: the winners weren't determined by arbitrary metrics like height or fashion choices, but by how well they completed certain challenges. He could be anyone or anything he desired, restart a difficult level, and bounce back from failure as if it were a trampoline. In the video game world, it didn't matter that his dad was always on the road, shooting training videos or hosting clinics for wannabe cowboys. Real life had a way of disappearing the moment Josh picked up his controller—an aptly-named tool for something that gave him the illusion of personal agency.

Over the next decade, he'd come and gone from Broken Bar Ranch so frequently that his mother set a place for him at the table every night, and at least once a month she'd set out an extra plate for the girlfriend he never brought home. His dad may have been a showman, but his mom clearly had a few acting skills of her own, judging by how happy she pretended to be each time Josh came strolling through the front door with duffle bag in hand.

But today, as he stuffed his clothes into the bag, Josh knew he wouldn't be coming back. He'd spent years waiting for some nudge from the universe to get out on his own and finally make something of his life, and the universe had responded. Only it wasn't a nudge—it was a full-on beatdown. If he didn't get out now, he'd never get another chance.

A knock at the door brought him out of his thoughts. When Josh turned around, he saw his mother, Soraya, standing on the threshold. According to his dad, she'd always been a natural beauty, her faintly olive complexion sprinkled with dark golden freckles. A sheet of gleaming black hair grazed the dip of her lower back, although she often kept it tied up in a bun when working around the barn or house. Tonight, she wore a baby blue satin blouse and a pleated white skirt. It was the kind of outfit she normally saved for hosting company, even though the only other people they saw these days were the ranch hands.

"Do you want me to wash your bedsheets?" she asked.

Josh smiled. His dad had taught him how to read between the lines, to look for clues that gave away a person's (or a horse's) true feelings. When his mother asked about the sheets, what she really meant was: *will you be coming back?*

"Okay," he replied, which was much easier than admitting he had no idea what the future held, or that his mother still laundered his bedsheets for him.

Part of him felt guilty for leaving her. Their house sat on nearly a thousand acres of rolling hills and pristine rivers, at the end of a driveway that snaked through a network of corrals and outdoor sand rings. His father's employees were housed in a series of outbuildings at the edge of an evergreen forest: each night, the smoke from their firepit would sweeten the air, casting its embers high above the twinkling glow of the city in the distance. So, his mother wasn't really alone, despite how empty the house felt most of the time.

Soraya sighed, a heavy smile etched into her face as she turned away from his room. "Dinner's on the table."

Their table could seat six people comfortably, although they'd managed to squeeze in twice that many guests one year when Josh was a baby and his mother's family had flown in from Argentina to spend Christmas at the ranch. These days, it was usually just the two of them, sitting across from each other under a row of pendant lights.

Josh picked at the salad on his plate and tried to ignore the empty chair at the head of the table. Soraya, sitting directly across from him, appeared to be doing the same.

He reached for his wine glass and took a sip. "I may have an opportunity to work in Colorado," he said as he set it down again.

His mother raised her gaze, expectant. "Oh?"

"It's not confirmed yet, but I was thinking I'd drive down there and rent an Airbnb for a few weeks to clear my head." Josh paused, his knife and fork poised over his plate. "I worry about you."

"Me?"

"I don't want you to be lonely when I'm gone."

"I'm not going to be lonely. And I don't want you to put your life on hold to take care of me." Soraya speared a slice of carrot with her fork. She chewed, swallowed, and asked, "What kind of work would you be doing?"

"Manual labour," Josh replied with a shrug. "It's not what I want to do, but it's something."

"All work has value. That's what your dad used to say."

"I know."

"He spent a lot of time in Colorado when you were young."

"I know," Josh said again. "That's why I'm going there."

They fell back into silence. Over the clinking of silverware, Josh could hear the men outside wrapping up their workday. The ranch hands were like family to him. In fact, it had been Ernesto, the foreman, who'd driven Josh to the hospital on the day of his accident. Mickey had recently purchased a green-broke mare at auction and planned to turn her into a bona fide ranch horse. He'd gone up to the house for a few minutes when Josh, then just three years old, had climbed daringly onto the animal's back. Startled, the mare had bolted across the sand ring, leaving Josh clinging to her mane like a burr for what felt like an eternity. When he'd fallen, he'd landed on his head, causing Ernesto to leap over the fence and into the path of the ill-tempered mare. Moments later, Mickey had come running out of the house, grabbed Josh out of Ernesto's arms, and unleashed the kind of scream that could only come from thinking his son was dead.

The PlayStation had shown up a few days after Josh was released from hospital. He'd never gotten back on a horse, which suited him just fine: these days, he had all the horsepower he needed in the garage, draped in a sheet and branded with the Ducati logo. Even now, as he was walking across the yard in the half-light of early evening, he wasn't sure whether he'd bought the bike because he thought it gave him an edge, or because he wanted to prove he wasn't a total failure, especially to members of the opposite sex.

It didn't matter, really. By this time next week, he'd be in another state entirely, scraping the bloodied pulp of his ego off the floor of rock bottom.

Josh approached the paddock and rested his elbows on the top board. His father's horses grazed peacefully beneath the trees, their hides a patchwork of colours muted by the disappearance of the sun. The sweet, cool scent of grass was heavy in the air, along with a buzzing cluster of hover flies singing their nightly soiree. Reaching into his pocket, Josh pulled out his phone, scrolled through his contacts, and clicked on a familiar number.

When the ringing ceased, he said, "It's Josh Hammond. I was calling to ask if your offer stands."

Four

Long before they became parents, Samantha and Terry had travelled the globe. Their goal, ultimately, was to visit all seven continents before they retired. They'd managed to cross five of them—North America, South America, Asia, Europe, and Australia—off their bucket list by the time Samantha received a Facebook message from a girl in British Columbia, saying she was pregnant and looking for someone to adopt her unborn baby. On that day, the entire focus of Samantha and Terry's life had shifted. They'd always wanted a family of their own, but after years of trying to conceive, that dream had faded away like smoke, leaving behind the bitter aftertaste of disappointment. At night, Samantha had cried for the baby that would never inhabit her womb. Her friends, coworkers, and siblings all had children by then, and she could tell they pitied her lack of progeny.

"It's so easy for everyone else," she'd complained to Terry one evening. "I swear, the women around me reproduce like weeds." Samantha hadn't recognized her own voice in that moment, or the anger flowing through it like venom. These were women she loved and admired—women like her sister, Beth, who had given birth to twin boys only three years earlier, at the age of thirty-seven. "I can't take this anymore."

Terry had been sitting on one of the bar stools in their kitchen. As the silence returned, he'd stood up and crossed the room to place his hands on her shoulders. "Let's get away for a while. We'll go wherever you want."

They'd decided on Rome, a city packed with tourists and historical landmarks. As they'd wandered along the cobblestone streets and tossed pennies into the Trevi Fountain, Samantha had known exactly what to wish for. A week later, Hannah had reached out, proving that sometimes, wishes actually came true.

Even though they'd desperately wanted a child, it hadn't made raising their daughter any easier. Not long after they'd brought Kyleigh home, those same friends and coworkers had warned them about the rocky years to come. How their savings would dwindle, and their wrinkles would multiply. How the rollercoaster of emotions would turn their daily routine into a theme park of horrors. How they'd regret their decision to adopt once Kyleigh became old enough to inquire about her origins.

"You're going to wish you had a time machine," a couple of Terry's friends had joked, adding that they knew a good marriage counsellor if the Varchuks ever needed one. Later on, Samantha and Terry had laughed: after all, these were the same people who'd felt sorry for them for not being able to have a baby. Now, they felt sorry for them because they did.

"If everyone knew how difficult it was," Beth had confided one afternoon, "no one would have kids." And Samantha thought her sister ought to know, given that her burden was double.

It *was* difficult, and the secret Samantha could never bring herself to confess, even to Terry, was that she did have regrets. She missed travelling and running marathons and being able to sleep until eleven the morning after girls' night out. She missed the rush of booking plane tickets and the tranquility of spending a rainy Sunday morning curled up on the couch, watching the streets of downtown Toronto transform into mirror balls of scattered light. She missed her daughter's innocence during those trying middle-school years, and everything up to the moment Kyleigh had learned her DNA wasn't rooted in the Varchuk family tree.

There was a lot to miss when a person became a parent. But in this moment, as Kyleigh nursed a broken heart over a bowl of chicken noodle soup, all Samantha could think was, *If I had a time machine, I'd do it all over again.*

"Derek's been trying to call me," Kyleigh said, dipping her spoon into the soup and lifting it out so that the broth trickled back into the bowl. "Do you think I should call him back?"

"What do you think he'll say?" Samantha asked.

Kyleigh shrugged. "That he's sorry. That he was wrong." She pushed the bowl away and folded her arms on the counter. "Maybe Anvi's right: I just need to shut the door on this and not think about it anymore."

She furrowed her brows. It was one thing to stop doing something; it was another to stop thinking about it. From across the kitchen, Samantha could see the tears welling in Kyleigh's eyes, catching the light at odd angles. She filled the kettle with water and placed it on one of the burners, then went to the cupboard and took down a pair of mugs.

As she dropped a teabag into each cup, Samantha said, "Wouldn't it be nice if love worked like that? If the pain disappeared one day and never came back?"

Kyleigh thought about this for a moment. "I'm kind of glad it doesn't. Some of the best songs wouldn't exist if it weren't for people wallowing in their misery."

Oh, Kyle. You can always see the bright side of anything, Samantha thought.

"How was Thailand?" Kyleigh asked.

"It was beautiful. You would have loved the old temples."

"And the food?"

"To die for. A little spicy."

Kyleigh picked up her spoon again. Across all cultures, one thing seemed universal: food had the power to heal, especially when prepared by a mother's loving hands. But fixing a broken heart required a stronger salve, and Kyleigh knew she wouldn't find it in this kitchen.

As Terry walked in, he tossed a handful of mail onto the counter and began weeding out the junk, creating a separate pile off to his right filled with everything from fast food coupons to furniture store catalogues.

"Now, who keeps sending us these?" Terry wondered, holding up a flyer for lawn care services. "Do they not realize we live in a condominium?"

"I don't know, dad. That hanging basket you got last week is looking pretty gnarly." Kyleigh hooked a thumb at the balcony: the closest they came to having a backyard. Her gaze rested on Samantha. "Wouldn't it be nice if junk mail worked that way?" she said in reference to their earlier conversation.

Samantha chuckled and poured water over the teabags, releasing their flavour in swirls of raspberry pink.

"I was just telling Kyle about our trip," she explained as Terry helped himself to some soup.

"Did you tell her about the monkeys?"

"I was getting to it."

"Let me guess: the temples were full of monkeys who were trying to steal the tourists' food," Kyleigh said.

"Among other things." Terry slurped a mouthful of soup. "You'd love it there."

"You know, it's funny you should mention travel. Because I've been thinking that I could use a change of scenery."

"Oh! How about Edinburgh? You've always wanted to go there," Samantha said, sliding a cup of tea across the island toward her daughter. "I could help you plan out your itinerary. Scotland is gorgeous, with all those old castles and green mountains…"

"It's okay. I'm sure there will be plenty of mountains in Colorado."

Samantha's gaze locked onto her. "Why do you want to go there?"

"Look, I love you guys, and I always will. But is it really so wrong that I want to know where I come from?"

"But you're not from Colorado—you're from BC," Terry put in.

"I know. I have my birth certificate, remember?" Kyleigh took a deep breath before continuing. "I'm not doing this to hurt you. You think I don't appreciate everything you guys have done for me? All the time, money, and sacrifice it took to make sure I survived this long? You know this isn't personal," she added with a glance at Samantha, "but I'd be lying if I said I wasn't a little bit curious to know the people who brought me into this world. If I have my father's eyes or my mother's sense of humour."

"I can confirm you have both," Samantha frosted. "And I also know you've been corresponding with Hannah since last year. We keep in touch occasionally, and she mentioned that you had reached out to her on Facebook."

"Yes, and she suggested we continue the conversation on WhatsApp." Kyleigh shook her head. "It's not like I'd be moving in with them. I'd just be going for a couple of weeks, seeing where they live, and coming home. I don't understand why this is such an issue."

And she never would, Samantha thought. If Kyleigh was lucky, she'd never know how it felt to be asked when she was having children by people who didn't know she couldn't; how it felt to look at the baby she'd fallen in love with and not see herself reflected in those big, beautiful eyes. She would never experience the sting of hearing that now twenty-five-year-old baby tell her that what she really wanted was to get acquainted with the people who'd given her up, when it would have been so much easier to shut the door on the past and not think about it anymore.

Samantha turned toward the stove, ladled some soup into a cup, and carried it to the bedroom. As the click of the latch echoed down the hall, Kyleigh turned back to Terry. "Are you sure you want to do this?" he asked.

"I was, but now…" Her focus shifted to the hallway in a combination of regret and irritation.

"Sometimes we can build people up in our minds to be more than they really are," he cautioned her. "Do Hannah and Ray know you're planning to visit them?"

"Yes."

"Good. In that case, I hope you enjoy your trip. That it… gives you closure."

Kyleigh slid off the stool, placed her bowl in the sink, and leaned over to give Terry a quick peck on the cheek. "Everything's going to be fine, okay? I'll text you guys as often as I can. If Derek calls, tell him I'm away on a business trip."

"Safe travels," Terry told her as Kyleigh swung her faux leather purse over her shoulder. "And remember: you can come home anytime you want. Our door's always open."

She smiled. It was getting late; Anvi would be wondering where she was. From the kitchen to the front door, Kyleigh thought about how she'd built Derek up in her mind, all too willing to overlook certain behaviours so she wouldn't have to face being alone. How a tiny part of her missed him, despite knowing the unforgiveable thing he'd done.

When Terry pushed open the bedroom door, he found Samantha sitting on the bed, flipping through the glossy pages of a photo book. Of the hundreds of pictures they'd posted to Facebook over the course of Kyleigh's childhood and adolescence, countless more had been hidden away from the public eye—not because they weren't worthy of being shared, but because they were too precious to risk being lost to a digital glitch. Some things in life deserved to be kept close to home, where no harm would come to them.

As he crossed the room to sit next to her, Terry said, "Kyle went back to Anvi's place."

"Did you talk her out of going on her trip?"

"No."

"You should have." On the page in front of her was a picture of Kyleigh at a friend's birthday party, her hair wet and matted from the water balloon fight she swore she'd won.

"She wants to know them, Sam. Kyle's not a little girl anymore."

"I know." Samantha turned the page. In this picture, Kyleigh was squatting down on the balcony, waving a dog treat in her fingers and teaching their old French bulldog how to rollover. For the remainder of Tank's short, canine life, he only ever showed his belly to her.

"And if it weren't for Hannah and Ray, Kyle wouldn't exist," Terry went on. "She's—"

"I know, Terry. She's not really ours. Even though we raised her, and gave her everything she could possibly need or want, it doesn't change the fact that she's someone else's daughter."

"If that's how you want to look at it."

Samantha raised her gaze to his. "How do *you* look at it?"

"Most kids only have one set of parents, if they're lucky. But Kyleigh has two, and they both want to be a part of her life. We're not competing with Hannah and Ray for Kyleigh's love—we're showing her that she has a home no matter what side of the border she's on."

He took the album from her and flipped through the pages. When they'd decided to adopt, they only told a handful of their closest friends and family members at first, knowing that adoption, while peddled as a viable option for couples who couldn't have children of their own, was often fraught with misconceptions. Terry's mother had criticized their decision to pursue an open adoption, saying it would be too confusing for Kyleigh to have contact with her birth parents. In the end, as both couples had become absorbed into their busy lives, the lines of communication had all but disappeared. But before they could close completely, Terry had snapped one final photo of Hannah and Ray during their last visit to Toronto: she in a green and white floral sundress, he in jeans and a pale blue button-down shirt, while Kyleigh showed off her new ballet slippers on the living room floor. To Kyleigh, this had been like any other family reunion: a chance to be showered with gifts and bask in the attention. What was so confusing about that?

"I forgot you took that picture," Samantha said. "They look so young, don't they? So… innocent."

"Exactly. They're not bad people, and I know they'd never do anything to hurt Kyleigh."

She nodded, her face pinched.

"We're not going to lose her," he promised, putting his arm around her shoulders. "When Kyle's ready, she'll come home to us like she always does."

*

Kyleigh wasn't totally convinced of the plan, but in light of everything it seemed to be the only one that made any sense.

Back at Anvi's apartment, she laid her suitcase out on the bed and began folding the contents of her wardrobe into its depths, creating a border around the inner edge using her socks. She thought about going back to Derek's apartment to fetch the remainder of her belongings, but ultimately decided to leave them where they were. She imagined him going room by room, discarding her hair products and collector's mugs as if she'd never existed at all. One day, maybe months from now when he thought he'd moved on, he'd uncover a small piece of her someplace unexpected and the pain of their breakup would come over him like a tornado, swift and destructive. Or so Kyleigh hoped.

"If you need a place to stay when you come back," Anvi had said earlier, "my door is always open."

"You say that now, but what if you get a roommate? Or a boyfriend?" Kyleigh had asked.

Anvi had laughed. "When do I ever have time to date?"

"I'm just saying, anything's possible."

"I'll make room. That's what friends do."

And family? Kyleigh wasn't exactly sure of the extent of their generosity, but she figured she had little to lose by reaching out. Maybe the people she knew the least would be able to help her the most.

Her eyes fell on her phone, lying face-down on the bed. She picked it up, her heart beating in the pit of her stomach from a combination of fear and excitement. Oversharing wasn't in her DNA, so she'd only told her biological mother as much as she needed to know, which was that she'd recently gotten out of a long-term relationship and wanted to use some of her vacation time to travel.

Hannah replied: *Of course, we'd love to have you.*

Kyleigh swallowed. "Love" and "have" weren't words she expected the woman who'd given her up to use, but she'd take anything she could get, if it got her out of Toronto.

Hannah: *When were you thinking of visiting?*

Kyleigh typed: *As soon as possible.*

Hannah: *I'll need a few days to get the house ready and shop for groceries. Ray's been busy putting in a new fence, so I need to help with that too. How does next week sound?*

Kyleigh: *Next week sounds great.* It also felt like an incredibly long time to wait, given the circumstances. Maybe she'd take it as an opportunity to learn how to make goulash—if she didn't rot away in bed first, that was.

Hannah: *We'll be in touch.*

Kyleigh tossed the phone back onto the bed, where it disappeared somewhere between the pillow and the comforter. Apprehension covered her in a cold wave. She barely knew these people. In fact, the last time she'd actually seen them was when she was six years old, and the only thing she really remembered about that day was the food. Hannah and Ray had kept in touch with her sporadically over the years, but not consistently enough for Kyleigh to carve out a permanent spot in her memories for their faces, much less feel a sense of connection. And yet, through the power of WhatsApp, a bridge between Toronto and Colorado was forming. She'd taken the first step tonight; next week, she'd reach the other side. After that, she didn't have a clue what came next.

Five

ASPEN, COLORADO

Even though it was barely noon, Ray felt as if he'd been working all day. His shoulders and lower back were sore, and the heat was making him drowsy. Setting down the fencing pliers, Ray pulled off his work gloves, picked up the bottle at his feet, and took several swallows of the warm water it contained. He could see his truck down in the valley, a three- or four-minute walk from where he currently stood on the crest of a hill looking out over the north pasture. At nearly forty acres, it was the largest of their enclosures and served as home base for their cattle during the winter and spring months. This meant that in the summer, when local cowboys came together to move their herds to public grazing land, the north pasture sat empty, giving Ray an opportunity to repair the fence—a task he'd been dreading for months.

"You all right?" Bernard called up to him.

Ray glanced down the hill and nodded. "And you?"

"Well enough. I'm almost out of water though."

"Here." Ray screwed the cap back on the bottle and tossed it in Bernard's direction. "I may need another break soon. For my leg."

Bernard drank until the bottle was empty. As he put the lid back on, he watched Ray take a few steps away from the fence and sit down at the base of a small tree. The shadows of the leaves flickered on his face as he removed his hat and set it upside down in the dry grass beside him, then leaned forward and cradled his knees in his arms.

"Maybe I'm getting too old for this," Ray said idly, squinting at the mountains in the distance. There was a time he thought he could move them, but those days were becoming harder to remember. His gaze drifted toward Bernard, whose snow-white hair was peeking out from under the edge of his cowboy hat as he hunched over a rotted fence post. "What was your retirement plan?" Ray asked.

"Didn't have one," Bernard admitted. "I figured I'd work until I couldn't work anymore, and if I was lucky maybe I'd die in my sleep one day. But a cowboy never stops being a cowboy, no matter how old he gets." He glimpsed Ray over his shoulder. "Jaxon will be able to help you, once school gets out for the summer."

"That's the plan."

"I thought you said you were going to hire someone to help you around the ranch."

"I did. He should be here in a few days."

Bernard grasped the post between his hands and gave it a sharp yank. The soil around its base was loose; all the wood needed was a good, firm kick, and the crumbling fencepost toppled to the ground. Just because the timber was old didn't mean it was useless: they'd salvage what they could for firewood later, a job Ray thought Jaxon was more than capable of doing. The problem was, although Jaxon *could* handle the work, he wasn't inclined to do it. At his age, he was far more interested in talking to girls and hanging out with his friends, but the fact remained that Ray wasn't getting any younger.

If only Jaxon was the only child he had to worry about, Ray thought as he pressed his hat back on his head and rose stiffly. He approached the fence again and picked up the pliers to cut away the dangling wire, studded with dozens of rusty barbs.

"It's the phones, you know," Bernard said suddenly. "Kids don't want to be outside anymore. They don't appreciate the value of hard, manual labour. And your boy's not going to develop a work ethic if you let him keep his phone."

"We got him the phone for emergencies," Ray explained as the first wire fell to the ground. "I had a phone at his age. It never stopped me from doing my chores."

"He won't learn his lesson if you keep making excuses for him."

26

"And what lesson would that be, dad? That you should honour your responsibilities instead of hiding from them?" Ray rested his gaze on Bernard. If his face were a map, then each wrinkle was a road to places Ray had never heard of: small towns where his father, propelled by grief over the death of his wife, had drifted and settled like dust.

After a moment, Bernard turned back to his section of the fence. He kept his head down so that his hat cast a shadow over his face, and used the toe of his boot to unearth the base of the fencepost. He said nothing further.

When the last wire had been removed, Ray wriggled the wood back and forth, loosening its hold on the dirt. Some fenceposts came out easily, while others put up more of a fight, determined to remain where they were. Children were like that too: if you planted them just right, their roots would keep them grounded for life.

*

Running for your life means only carrying the bare essentials.

Kyleigh couldn't recall where she'd heard these words—a documentary, maybe? She passed through a set of doors into an area designated for arriving passengers. Jetting off to a small American town in hopes of getting to know her biological parents was hardly a matter of life or death, but it couldn't be denied that she was travelling light. In fact, she was so underprepared for the occasion that she didn't even have an up-to-date picture of her birth father saved in her phone. But if he was really a cowboy, then surely there'd be an easy way to identify him… assuming he lived up to the usual stereotypes.

She scanned the crowd. Lots of cargo shorts, t-shirts, and leggings. A few Patagonia jackets. Hiking boots. What did cowboys wear when they weren't on horseback? She had no idea, but she was reasonably confident it involved jeans and maybe a belt buckle. Kyleigh wondered, just for a second, if she'd be able to pick Ray out based solely on eye colour—like catching a glimpse of herself in the mirror as she pushed a shopping cart through the shoe section at her local Walmart.

From across the lounge, she spotted a man fording the trickle of people headed toward the exit. Kyleigh remained where she was, taking in the old jeans, dusty boots, and green plaid shirt with buttons that went all the way up to his throat. His hands were tucked in his pockets, and his hair, once the pale brown of a fawn's hide, was streaked with grey. When they were ten feet apart, he stopped and looked her over slowly, as if his mind were calculating the same probabilities.

Ray smiled. "You look just like your picture."

"You have a picture of me?" As Ray pulled out his phone and turned the screen toward her, Kyleigh felt her cheeks warm. "Facebook. I should've guessed."

"Haven't you heard? It's where all the old people like to hang out."

"I'm surprised it's still around. Normally anything millennials touch, dies."

Ray laughed, his eyes softening. "You have your mother's sense of humour," he told her, glancing down at the blue shell of her carry-on. "And her taste in suitcases, from the looks of it."

Kyleigh nodded. She'd never understood the people who overpacked, stumbling through the airport with multiple bags in case they got the urge to wear their entire wardrobe while on vacation.

"Well," Ray said, "shall we go home?"

Kyleigh wrapped her hand around the carry-on's handle and gestured to the doors. "Lead the way."

She wasn't sure how she'd expected Colorado to look. For a state known for its mountains, there were plenty of flatter areas where the land seemed almost barren. As they drove, Ray explained the various regions as best he could, beginning with the plains to the east and south and ending with the desert on the west, where the iron-rich groundwater had painted the rocks sunset red. The ranch was located somewhere in the middle, tucked away amid thick pine forests in the beating heart of ski country. "We have plenty of open spaces too, but they're all surrounded by mountains of some sort," he said. "The weather's more unpredictable up here, especially around this time of year."

"I only brought one sweater," Kyleigh admitted.

"That's okay. Hannah probably has something you can wear if it gets cold enough."

She nodded, glimpsing the driver's seat. "Do you like it out here?"

A wrinkle formed at the corner of his mouth as he smiled. "Most of the time."

"I'm not much of a country girl. I mean, we used to visit my grandparents' cottage in the summer, but after two days I'd be begging to go home. Too many bugs, not enough AC." Kyleigh glanced at the passenger side window, her reflection superimposed on an endless panorama of foliage. A person could get lost out here without even trying.

"I can't promise there won't be bugs," Ray said. "And our house doesn't have AC, so we leave the windows open at night to cool it down."

"Right, so all the bugs will fly in."

Again, Ray laughed. Was she really that funny, or was he just nervous?

"We're almost there," he said a couple minutes later. The mountains closed in on them from all sides, an evergreen invasion.

Kyleigh tried to ignore the prickle of apprehension in her stomach. When at last they turned off the main road and down a gravel driveway, she picked her backpack up off the floor and balanced it on her knees. The act reminded her of riding the bus downtown, trying to protect her little island of space in the sea of apathetic commuters. She'd never stayed anywhere as remote as the ranch: even family vacations she'd taken as a kid involved some form of public transit, something she hadn't seen since Ray picked her up from the airport.

He parked the truck outside the house, a modest, two-storey dwelling with a roof badly in need of re-shingling and a wooden porch spread like wings on both sides of the front door. The lights were on in the kitchen, and through the window Hannah could be seen looking down at something in the sink. A hot ball of nerves climbed up Kyleigh's throat as she took in the scene. This was home for the next few weeks, and it couldn't have been more different than the fast-paced life she knew back in Toronto.

Kyleigh was so engrossed in her thoughts she hardly noticed Ray staring at her. He looked away as soon as she turned her head, letting his gaze rest on the front door instead.

"That driveway's really something," she ventured. "I'm guessing you guys aren't big on company?"

"Actually, we entertain all the time. If you hang around here long enough, you're bound to be invited to something." Ray reached for the driver's door and pushed it open. "I'll grab your bags if you want to head inside."

"Okay."

As Kyleigh stepped out of the truck, Hannah dried her hands on a towel and temporarily disappeared from view, only to reappear a moment later on the porch wearing a light grey cardigan, blue jeans, and a pale pink smile.

"Welcome," she said, taking Kyleigh into a Palmolive-scented hug. "How was your trip?"

"I survived it." Kyleigh's gaze swept over the front yard again, its corrals standing tall and dark against the waning glow of the sun. The ripe smell of livestock crept into her nose and settled there. "So, this is the real deal, huh? An actual ranch, with actual horses and cows."

Hannah nodded. "Just like I said."

"It's a slower pace of life, but you get used to it," Ray said as he carried her suitcase up the steps. "In fact, by the end of your trip, you might not want to leave."

"Come inside," Hannah urged. She laid a hand gently on Kyleigh's arm, like she was trying to confirm this wasn't a dream—that the daughter she thought she'd never see again had finally found her way home.

"Jax, could you come down here for a minute?" Ray called out as he closed the door behind them.

As footsteps creaked across the ceiling, Kyleigh directed her attention to the far side of the room. Hannah had mentioned they had a son, but it hadn't occurred to Kyleigh until this very moment that the teenage boy loping down the stairs was her biological brother. Jaxon was tall, like Ray, with a sturdy build that filled out the black t-shirt and faded jeans he wore. He had his mother's defined cheekbones and thick bronze hair that fell over his forehead in waves, forcing him to shake his head slightly in order to see Kyleigh clearly.

"Jaxon, this is Kyleigh," Ray said, setting her suitcase down beside the bench. "She's going to be staying with us for a while."

Jaxon pocketed his hands and smiled warily. "Hey."

"Hey. You can call me Kyle. Everyone does." Kyleigh glanced at his shirt, hoping they listened to the same music, or at least supported the same causes. Anything to bridge the absurd, nine-year age gap that separated them. "Never Kill Dogs?" she guessed, gesturing to the acronym 'NKD' that was spelled out in yellow across the front. The vertical stem on the *K* was shaped like a warhead pointing up at Jaxon's throat.

Jaxon followed her gaze, confused. Then he laughed and said, "Oh, you mean 'Nuked'. It's a channel I watch on YouTube."

Kyleigh nodded, feigning understanding. "Of course. Who doesn't love *Nuked*?" Whatever the hell that was.

Hannah chimed in, "Dinner's not quite ready yet, so why don't we show you where your room is?"

"Sure." Kyleigh started to reach for her suitcase, but Ray beat her to it and led the way upstairs.

"Could you set the table, please?" he asked Jaxon. His son nodded and disappeared into the kitchen, where the clatter of plates quickly drowned out the awkward silence that followed their family reunion.

Kyleigh trailed Ray upstairs, with Hannah taking up the rear. There must have been some unspoken rule that all ranches had to be decorated the same way, with leather furniture and cowhide rugs and thick wooden banisters. Lining the hallway on either side of the stairs were numerous old photographs in cloudy metal frames, including an image of a woman clutching the halter of a ruddy brown horse.

"That's Emma, your biological grandmother," Hannah explained. "I never met her, but Ray keeps her memory alive with stories and pictures. So does his father, Bernard, who lives on the property not far from here."

They continued up the stairs and down the hall, drawn by the sounds in the guest bedroom. Ray had deposited Kyleigh's luggage at the foot of the bed and was fighting with the latch on the window to let fresh air flow into the room. As she crossed the threshold, Kyleigh's gaze drifted to the queen-size bed, draped in a vintage floral quilt with a thick blue border. The dresser featured three rows of drawers and an antique oval mirror, and directly across from it was an armoire with small horseshoe knobs jutting out of the wooden doors. The chemical odour of mothballs filled the room.

"I know it's not much," Hannah began, sounding apologetic, "but the bed's actually very comfortable. And the sheets were washed this morning."

Ray added, "The bathroom is next door. If you need extra towels, you're welcome to take them out of the linens closet in the hall." He exchanged a look with Hannah before saying, "We'll give you a bit of time to settle in."

Halfway down the stairs, Hannah stopped and turned to look back up at the second floor. It seemed like just yesterday she was settling into that very same room, a year after she and Ray had started dating. Back then, her greatest worry was that he hadn't kissed her yet—she'd even gone so far as to call her roommate, Joanna, for fashion advice, thinking that perhaps Ray's attraction to her was already fading. Now, it was twenty-six years later, and the daughter they'd never planned on having was laying her clothes in the same dresser, scrutinizing her reflection in the same mirror, and no doubt wondering what kind of summer she had to look forward to.

"She'll be fine," Ray said. "She just needs a bit of time to adjust."

"I know." Hannah descended the last few steps and crossed to the kitchen, where Jaxon was sitting in his usual seat at the table staring at his phone. He'd laid out five place settings and a basket of dinner rolls, still hot and steaming from the oven, before deciding to reward himself with another video.

"So, I guess we're not going to talk about it," Jaxon said suddenly.

Ray turned away from the fridge. "Talk about what?"

Jaxon pointed to the ceiling. "*That.*"

"'That'? You mean, your sister?" Setting a pitcher of water on the table, Ray said, "Kyle has as much right to be here as you do. Just because we haven't seen her since she was six doesn't mean she isn't part of the family."

"Yeah, but you have to admit it's pretty weird, right? I mean, she's had all this time—"

"I don't see any butter," Ray interrupted, finally realizing what was missing.

Jaxon sighed and slipped his phone into his pocket before getting up to finish what he'd started.

"I'm just saying," he continued, picking up the butter dish and setting it on the table, "people might ask questions."

"People can ask all the questions they want. Doesn't make it any of their business." As the salad, mashed potatoes, and roast beef were presented, Ray slid into the chair across from his son. Jaxon knew better than to have his phone at the table but couldn't resist one more peek to see if his favourite creator had posted anything new. Ray scraped together as much patience as he could before saying, "Frankly, you have more important things to worry about this summer than the local gossip."

"Like what?"

"Like working for me. Bernard and I will need all the help we can get to repair the fences in the north pasture, so I suggest you cancel any plans you might have."

"But it's summer vacation," Jaxon argued. This, at least, was enough to make him forget about whatever was on his phone for a few seconds.

"Come on, Jax," Ray said, "you know we don't take vacations on a working ranch."

Just as Jaxon was set to counter this, the front door opened and Bernard appeared wearing a flannel shirt, old jeans, and a pair of cowboy boots caked in fine, yellow dust. Before coming to live on the ranch, he'd been hitchhiking across the Midwest, sleeping in motels, truck stops, or, more often than not, a tent under the stars. This insatiable wanderlust had turned his skin thick and brown like leather so that even when he was freshly washed, he never looked totally clean.

"Sorry I'm late," Bernard said as he rolled up his sleeves. At the kitchen sink, he pumped several globs of the lemon-scented hand soap into his palm and worked it into a lather. It wasn't until he'd dried his hands and sat down at the table that he noticed the extra plate and set of cutlery. He turned a quizzical look on his son. "Didn't know we were having company tonight."

"Mom and dad didn't tell you?" Jaxon asked, quirking a brow. "Kyleigh's upstairs."

Bernard's eyes narrowed on Ray again. "Kyleigh? You mean, your daughter?"

"Is that a problem?" Ray asked.

"Not for me. I just thought maybe you had your hands full enough with the fences and such." Bernard shrugged and helped himself to a roll. "How long is she staying?"

"A few weeks." Ray looked at Hannah. "Is she not eating with us?"

"I'll go let her know dinner's ready."

Ray ran a hand through his hair. Deep down, he knew Bernard was right: he didn't have time to bond with Kyleigh. These days, he hardly had time to spend with Jaxon, although he secretly hoped working on the fences together might give them a chance to talk the way they used to when Jaxon was younger. What happened to that little boy who used to follow him around all day, begging Ray to show him how to hogtie a calf or make a halter out of a length of rope? Ray looked across the table again, but he didn't recognize the teenager at the other end of it.

"Sorry, I didn't realize you were all waiting for me," Kyleigh said as she entered the room. Her gaze landed on Bernard, who paused in the middle of spreading butter on his bread. "Hi. I'm Kyle."

He brushed the crumbs from his fingers, stood up, and offered his hand to her. "I'm Bernard. Your grandfather."

"It's nice to meet you." Kyleigh took a seat in one of the chairs and surveyed the various offerings laid out in front of her. "Do you do this every night?" she asked as the potatoes made their rounds.

Hannah glanced at her and replied, "Of course. It's important for families to eat together."

Little by little, Kyleigh's plate filled up with meat, potatoes, and bread—far more food than she was used to eating at home, where sit-down dinners were reserved for special occasions like Christmas and Easter. These were the only times multiple generations dined together, although Kyleigh couldn't recall the last time Samantha's parents had made the trek from Halifax to join them.

"My new ranch hand should be here sometime tomorrow," Ray said to no one in particular. "I'm thinking I'll just show him around a bit, and we can start fresh with the fences on Friday."

"What's his background?" Bernard asked, going in for his second roll.

"He grew up on a horse ranch in Montana. I don't think it'll take him much time to become acclimated here."

"Are you paying him?" Jaxon asked.

"Of course."

"How much?"

"That's confidential."

Jaxon switched his attention to Bernard. "How much is he paying *you*?"

Bernard chuckled and mopped up the drippings from the roast with a hunk of bread. "Enough to make sure I don't run off again."

"I'm sorry. Run off?" Kyleigh repeated.

Taking in her puzzled expression, Bernard's mouth twisted into a rueful smile. He set his half-eaten roll on the edge of his plate and met Ray's gaze before offering up his best attempt at an explanation.

"There's a lot of history in this place." Bernard made an encompassing motion with his hand toward the food and the people gathered around it. "People are always coming or going. Like you, for instance."

"I'll keep that in mind," Kyleigh said uneasily, wondering what kind of force had propelled Bernard away from a place that seemed, for all intents and purposes, like a refuge from the rest of the world. Or had she already built the ranch up in her mind to be more than what it really was: an establishment geared toward the cultivation of livestock?

"Jaxon," Ray said near the end of the meal, "chores."

Jaxon sighed. As the last of the dishes were cleared away, he stood up and placed his plate in the sink, then trailed Ray to the door.

"Chores?" Kyleigh asked Hannah, who was packaging the leftover roast.

"Bringing the horses in, feeding and watering them, that kind of thing. You're welcome to join them if you want."

"Would that be okay?"

"Of course. Why wouldn't it be?"

"I mean, I'm not exactly what you would call 'handy' or 'outdoorsy.' I had a dog growing up, but he was basically a lap dog, and half the time we just let him out to pee on this little patch of fake grass on the balcony."

"Well, I don't think you'll break anything out there. Running a ranch is a lot of work, but it's pretty straightforward once you get used to it."

Hannah looked toward the kitchen window at her husband and son's receding figures. Bernard had left a few minutes earlier to turn on the lights down at the barn and do whatever else needed doing to close the ranch down for the night.

She added, "I know it may not seem like it, but Ray's excited to spend time with you. When I was pregnant with you—before we made the choice to pursue adoption—he was fully prepared to raise a family."

"But... you weren't."

"Giving you away was one of the hardest things I've ever had to do. Sometimes I wonder if we really did the right thing, or if we took the easy way out and blamed it on being young."

"You know, sometimes I wonder that too." Kyleigh turned toward the stairs. "On second thought, I better finish unpacking."

As she retreated to the guest bedroom, Hannah piled the remaining dishes in the sink and tried to get a handle on her thoughts. If she'd known opening their home to their estranged daughter would tear open so many old wounds, she might've thought twice about answering Kyleigh's message. But it didn't matter now: what was done was done. As a parent, she could only do so much to ensure her children ended up happy and well-adjusted. The rest was up to them.

Setting aside her usual domestic distractions, Hannah walked over to the front door. She threw her hair into a quick ponytail, slipped her feet into a pair of dusty old paddock boots, reached for the door, and headed outside to lend a hand down at the barn.

Six

"It could be worse," Mickey had said three days before his death.

Josh had looked at him uncomfortably, trying to focus on the words coming out of his father's mouth rather than the pasty quality of his skin. "How so?"

"I could've been struck by lightning. Or hit by a bus. Instead, I got to spend the last weeks of my life with you."

Forcing himself to smile, Josh had stared down at his ice-cold cup of tea. So far, the oncologist's timeline had been accurate: patients with this form of cancer usually succumbed to their illness within four months, and the chemotherapy had stopped working after three. On that day, Mickey had been offered a more aggressive treatment option and declined. "If I'm going to die," he'd told the doctor, "I want to do it at home." Two days later, the Hammonds had received a visit from a company that outsourced medical equipment for end-of-life care. They'd installed a heart rate monitor next to the bed in the guest room, which had a large picture frame window overlooking the paddocks, and stacked boxes of sterile gauze and syringes in the corner next to the dresser. Twice a day, a hospice nurse named Clara came in and administered hydromorphone through a port in Mickey's upper arm, drained his catheter bag, and rearranged the pillows to prevent skin breakdown. The rest of the time, Josh and Soraya took turns providing care.

That day, it had been Josh's turn to sit with Mickey while he faded in and out of sleep. One by one, each of the ranch hands had stopped by the house to say goodbye. Only Ernesto had dared to stay longer than five minutes, perched on the edge of a wooden chair holding his cowboy hat between his knees.

Mickey had reached out and placed a bony hand on Josh's arm. "Best weeks of my life," he'd rasped.

Setting his tea on the windowsill, Josh had cleared his throat and glanced at the TV across the room. He'd always hoped that one day he'd be able to introduce Mickey to his girlfriend or his first child, and now he was realizing he'd waited too long to grow up. What were the years ahead going to look like, as a fatherless adult son?

Josh had turned his chair toward the bed. Cancer had eaten away at every corner of Mickey's body, hollowing out his chest and cheeks and whittling his bones down to brittle lines. His inability to swallow liquids had caused his lips to become dry and chapped, so Soraya had dabbed Vaseline on them in an effort to ease his discomfort. Soon, Clara had warned, Mickey would slip into a prolonged state of unconsciousness and his blood pressure would drop, signaling that death was imminent.

I'm not ready, Josh had thought. He felt dizzy, like he was standing at the edge of a cliff staring down at the blue thread of a river below. Every breath of stale air made him feel like he was going to be sick.

"I'm sorry," he'd whispered around the knot in his throat. "I'm sorry I wasn't more." Josh wilted forward, draping himself over the withered shape of his father's body.

Mickey had lifted one hand and placed it weakly on the back of Josh's head. "The best thing you ever were… was my son."

Josh had kept his head down, praying to the only god he'd ever believed in that this was true.

*

It was mid-afternoon when Josh pulled into the driveway, a choppy shoelace of gravel that vanished over the hill and into a crease where the mountains met the sky. Josh kept to the road's edge, avoiding the rougher patches as the Ducati's engine purred in the silence of a lazy summer day.

When he eventually came upon a house, he parked his bike under a nearby maple tree, turned off the ignition, and removed his helmet. As far as workplaces went, this one wasn't terrible: the barn might've been old, but it looked well preserved. The hayloft door stood open, and through the rectangular opening he spotted a wall of hay several bales deep. Hay was a natural insulator and storing it above the barn meant that even during the bleakest winter months, the horses would be warm and toasty in their stalls below. Along with repairing the broken fences and digging holes for new posts, Josh knew he'd be expected to haul hay and ensure the loft above the barn was fully stocked by the end of the summer. After that, Josh wasn't exactly sure where he'd be, but he was pretty damn sure it wouldn't be anywhere near Montana.

As he was admiring his new workplace, the screen door whined on its hinges. He turned sharply toward the sound to find a woman in white shorts and a blue tank top emerging from the house, her hair pinned in a messy bun on top of her head. She held her phone in one hand and a mason jar of iced tea in the other, and was carrying both over to the bench swing beneath the kitchen window.

"Hi," Josh called out.

Kyleigh acknowledged him with a nod. "Hi."

Swinging a leg over the bike's seat, he tucked his helmet under his arm and watched as she settled on the wooden bench, the glass jar that held her refreshment studded with shining droplets of moisture.

"If you're looking for Ray, try the barn," she said without looking at him. "I hear he spends the majority of his time there."

"Do you work here too?"

"Just visiting."

Josh nodded and turned away. "Thanks."

He followed the dusty path to the barn. Most of the day-to-day equipment was stored in a large shed with a corrugated tin roof. Josh poked his head inside and spotted a pair of rain barrels in the corner, a couple months' worth of firewood, various attachments for the tractor, a stack of wooden pallets, and an old paint bucket containing a jumble of tools. Josh had grown up around cowboys, even if he didn't consider himself one, and he knew that everything on a ranch had its place and purpose. Same went for people, although it was still too early to tell just how useful Josh would be here.

He kept walking. Eventually, the sound of voices drifted into his ears, and he followed that too, straight past the barn and over to a small round pen. The man at the centre of it had a wiry, stooped frame suggestive of advanced age and poor posture, although it was difficult to tell through the clouds of dust precisely how old he might've been. Clutched in his weathered hands was a thick length of rope, which he fed through his fingers to keep the yearling on the opposite end of it at a safe distance.

At the sound of Josh's approaching footsteps, Ray angled away from the fence and smiled.

"You made it," Ray said, repositioning his hat in order to see Josh more clearly. His gaze fell on the helmet tucked under Josh's arm. "I didn't peg you for a motorcycle guy."

"I thought it might give me an edge," Josh confessed. "It was a stupid move, I know. Even the ranch hands back home won't stop teasing me about it."

Amusement flickered across Ray's face. "Well, you're here now, and that's all that matters." He indicated the sand ring. "That's my dad, Bernard. I've asked him to help me break a couple of my younger horses so I can focus on the more mundane aspects of running a ranch. Gives him a break from fixing fences, too."

Josh nodded, picturing Ernesto in the sand ring at Broken Bar. Once upon a time, he'd been working at a livestock auction in Billings, Montana, where his days consisted of facilitating the flow of cattle and horses through the stockyard. Mickey hadn't been looking to hire anyone when he spotted Ernesto in one of the pens, soothing a visibly agitated one-eyed mare. According to Ernesto's version of the story, a young cowboy named Dale had approached the horse on her blind side, startling her, and she had struck out reflexively, nicking him in the shin with her hoof.

"His pride suffered more damage than his leg," Ernesto had said in a grave tone. "For some men who call themselves cowboys, that's all it takes for them to go off." Wounded (but not mortally so), Dale had grabbed a cattle prod and rammed it through the bars of the pen, delivering a five-thousand-volt shot to the mare's shoulder that caused her to squeal in pained surprise. Ernesto had seen no choice but to intervene, and by the day's end he had a new job working for Mickey, who also ended up buying the one-eyed mare. If it weren't for Ernesto, Josh thought now, Mickey might have never become The Horse God. After all, someone had to stay back and run the ranch while his dad was on the road. Yes, cowboys had to be tough, but the real ones were gentle too.

As Josh set down his helmet and rested his elbows on the fence, Ray nodded to the filly. "She won't be ready to ride for another couple of years, but she's old enough to learn her basic paces. The lunging is really just to teach her how to follow directions, not for physical conditioning."

"Yeah. And the line is attached laterally to mimic the pressure of a bit." Josh shrugged. "Dad never liked using a bit. The more natural the connection, the better, he said."

"I agree. Unfortunately, most people don't have the time or skills to get to a place where a bit isn't necessary. They want to be in control at all cost."

Ray winced and shifted his weight to his left leg.

"I noticed you had a couple of dead trees out by the road," Josh said as the pain smoothed off of Ray's face. "I'm guessing you'll want them taken care of at some point?"

"Eventually, but right now I'm more concerned with what's going on out there." He indicated the trees to the north, which served as a natural barrier between the ranch and the range. "Bernard and I have already started tearing down the old fence. Once the new posts go in, the entire perimeter will need to be restrung with new wire. Getting all that done before the fall isn't going to be easy. To tell you the truth," Ray added with a smirk, "I don't think I can physically handle the workload this year. Between fixing the fences, running the ranch, and taking care of my family, I'm maxed out."

"What about your son?"

Ray put a hand to the crown of his hat and tipped it forward to shield his eyes from the sun. He said nothing as the filly trotted past him again, encouraged by the soft clucking noises of her handler.

After a minute, he said, "Jaxon's a good kid, but he doesn't seem to want anything to do with me lately. That's why you're here." Ray stepped back from the round pen, telling Josh, "Come on, I'll give you a tour of the place."

Josh had already seen much of the yard, but there were plenty of things still to be discovered, like the manure pile on its concrete pad behind the shed and the storage-room-turned-office in the barn, where Ray spent his evenings replying to client emails and fretting over his family's financial future. He explained that most ranches operated on razor-thin margins, with good years often followed by bad ones. Out here, success or failure was a matter of adaptability, and he'd seen plenty of cattlemen go broke because they refused to embrace the changes that were sweeping the industry.

"I was skeptical about having a YouTube channel when I was younger," Ray said as they concluded their tour of the hay loft. "I didn't think people would honestly want to see what went on here on an average day, but I guess there's an audience for everything. I have your dad to thank for that."

Josh smirked. "Dad did love an audience, so long as they weren't looking at me."

"He never took you on tour?"

"No. After my accident, he made sure I never got within a hundred yards of a camera crew again. Ironically, he thought the safest place for me was on the ranch. My mom more or less raised me alone, and I think toward the end of his life, my dad regretted that."

Josh took a couple steps toward the hay loft door. It was cooler up here than it was down in the main barn area, with the steady breeze funneling through the high wooden rafters. Tucked into the angles of the joists were several swallows' nests, made from mud and hay that dangled like tinsel above the grey-green bales.

He went on, "Dads miss out on a lot trying to give their kids the best life. I don't hold the touring against him. I just wish we'd had more time together as I was growing up."

Ray joined him at the edge of the loft and looked toward the sand ring in the distance. Since Bernard's reappearance seventeen years ago, Ray had been trying to make up for the lost years by giving Bernard a place to live and a chance to bond with his grandson. But it was all just damage control at this point: one day, Bernard would be gone, and the only thing Ray would really remember about his father was that he'd loved his horses more than his sons.

When the wind lifted again, it brought with it the earthy scent of the mountains along with the sound of two people talking. Josh glanced toward the house and saw Hannah and Kyleigh making their way out to the metallic blue sedan parked near the corner of the veranda. Hannah tossed her reusable grocery bags into the backseat before ducking behind the wheel, leaving Kyleigh to slide into the passenger seat beside her.

"That's our daughter, Kyle," Ray said as the car's taillights came on.

"I didn't know you had a daughter."

They watched the car pull away from the house, churning up a low fog of dust as it rolled down the driveway.

As they lost sight of it behind the trees, Ray replied, "Not many people know that Hannah and I have two kids. Kyle lives in Canada now, so we're hoping she'll pursue dual citizenship. But I don't think she's a fan of the idea of living on a ranch."

He turned away from the door, his thoughts already moving in a new direction. As he led Josh back across the hay loft, Ray asked, "Do you have a place to stay tonight?"

"A buddy of mine's got an Airbnb not too far from here. It's sort of being renovated, so he's agreed to rent it out to me at a discount."

"I'm glad. Unfortunately, we don't have any extra rooms at the moment, otherwise I'd move Bernard into the guest room and let you take the bunkhouse."

Josh climbed down the ladder after him. He thought about the bunkhouses at Broken Bar, with their knotty pine floors and wooden bunks, and the small card table in the kitchen where the ranch hands ate their meals and gambled away their earnings in poker. Inevitably, one of them would insist on playing guitar, and another would join in on the harmonica. As a kid, Josh loved listening to the warm notes of their spontaneous compositions, carrying far and wide in the stillness of a summer night.

The heat of the day was rising fast. Josh felt the worst of it on his face and the back of his neck, where his leather jacket didn't quite cover his skin. They walked over to the round pen, where Bernard was stroking the filly's muzzle and speaking to her in a low, soothing murmur.

Josh picked up his helmet. Bernard's back was to him, and for a moment all Josh could see were the old cowboy's hands, browned from the sun. Before Mickey died, he'd made Josh a promise: *Wherever you go, I'll be right there with you.* So far, Mickey had found him in the most unexpected places: in busy coffee shops, in conversations between strangers, and now, in the masterful motions of a horseman who had never forgotten his mother tongue.

Bernard turned around, noticed Josh watching him, and said, "You all right, son?"

Josh snapped out of his stupor. "Yeah. I was just leaving." He tucked his helmet under his arm and cut a beeline back to the Ducati.

"Tomorrow's going to be a long day," Ray said as Josh swung a leg over the bike's seat. "Wear layers. You want to be warm *and* protected from the sun up here."

"Got it."

"For what it's worth, I'm glad you called. I know these past few months haven't been easy for you and your mom, but hopefully this helps you out a bit." Glancing back at the barn, Ray said, "I better get back to work. I'll show you around a little bit more tomorrow, although it'll still be dark at five."

"Five A.M.?"

Ray smirked. "We start early on a working ranch. Of course, if that's not your cup of tea…"

"No, no, five's… great."

As his new employer strode back to the barn, Josh sighed and started up his bike. "Welcome to the real world, champ," he muttered to himself, channeling Mickey through the cool shell of his helmet. Like Ray had said in the barn: there were those who adapted, and those who didn't, and Josh was determined not to fall into the second group. He would do whatever it took to survive out here or die trying.

Seven

"No, I'm not telling you where I am. Why? Because the last thing I need is you showing up here thinking you can win me back or something."

Kyleigh paced around the bedroom, her stomach in knots and her hands ice-cold. Ever since she'd arrived in Colorado, she'd been too busy adjusting to her surroundings to think about Derek, much less take his calls. But she could only ignore a problem for so long before it blossomed into a crisis, and now, alone in the house for the first time in days, Kyleigh wondered how she would ever return to Toronto without tumbling into the same dysfunctional relationship that had driven her out.

"I'm not trying to win you back," Derek said in an infuriatingly calm voice, "I'm just worried about your safety. I mean, you left the country on a whim—"

"Who told you I left the country?"

"Your dad said you were on a business trip. Aren't you?"

She inhaled sharply, curbing a hot wave of anger. "What do you want, Derek?"

A door downstairs closed, prompting Kyleigh to turn away from the window. Soon, she heard the telltale creak of old floorboards as someone crossed to the stairs, the alternating tempo of their footsteps echoing off the old, picture-lined walls.

"Just tell me where you are," Derek replied with a sigh.

"No."

"Are you in Atlanta?"

"Why the hell would I be in Atlanta?" Kyleigh asked before remembering that her employer had an office in Georgia.

She glimpsed the hallway again and locked eyes with Jaxon, who paused with his hand on the doorknob of his bedroom. Kyleigh crossed the room and shut the door before returning to her conversation.

"Kyle, you're freaking me out. I know what I did was inexcusable, but that doesn't mean you should take it as an invitation to disappear. What about your job? What about your life in Toronto?"

"My job is not your concern. And I don't think you should be commenting on *my* personal affairs when you were the one to destroy everything we worked for." She shook her head, fighting against the dull ache in her throat that threatened to make her voice splinter. "Why Leanne?" she asked.

"I told you: we got put on a project together, and it involved a lot of late nights."

"Funny. I work a lot of late nights too, and not once have I ever considered sleeping with one of the guys on my team. What I want to know is, what does Leanne have that I don't?"

"Kyle…"

"Derek," she countered firmly, "I want to know. I *need* to know."

The line went silent. After a few moments, Derek replied, "Time."

"What?"

"She had time for me. I know it sounds like bullshit, but it's true. You were working all the time, and even though we lived together, I hardly ever saw you." Derek cleared his throat, embarrassed. "I know what you're thinking, okay?"

"Believe me, you have no idea what I'm thinking. Am I supposed to apologize because I'm building my career instead of pandering to your insatiable male ego?"

"I'm not asking you to apologize for anything. But you asked me for a reason, and I'm giving you one. When you got promoted and started spending all your time at work, I became resentful. Eventually I opened up to Leanne about these feelings, and she made me feel seen and heard."

"I'm not against you talking to other women, but how did she end up in your bed? Did you invite her over?"

"Kind of."

"Kind of?"

"Look, why does it even matter? The point is, I let a single, stupid decision destroy our relationship, and I feel like a complete jackass about it."

"It matters because I cannot, for the life of me, figure out how I missed all the signs." Kyleigh snarled, if only to keep herself from dissolving into a puddle of angry tears. "I know I work a lot and I know I'm not around as much as I should be, but I thought I knew you better than this. I thought, just maybe, you were the man I'd spend the rest of my life with."

"I could be…" he said in a small voice. "I know I don't deserve a second chance, but I'm asking you for one. I promise, this will never, ever happen again."

As tears clouded her vision, Kyleigh stared out the window at the aspen trees behind the house. Yes, she worked too much, but only because she was a woman in a man's world trying to prove that she belonged. And when all that had deteriorated, where had she gone? Deeper into a world dominated by the opposite sex, where the women cooked and cleaned while the men enjoyed the fruits of their labour at the dinner table each night.

"Kyle, please," Derek croaked, "just tell me where you are so I can finally get some sleep."

"I've got to go," she said tightly, turning back to the room and its outdated décor. She hung up the call and tossed her phone onto the bed. It sank gently into the old quilt, landing in a strip of sunlight that made the microscopic particles drifting through the air sparkle like glitter. For several moments, Kyleigh merely focused on breathing in and out, letting her feelings about the breakup rise and settle like dust. Cheating seemed so one-sided, but what if it wasn't? What if she'd been so blinded by her own goals and aspirations she'd forgotten Derek had needs, too?

But no, she would've noticed things were different between them, or his betrayal wouldn't have come as such a shock.

One thing was clear, though: she wasn't interested in any sort of reconciliation. Pushing away her guilt, Kyleigh checked her reflection in the mirror. There was a reddish tinge to her eyes that she blamed on not being able to sleep, but she appeared otherwise healthy and strong. She pictured Ray and Bernard out in the fields, methodically installing the new fenceposts and connecting them with a shiny spool of wire. It seemed like a monumental undertaking for such a short span of time: summers were short in the mountains, so they needed all the help they could get.

Crossing the room, Kyleigh opened her door to find the door to Jaxon's room was open as well. She steered herself toward the stairs and headed down to the main floor to find him sitting at the kitchen table, munching on a Pop Tart covered in a thick layer of white frosting.

His gaze flashed upward, catching her face as she strode into view. "Trouble in paradise?" he asked, the Pop Tart crumbling as he bit into it again.

"Were you eavesdropping on my conversation?"

"Not intentionally," Jaxon replied defensively. When Kyleigh continued to stare at him, he explained, "It's an old house. Every time my parents argue, I swear it's like I'm right there in the room with them even if I'm on a different floor."

"I can only imagine what else you hear." She faced the window and scanned the yard unseeingly. "So, how much did you accidentally pick up on just now?"

"Not much," Jaxon admitted, waving his second Pop Tart to indicate that his desire for a snack was a greater priority than sticking his nose in Kyleigh's business. That didn't mean he wasn't curious to know what was going on. "Was that your husband on the phone?" he asked.

"Boyfriend. *Ex*-boyfriend. By the way, where is everyone?"

"Mom went into town. Dad and grandpa are out working in the north pasture, along with that guy dad hired last week."

"Do they need any extra help?"

Cramming the last bite into his mouth, Jaxon picked up his plate and carried it over to the sink. "Are you offering to take my place?"

"Take your place, no. Assist, yes."

He looked her over quickly, stoking the anger still smoldering in the pit of Kyleigh's stomach.

She told him, "Look, I just want to feel useful, okay? I need something to do."

"Fine, you can come. But not like this." Jaxon indicated her jeans shorts and white t-shirt. Her feet, as usual, were bare save for a small tattoo of a daffodil on her right ankle. He inclined his head toward the mudroom and said, "I'll see if I can find you some boots."

"Great. I'll go get changed."

She headed back upstairs while Jaxon rummaged around in the assortment of footwear. When she was packing her bags at Anvi's apartment, her wardrobe had been the furthest thing from her mind: half her clothes were still at Derek's place, and there was no way in hell she was going to reveal her precise location by asking him to mail them to her. In the guest room, she stepped into a pair of olive-green jeans and white crew socks, pulled on a black hoodie, and smeared sunscreen on her face and neck. When all was said and done, she studied her reflection in the mirror and realized exactly what was wrong with it.

This was Derek's sweater, the one she'd borrowed on their third date and never returned because she liked the way it smelled. Even after countless washes, the memory of his scent still lingered on the pilled fabric, forcing the hot burn of tears to return to her eyes. There was nothing to be none for it now though, except to drive out to the middle of nowhere and get this sweater as filthy as she possibly could.

"Okay, here I am," Kyleigh said as she trotted downstairs a few minutes later. As Jaxon looked up from his phone, she spread her arms, asking, "What do you think? Do I look like a rancher's daughter?"

"I think there's potential," he answered. He reached down and picked up a pair of roping boots that were so old, it was impossible to tell what colour they used to be. "I don't know what size you wear, but these might fit," he said as Kyleigh eyed the parched leather.

"Only one way to find out." She took the boots from his hands and wrinkled her nose in disgust. "What's that smell?"

"Manure, probably."

"Lovely." Nevertheless, she pulled them on.

They headed outside, with Jaxon leading the way to the old shed that housed their tractor and other farming equipment. He opened the driver's door to Ray's old Chevy and slid behind the wheel before lifting the key off the rearview mirror. As she climbed into the passenger seat, Kyleigh gazed around at the vehicle's interior, from its bare-bones instrument panel to the sheet of plywood that appeared to be the only thing separating her feet from the ground. The glove box was bursting with faded maps, crumpled receipts, and a waterlogged book, *Edible Plants of Colorado*, which boasted over a hundred varieties of ostensibly nutritious local flora.

"You're sure this old rust bucket still runs?" she asked.

"Yup. They don't make trucks like this anymore—at least, that's what my dad says." Jaxon fired up the engine, put the truck in gear, and drove toward the north pasture. The ancient Chevy lumbered over the rough terrain, slashing through the trees overhanging the trail.

Kyleigh pulled the forager's handbook from the disarray and flipped to a random page. "With few exceptions, the leaves of most coniferous trees are safe to eat," she read aloud. Next to the paragraph of text was an image of a Southwestern pine accompanied by a black-and-white illustration of its needles—a visual reference for the discerning consumer. "As if anyone would be *that* desperate."

She met Jaxon's gaze. Before long, he turned his attention back to the rutted path and shook his head.

"What?" Kyleigh asked.

"You didn't do your research, did you?"

"My research?"

"About this place. About my dad." As they drove over a tree root, the truck's frame juddered violently. Kyleigh grabbed the door to steady herself. "If you ever get bored of arguing with your boyfriend, Google the Bionic Cowboy Tour."

"*Ex*-boyfriend," she clarified. "And why should I Google that?"

Jaxon couldn't help it—he laughed.

"What?" she demanded again.

"Why are you even here? No offense, but it's kind of weird how you just woke up one day and decided you wanted to be part of our family despite not knowing a single thing about us."

"I didn't wake up one day and decide anything," she snapped back. "It was a gradual process of accepting that half my life is in Canada and the other half of it is here. I should be allowed to visit every once in a while, even if I don't know the first thing about cows or trucks or—" Kyleigh waved a hand at the field guide to edible plants "—how to survive in the wilderness."

"Right, but you should still do some research," Jaxon replied.

The tree cover thinned as they emerged at the edge of a wide, green plateau. Parked in the shade of a nearby tree was Ray's truck, the bed of which was filled with barbed wire: great, glistening bales of silver armed with steel teeth. Scattered at regular intervals around the pasture's perimeter were piles of fenceposts waiting to be installed. Pine was the preferred wood for these purposes: when properly treated, these posts could last thirty years, even when exposed to the harsh elements the back country was known for. *With any luck,* Ray had thought earlier, *this fence will outlive me.*

He was currently hammering a fencepost into the ground. Bernard was standing across from him, holding the post steady as Josh measured out the distance to the next hole. Jaxon parked behind Ray's truck and killed the engine, prompting Ray to turn around.

Jaxon raised his hands as he and Kyleigh stepped out of the vehicle. "It wasn't my idea," he said.

"I believe you." Ray looked at Kyleigh again and offered a smile. "Nice boots."

"Thanks." Kyleigh pocketed her hands. She was all too aware of how everyone was staring at her, and who could blame them? She started toward the fence and examined the steel barbs twisted around each length of wire. "Does this hurt the cows?" she asked.

"Not too badly. Their skin is tougher than ours, but it gives them just enough of a poke to think twice about trying to escape." Ray nodded at her hands, still balled up in her—well, Derek's—sweater. "The boots are a good start, but you're going to need something to protect your hands, too. Jaxon, why don't you see if you can find Kyle a pair of work gloves in my truck?"

As Jaxon ferreted around in the glove box, Ray turned back to the rest of his team. "You already know Bernard, of course," he told Kyle. "And this is Josh. I used to be good friends with his dad."

"We met briefly the other day," Josh reminded her as he approached them. "But it's nice to meet you… again."

"Likewise."

Soon, Jaxon trailed Ray over to the fencepost he'd been working on a few minutes earlier. Their voices mixed with the steady breeze to form a broken string of chatter that Kyleigh found difficult to follow. She waited for her introductory lesson on fixing fences to begin, but it was clear neither her father nor her brother had any intention of bringing her up to speed. She turned back to Josh, hoping he would be slightly more forthcoming.

"So," Kyleigh said as she slipped on Ray's gloves, "where do we start?"

Josh's smile widened incrementally. He pointed to his section of the fence and said, "I've been trying to stay at least a couple sections ahead of Ray here, but he's catching up pretty quick."

"I imagine he's had a lot of practice."

He indicated her shirt. "Guess no one ever told you not to wear white around horses."

"I don't see any horses out here. Or cows, for that matter."

"Every summer Ray moves his herd to public grazing land so they can put on weight before going to market. Saves having to send them to a feedlot."

"Seems like you know a lot about this stuff."

"I should hope so. I grew up on a ranch, after all."

They began walking along the fence, away from where Ray, Jaxon, and Bernard were struggling to get the alignment of the fencepost just right. Josh may not have been a cowboy, but he clearly knew how to dress for the occasion, with his jeans, work boots, and faded red t-shirt that showed off the definition in his upper arms. His skin was a couple shades darker than Ray's, whose tan had developed over a lifetime of working outdoors. When Josh turned his head to look at her again, Kyleigh saw a wave of blue pass through his shock of jet-black hair.

"So, what did you do to end up out here?" she asked.

"It was kind of a personal favour," he said sheepishly. "My dad passed away about four months ago. I needed an excuse to get out of Montana for a while, and Ray said if I ever needed work, I could come here."

"I'm sorry about your dad."

"Me too. He was…" Josh struggled to find the right words to express the murkiness of his grief. In addition to being an entertainer, Mickey Hammond had been a man plagued by inner demons. At various times throughout Josh's life, he'd wished his dad would drop the whole tortured cowboy bit and focus on what was really important: his family. "He was a great person. He wasn't perfect, but who is?" He figured now would be a good time to shift the focus of the conversation back to Kyleigh, before the wave of pain broke through the thin barrier of happy memories. "I'm assuming something brought you out here, too."

Kyleigh followed Josh's lead as he began arranging the fenceposts at regular intervals, marking the places where they would eventually stand. "I have two reasons: the real one, and the one I want people to believe. Which one do you want to hear?"

Josh dropped his end of the post and straightened to look at her. "The real one."

Kyleigh pressed her lips together. "It's kind of embarrassing."

"My answer's the same."

"I found out my boyfriend of five years was cheating on me and had to move out of the apartment we shared. My parents—my adopted parents, I mean—offered for me to stay with them until I got back on my feet, but instead I decided to come out here so I could get to know my biological family."

"I'm sorry about your boyfriend."

Kyleigh shrugged and swallowed the stab of pain at the back of her throat. "It's okay. We're both young, and I'm sure we'll find other people eventually."

He nodded, smiling kindly. "Him, I'm not so sure about, but you… definitely."

Just then, Ray sauntered over to them.

"How's the fence coming?" he asked.

Josh replied, "So far, so good. We're ready to start digging holes anytime."

Satisfied by his answer, Ray headed back over to where Jaxon and Bernard were working on opposite sides of a neat line of pale yellow fenceposts.

Josh turned back to Kyleigh, her cheeks still warm from the unexpected compliment.

"Well," he said, "I guess we should get started."

Eight

Hannah was in no hurry to go home. Instead, as she sat in the parking lot of Whole Foods and watched the sun set behind the mountains, she thought of the family waiting for her back at the ranch: her husband, a lifelong cowboy quietly struggling with his deteriorating health; her father-in-law, a mountain man who'd never fully adjusted to modern life; her son, yearning for the things all teenagers craved; and now, her daughter, who'd washed ashore on their little island and no longer knew which way was home.

Putting the car in gear, Hannah pulled out of the parking space and headed for the exit. Last night, when she'd invited Kyleigh to help make dinner, Kyleigh had sat on the wooden stool in the corner of the kitchen and, instead, talked about her job, where she was one of only two female engineers. Hannah hadn't minded the company, but listening to Kyleigh wax poetic about her career was a painful reminder of the plans she'd abandoned when she decided to marry Ray. If she could go back in time and choose a different path, what would her life look like today?

Hannah followed the road out of town, passing the places that had become woven into the fabric of her life: a Starbucks, a gas station, a burger joint, an autobody shop. They'd carved out a good life for themselves here, despite the skyrocketing cost of living that kept most people from enjoying the usual mountain town luxuries. During the pandemic, the ranch had been the ideal place to hide from the world: they'd had plenty of food, firewood, and supplies to carry them through the worst of the shortages. Plus, with a baby at home, they hadn't had time to socialize even if they wanted to.

How times have changed, Hannah thought as she pulled into the driveway of Fitzgerald Farms. The once beautiful property hadn't been the same since Laney's passing eight years ago, leaving Jim the sole occupant of the now-defunct horse boarding facility. As she drove toward the house, Hannah understood why Ray never visited, despite her constant nagging. It would've broken Laney's heart to see her home in such a state: the driveway choked with weeds, the garden destroyed by pests, the trees sick or dying or dead. It had taken some convincing, but eventually Jim had agreed to let Hannah come in a few times per month and tidy up the house, even if it was just to ease her own mind.

Hannah stepped out of her car and navigated the tangle of nettle blanketing the walkway. Stopping just long enough to collect the packages that had accumulated on the front porch, she slotted her spare key into the lock and shouldered through the door. That was when the smell hit her: it was a rancid concoction of rotting food and general uncleanliness, mixed with the more subtle reek of gin and mould. Hannah unloaded the packages onto the glass table just inside the door, where guests used to place bottles of wine and winter gloves before Laney inevitably swooped in to welcome them to her humble abode.

Hannah tried the light switch closest to her. The electricity had been shut off a couple of times, forcing Ray to step in and manage Jim's finances. Whatever money was left over after the bills had been paid went toward funding Jim's growing list of vices.

As a bright glow filled the living room, Jim, who'd been napping in his armchair, startled awake.

"Who's there?" he barked, bleary-eyed.

"It's just me, Jim," Hannah said as she crossed the room.

His gaze fixated on her with palpable acrimony. "Weren't you just here two days ago?"

"I was here two weeks ago, although it smells like no one's cleaned in a month."

She took a seat on the sofa. Scattered across the coffee table were old pizza boxes, some magazines Jim had been using as coasters, and an empty bottle of Jack Daniels. Hannah picked it up and eyed the black label.

"There's more in the kitchen if you want some," Jim told her, rubbing his left eye.

Hannah shook her head and set the bottle back on the table. "I haven't had a drink in five years, but thank you for your hospitality."

He chuckled, shifting in his chair. "Now there's a word I haven't heard in a while. To think of the parties we used to throw… the food I used to cook…"

A nostalgic smile surfaced on Hannah's face. It was hard to see it in the growing darkness, but just beyond the patio door was the gazebo where she'd once told Ray the story of how her first boyfriend had died nearly thirty years ago. Their lives were unrecognizable now, although some things—like their love and devotion to one another—hadn't changed at all.

"I know why you're here," Jim said, drawing Hannah's attention back to the armchair. "I see you taking your pictures when you come in to clean. But I'm not leaving this house, and you know good and well that I'm not selling this place to some goddamned developer."

"The way you're going, you might die before anyone tries to take this place from you," Hannah said bluntly. "Is that what you want?"

"I don't want anyone coming in and telling me what to do. That includes Ray."

"You know he's only trying to help."

"The hell he is."

"If you let us, we can find you a nice, relatively inexpensive place to live—someplace like an assisted living facility where you'd get the support you need but could still have your independence."

"I'm not going to die in some godforsaken facility like Laney did," he bellowed, leaning forward in his chair and jabbing a sausage finger at Hannah. An inebriated flush filled his cheeks, highlighting the indignation that flared in his eyes. "The last time I saw her, she was skin and bones. And bedsores! Didn't recognize me or anyone else. I promised her right then and there that I'd make sure Fitzgerald Farms didn't fall into the wrong hands, and I'll keep that promise 'til my dying breath."

"If you want to do right by Laney, then you need to take care of yourself. Ray and I don't mind managing your bank accounts, but if anyone other than me were to walk in here and see what's become of the place—" At this, she waved a hand over the clutter. It was one thing for a house to be a little messy, but the odour told her the damage was more extensive than it appeared on the surface. "They'd be on the phone to Adult Protective Services. And APS would remove you from the house for your own safety."

"My own safety?" Jim barked, his face turning markedly darker. "Now, you listen to me: I started working when I was thirteen, and I didn't stop working until Laney went to live at Alpine Terrace. I've never taken a handout, and I've never needed anyone to protect me."

"That might've been true a few years ago, but we're talking about *today*, Jim. We're talking about right now." Hannah reached for the bottle again, only for Jim to snatch it out of her hand.

His glare settled on her, his eyes black as coal in the lamp's rosy glow. "You want to do some good, then know your place."

Hannah rose and headed toward the kitchen. "We can talk about this another time, when you're not quite so defensive." But when would that be? Jim had become more belligerent in recent years, taking his anger and helplessness out on anyone who dared to set foot in his lair. Victor and Adrianna generally kept their distance, while Marcus and his longtime girlfriend, Cindy, rarely came to Colorado. This left Ray, the youngest of the three brothers, to bear the burden of his aging godfather's health alone.

Hannah worked from one end of the counter to the other, tossing TV dinner trays, empty beer cans, pizza boxes, eggshells, old dish rags, mouldy sponges, plastic bread ties, and the odd broken lightbulb into a black garbage bag. A toxic-looking sludge coated the bottom of the coffee pot. She rinsed it out, filled it with hot water and dish soap, and set it aside to soak while she tackled the dishes that had piled up in the sink. She remembered being a young mom and spending what felt like hours in the kitchen each day, cleaning bottles and soothers and pureeing batches of baby food to store in the freezer. Needless to say, she knew her way around a kitchen, even if it wasn't her own.

Hannah rinsed the last Tupperware lid and added it to the mountain of dishes in the drying rack before turning her focus to the coffee pot. By some miracle the coffee maker still worked, so she set about preparing a fresh pot while continuing to throw away virtually everything in the fridge.

"What are you doing?" Jim asked from the living room.

"Trying to prevent you from getting food poisoning." She pulled out a jar filled with a mysterious grey substance and carried it over to the armchair, where Jim was watching the news on the flatscreen TV above the fireplace.

Hannah held up the jar and asked, "Would you like to take a guess at what this is?"

His lips puckered. "Is there a date on it?"

"Sure. But the fact that the contents now resemble raw sewage makes the expiry date redundant."

"That's a good jar," Jim told her as he turned back to the TV, "keep it."

Hannah, at last, lost her patience. "I'm not keeping this! I don't care how good the jar is—the stuff inside is rancid. Do you really think Laney would have wanted you to hold on to trash?"

"Don't talk about my wife like you knew her. And the things you see around here are not 'trash'… This is exactly why I didn't want any help. People come in and start making decisions, and if I disagree with those decisions, they look at me like that." Jim pointed the remote at Hannah's face, her expression caught somewhere between pity and exasperation. "I can take care of myself, damn it."

"You know what, you're right," Hannah said, setting the jar on the coffee table. "I'm overstepping. If you don't want the help, I can't force it on you."

"You tried to do the same thing to Laney when she was still alive," he reminded her, "you and Ray both."

"I don't remember it quite like that, but I'm not in a mood to argue anymore. I'm going home now, but if you *do* need anything, you have our number."

Before Jim could lay into her again, Hannah stepped around the couch and strode toward the front door. She picked up the black garbage bag, its contents clinking as she wrapped the neck around her wrist and hauled it out to the shed, where at least five other, identical black bags were already waiting. If she had Ray's truck, she could've loaded it up with garbage and driven it over to the landfill. But she didn't have Ray's truck. What she had were a splitting headache from the ungodly smells inside the house and the stress of arguing with a brick wall.

She didn't need this.

Hannah sighed, threw the bag she was carrying on top of the pile, and closed the shed door before returning to her own, uncluttered life.

*

A year after Jaxon was born, Ray had hosted a socially-distanced clinic in Ouray, Colorado for a group of ten aspiring horse trainers looking to fine-tune their approach to starting colts. Most of his students had grown up in the industry: they were the sons and daughters of established ranchers who still used the tried and true methods most people thought about when they heard the phrase "breaking a horse." But in a world that was shifting toward compassion and the ethical treatment of animals, this small group of cowboys and cowgirls were hoping to change the narrative—to go against the teachings they'd been raised on, even if it meant being teased by the older generation for being "too soft."

Little did Ray know at the time that while it seemed easy—even necessary—to break out of the mold his father had set for him, it was nearly impossible to watch his son doing the same. So many of the things Jaxon did made no sense to Ray, from how he talked to his friends to the way he felt about school. There was suddenly a stranger in his house that looked a little bit like him, but who was determined to act like they'd never met. It worried Ray to think about what might happen to the ranch once Jaxon became of age: his generation simply didn't value tradition or hard work the way Ray's or Bernard's had. In fact, the only thing Jaxon seemed to care about at any given moment was whatever was on his phone. Unfortunately, Ray wasn't the only one to notice this.

"You ought to take that thing away from him," Bernard said the morning after Hannah had gone to Fitzgerald Farms to check on Jim. "I've never seen a young person spend so much time staring at a screen. Imagine what it'll do to his brain."

Ray hoisted one of the fenceposts onto his shoulder and carried it over to the section they were currently working on. They'd been out in the north pasture since dawn, taking advantage of the cooler mornings before the sun and higher elevation turned the open plateau into an oven. Jaxon's response to being dragged out of bed so early was to whine, drink too much coffee, and watch videos on his phone until he "woke up a little more." Unlike his sister, who seemed to welcome the fresh air and a chance to get her hands dirty, Jaxon used any excuse he could think of to take a break.

Ray positioned the post in the hole, twisting it back and forth for a better fit. A few sections down, Kyleigh and Josh were unspooling the barbed wire while Jaxon stood off to the side, his thumbs tapping on his phone screen.

"Like I said, it was supposed to be for emergencies only," Ray said once the post was straight. "I can't help it if today's phones are more sophisticated than your average computer. And I also can't do anything about the fact that Jaxon's friends are way cooler than I am. That's just the way it goes."

"You're being too soft on him. Do you think my father would've let me slack off like that?" Bernard threw another hardened glance at his grandson.

Ray avoided looking at Bernard as he said, "I don't think grandpa Dustin would've approved of you taking a twenty-year hiatus from running the ranch, had he been alive to witness it."

"Jesus Christ. You're never going to let that go, are you?"

"What do you think?"

Bernard sighed. If there was one thing every generation had in common, it was the belief that the generation after theirs was doomed. Ray couldn't recall ever being so caught up in the online world that it changed how he behaved in the real one: out in the fields, where very little had actually changed since his great-grandfather had put down roots, nothing seemed more important than being aware of his surroundings. Why would anyone want to be distracted when they had all this natural beauty at their fingertips instead?

The distant thrumming of a helicopter caught Ray's attention. He looked up and saw its bulbous body gliding above the trees that separated their land from their neighbour's.

As it passed overhead, Kyleigh raised her gaze from the fencepost and squinted. "What is that?"

"It's a helicopter," Jaxon deadpanned, "you never seen one before?"

"Of course I have. I'm just wondering why it's flying so low."

"Must've just taken off," Bernard offered, tracking the chopper as it headed toward a tract of public grazing land near the mountains. As his gaze returned to Ray, he said, "That's the second one this month."

Ray nodded. On the spectrum of things that might pose a threat to his family or way of life, the helicopter was somewhere in the middle. He was more concerned about an unattended campfire burning out of control, or some viral trend urging local teenagers to vandalize private property, but two helicopter sightings in one month, especially this far from an airport or base, was certainly noteworthy.

As the helicopter faded to a speck, the group resumed their work. Ray had just planted another post in the ground when a dark green pickup truck appeared on the narrow dirt path that linked the Fishers' property to the one next door. Two winters ago, when the Hoyts' barn roof had collapsed, Waylon's youngest son, Bellamy, had ridden next door seeking Ray's help to rescue the cows trapped inside. Since then, the trail had become a lifeline for both families: a way to shuttle hay, building supplies, and intel between homesteads when the main road was impassable.

The truck came to a stop, the driver's door swung open, and out stepped Waylon Hoyt, a brawny man in his sixties who'd succeeded in being shorter than all four of his sons despite being over six feet tall himself. He wore a grey pinstripe shirt, dark blue jeans, and black snakeskin cowboy boots with pointed toes rather than the more common roper boot, which was as popular for riding horses as it was for working around a ranch. Set in the broad, suntanned face were a pair of almond-shaped eyes and a long, angular nose that had been broken three times: once in a bar fight, and twice during two separate cattle drives. The result was a slightly crooked septum and a handful of stories he loved to rehash in gruesome detail, painting himself as the victor in every retelling.

"Morning, folks," Waylon said as he closed the driver's door.

"Morning, Waylon." Laying the fencepost on the ground, Ray walked over to meet his neighbour. Gradually, the rest of his party came forward until they'd formed a loose circle around their visitor.

Waylon nodded to the tangle of wire in the background. "Putting up a new fence, I see. Didn't realize you'd torn the old one down."

"A lot of it was rotted, so we didn't have much choice. Anyway, what brings you over to our side of the tree line?" Ray asked.

"Well, to tell you the truth, I came over here to warn you."

Ray faltered. "Warn me about what?"

"The helicopters." Waylon pointed his index finger toward the sky. "They're BLM choppers. I called them because when my oldest, Roman, was out checking on the herd the other day, he noticed what appeared to be stray horses out by the old stock tanks. When he got within fifty feet of them, he noticed they had no brands. And they were small, too—not like the horses you normally see around here." He waggled his brows, leaned forward slightly, and in a conspiratorial whisper, told his audience, "He thinks they might've been mustangs."

"Mustangs," Josh repeated with a glance at Ray. "Out here?"

"That's what I mean," Waylon said, visibly annoyed at the interruption. "The BLM has a few herd management areas around

Colorado, but Aspen isn't one of them. So, Roman put in a call to them, and they agreed to come out and deal with the situation."

"Deal with the situation," Ray repeated. "That's a pretty mild way to put it, given the BLM's reputation."

Waylon waved his hand. "Well, they're not saints, but they know how to take care of the land. Their plan is to round up the mustangs and transport them to an off-range facility to be processed at a later date."

"I don't know how the BLM operates these days," Bernard put in, "but when I was in charge of running this place, there was still a stigma around mustangs. A lot of people thought of them as pests, especially local ranchers who relied on public land to graze their herds. Wouldn't surprise me one bit if the BLM is still using the same tactics, but hiding it behind family-friendly language like 'off-range facility.'"

"Do you think there are mustangs on our property, dad?" Jaxon asked. His eyes were wide, enticed by the possibilities.

Ray answered, "I've never seen any, but that doesn't mean much when they're always on the move."

"If you do happen to see them, give the BLM a call. Mustangs aren't good for the environment, and they're no good for business when they're grazing the land down to nothing," Waylon said. He panned his gaze over the meadow again. A spread this size could easily sustain the four hundred head of cattle Ray relied on to keep his family fed and housed, but only if the wild horse population remained in check. In Waylon's opinion, the ideal number of mustangs on a working ranch was a solid zero.

"Anyway," he said after a moment's thought, "I'll let you get back to it. If you ever need a hand around here, give me a holler."

"Thanks, Waylon. And thank you for the heads up about the chopper."

Waylon tipped his hat in a farewell gesture and strode back to his truck. As the vehicle pulled away, Ray's mind shifted back to the fence, rising and falling with the natural undulations of the land. Since the dawn of time, people had been carving out designated areas for livestock and human habitation with little regard for the ecosystems that had preceded their arrival. When his great-grandfather had left West Virginia for better economic opportunities in Colorado, Ray was almost certain he hadn't been thinking about the effect his ranching ambitions would have on the local mustang population. It was called the Wild West for a reason: the further one ventured into the unknown, the bloodier the fight for survival.

"We should get back to work," Ray said, picking up the fencepost he'd laid down earlier.

"But what about the mustangs?" Jaxon asked.

"What about them?"

"We're not just going to let the BLM round them up, right? Like grandpa said—who knows what 'processing' actually involves?"

"I appreciate your concern for the mustangs' welfare, but you're forgetting two very important things. One, the mustangs are on private property, and two, I rely on the BLM for my grazing permits, so you'd do well not to antagonize them or interfere with their operations in any way." Ray raised his brow. "*Capisce?*"

"Yeah. Totally."

Ray smiled to hide his worry. "Good. In that case, I won't hold my breath on a call from Waylon saying he caught you sneaking around his stock tanks."

"No, sir."

"Good," Ray said again, feeling the tension leave his chest and shoulders at last. "Back to work... all of you."

Nine

It was tough to focus when so many things demanded Jaxon's attention. For the past few hours, he'd been flipping back and forth between his phone and his laptop, trying to respond to his friends' messages while simultaneously educating himself on local history. Following Waylon's visit, Jaxon had gone down a rabbit hole of reading about mustangs, the BLM, and the role so many ranchers had played in the decimation of America's wild horse population. And what he'd learned was horrifying.

When Spanish settlers had arrived on the shores of what was now the United States, they'd brought several varieties of European horses with them. Over time, as these domestic horses had either escaped or been released by the colonists, they'd reverted to a feral state and established small herds that proliferated across the country, giving rise to a new breed that was tough enough to survive on the open plains of the Wild West.

Of course, not everyone saw the mustangs as a symbol of freedom. To the men and women who relied on the land to support their ranching practices, the untamed horses were no better than the rats and roaches taking over the cities. Their growing numbers meant a greater need for food, and this strain on the ecosystem was bad for business. Faced with the threat of losing their cattle to starvation, local ranchers had decided to take matters into their own hands and eliminate the problem for good.

Chased off cliffs. Gunned down at a gallop. Rounded up in pens and slaughtered with buckshot. These were just a handful of the ways thousands of mustangs had met their cruel and bloody death. Exhausted, malnourished, and separated from their herds, stragglers were tied to old tires in the scorching sun, where they waited to be collected by rendering trucks. America's wild horse, once a common sight across the new world, was rapidly disappearing from the face of the earth.

Then, in 1971, everything changed with the passage of the Wild Free-Roaming Horses & Burros Act, which granted mustangs federal protection from illegal capture and poaching. The subsequent repopulation efforts became the purview of The Bureau of Land Management, whose primary responsibilities included maintaining the land for public enjoyment, resource extraction, and energy development projects. The mustang population, once teetering on the precipice of extinction, quickly rebounded. All appeared well, until Jaxon got to the part of the article that mentioned the helicopters, the roundups, the off-range facilities. How could a governing body that issued grazing permits to local ranchers also be in charge of looking after the animals that were directly threatened by those operations?

He looked up from his computer as a figure darkened his doorway. Kyleigh smiled tightly, her arms folded across her chest.

"What are you doing?" she asked.

Jaxon's gaze returned to the screen. "Research." He glanced at his phone, picked it up, tapped out a brisk reply, and set it down again.

"May I come in for a minute?"

"Sure."

She crossed the room and took a seat on the wooden desk chair. Now that school was over, the workspace seemed almost barren, with the white board on the wall wiped clean and the handful of textbooks turned in for the year. A chipped coffee mug held a handful of writing instruments, most of which were still full of ink. Kyleigh reached for a ballpoint pen and uncapped it, prompting Jaxon to look up from his laptop.

"I wasn't expecting your room to be so neat," she admitted as she put the pen back. "This place is practically sterile."

"Just because I'm a guy doesn't mean I live in a dumpster. Besides, my mom's got a system for everything."

"So I noticed."

"Is there a reason why you came in here?" Jaxon asked. Another bubble popped up on his phone—not a message from his best friend, Bodhi, but a YouTube notification from a channel he'd been subscribed to for years. Jaxon swiped it away, then scrolled down the page he was reading on his computer until he came across a picture of a herd of mustangs grazing peacefully beneath a cloud-dabbed sky.

"Actually, yes. I was hoping you could tell me more about Ray."

"What do you want to know?"

Kyleigh stood and pulled her phone out of her back pocket. On the screen was a picture of Ray, sitting on the bench swing outside their house and looking at something slightly above the camera. Dressed in beige cargo shorts and a white t-shirt, his prosthetic leg was clearly visible, and so was the look of discomfort on his face at having been posed in such a vulnerable manner.

"When I Googled the Bionic Cowboy Tour, this was the first image that came up," she said, turning her phone so Jaxon could see the screen.

"You know you can just click on the picture and it'll take you straight to the article."

"I don't want to read the article. I want *you* to tell me exactly what I missed."

He sighed. "Fine."

Kyleigh sat down in the chair once again, eager to hear the full story.

"When my dad was a little kid, grandpa walked out on the family," Jaxon began. "He was gone for about twenty years. Then one day, my dad found him camping in the woods on our property. It was in this remote place in the mountains and dad thought he could talk him into coming home, but along the way he fell off his horse and hurt his leg. He was missing for three days. Eventually, a canine search-and-rescue team found him and took him to the hospital."

"I'm guessing he was in pretty bad shape."

Jaxon nodded. "He got really sick from the infection in his leg. The doctors tried to save the limb, but in the end, they had to amputate it in

70

order to save his life. My mom said my dad was off work for over a year. It was hard for him, mentally and physically, but eventually he started hosting horse training clinics again. Rather than act like the accident hadn't happened, he rebranded himself as the Bionic Cowboy and went on tour across the country. For about three months, it was just me and my mom living here. And my grandpa."

"Wait. You're telling me that after he abandoned his family and essentially caused your dad to become an amputee, you guys let Bernard stick around?"

"Yeah. My Uncle Marc was pissed about it, but mom convinced him that people deserve a second chance." Jaxon shrugged. "I don't really like to talk about what happened to my dad, and he doesn't like to talk about it either. That picture of him on the porch was taken a few weeks after he came home, I think, but you could always ask him."

Kyleigh made a mental note to do just that. It seemed strange that in all the messages she'd exchanged with Hannah, Ray's accident hadn't come up even once. Then again, how much did Hannah and Ray really know about *her*?

That was a question for another day, Kyleigh decided. Jaxon had gone back to staring at his computer, so she asked, "What are you researching?"

"How to deal with my older sister dropping in unannounced."

"Ha. Very funny."

A smirk flickered across his face. "I'm reading about the BLM." He turned the laptop toward her. "Basically, their job is to look after the mustangs, but according to this article, they've come under fire for some pretty questionable herd management tactics."

Kyleigh leaned forward to get a closer look at the image he'd presented her with. "Are those the same mustangs that dude in the pointy boots was talking about?"

"I don't think they were from this herd specifically. I found a few other articles too, including one in which the BLM was accused of causing injury to a couple of mustangs during a roundup. The main way they gather the herds is by helicopter. All the noise and chaos basically sends them into a blind panic, causing a stampede."

"That doesn't sound very humane."

"It's not. There are more ethical ways of curbing overpopulation, but I guess the helicopters get the job done faster." Jaxon clicked off the article and pulled up another. "Wild horses have been known to travel for miles in search of fresh water. That's why their hooves are so tough. But they're not made to be chased all over the state for the sake of human convenience. The writer of this article talked about visiting one of those off-range facilities Waylon mentioned and seeing that several of the mustangs' hooves had been worn down to the bone. Imagine working on the fences without gloves—that's essentially what's happening here. Those guys in the helicopters are literally running the mustangs off their feet."

Jaxon looked up at Kyleigh, whose face was almost totally devoid of emotion. Why wasn't she angrier about this? Even Ray, who'd built his reputation around rescuing slaughter-bound horses and transforming them into willing, trainable partners, had seemed unperturbed by Waylon's visit when he should have been seething at the implications instead.

Jaxon added, "There's another article, but I can't stand to look at the pictures. There's one where this foal has a broken leg—"

"Thanks, but I've heard enough. To tell you the truth, I'm still trying to process the fact that my biological father went missing for three days and lost his leg to an infection. I know I'm not really part of the family, but it would've been nice if someone had filled me in."

"I don't get it. Why do you care so much about our family all of a sudden?"

"Because I do. Why do *you* care what the BLM does to a bunch of wild horses?"

"Because," Jaxon replied testily, "what they're doing is wrong, and if we don't talk about these things, then they're just going to keep happening."

His phone buzzed again, this time with a message from Bodhi asking him if he'd seen the latest *Nuked* video where the channel's hosts, Cory and Rory, attempted to blow up a watermelon using a pair of jumper cables. In just three years, they'd gone from conducting experiments in their parents' garage to collaborating with big-name YouTubers, selling merchandise, and landing sponsorship deals with major brands. What started out as a mostly educational platform had quickly transformed into an endless stream of increasingly absurd stunts. It was the kind of content that was sure to get hits, and that people like Bodhi, an amateur bull rider, were guaranteed to be drawn to. When it came to things like wacky science experiments and riding dangerous animals, the more unpredictable the outcome, the better.

Kyleigh's expression softened. "I hate to tell you this, but people don't want to talk about that sort of stuff. They want to hear the latest celebrity gossip and who won the hockey game—stuff that makes them forget about their miserable lives."

"I know."

Kyleigh stood up, her mind still reeling with questions as she headed downstairs. Out of habit, Jaxon clicked on the YouTube link from Bodhi. Cory and Rory appeared, dressed in lab coats and safety goggles. Cory, the shorter of the two, gave the audience a rundown of what they were about to see, just like he did at the start of every video. Rory explained their watermelon-and-jumper-cables-setup while cheery banjo music played in the background. The longer Jaxon watched, the more frustrated he became with both the over-the-top special effects and his own inability to look away.

Then the countdown began, with Cory manning the detonator and Rory, crouched down behind a sheet of plywood for safety, flashing the cameraman an enthusiastic thumbs-up. *Five, four, three, two, one…*

As the watermelon exploded in a bright pink mist, Jaxon once again glanced at his laptop. The black-and-white image showing dozens of culled mustangs sickened and enraged him. It was like some people had been born with their finger on a detonator, and all it took was an audience for them to do their worst.

He received another message from Bodhi: *Did you watch it?*

Jaxon: *Yeah.*

Bodhi: *Sydney and I are getting together with a few people this Saturday. You should come.*

Jaxon considered Bodhi's offer. It was no secret that Bodhi's girlfriend, Sydney, had all the right connections, mainly thanks to her dad owning several chalets in town. Among them was the Mountain Jewel, which featured an eight-person hot tub, vaulted ceilings, and palatial windows offering panoramic views of Aspen's most famous ski hills. As a rising star in the world of professional rodeo, Bodhi also had a fair number of connections and a rapidly growing online fanbase to boot. At a time when it seemed like everyone had a platform, it irked Jaxon that neither of his friends had bothered to raise awareness about the things that truly mattered, like eliminating poverty or saving wild horses.

He typed out his reply: *I would, but my dad's making me work for him all summer and doesn't want me making plans.*

Bodhi: *ALL summer?*

Jaxon: *Yup. Fences.* He added: *Our neighbor came by today. He said his son saw a few mustangs on his property.*

Bodhi: *I didn't think there were any mustangs around here.*

Jaxon: *Me neither. The BLM currently has four herd management areas in Colorado, but they're mostly on the western slope.*

Bodhi: *Weird. Maybe they were domestic horses that escaped from a local ranch?*

Jaxon: *I doubt it, if the BLM is involved. But if the BLM is involved, it could mean trouble.*

Rather than explain himself, Jaxon pulled up the article he'd been reading, copied the link, and pasted it directly into their conversation. Bodhi wasn't much of a reader—his information diet consisted largely of TikTok videos, Reddit feeds, and whatever distorted truths Sydney whispered in his ear—but like Jaxon, he'd grown up around horses and was more than qualified to opine on the BLM's hypocrisy.

For several moments, Bodhi didn't reply. While he waited, Jaxon continued to Google any articles or news stories involving the wild horses. Of course, the best way to learn the truth was to witness a roundup for himself. They'd lived next door to the Hoyts for as long as Jaxon could remember. Surely, Mr. Hoyt wouldn't mind if he dropped by, would he?

At last, Bodhi said: *Sydney's dad can get us tickets to VidCon next year. Nuked will be there. Wanna go?*

Jaxon: *Did you even read the article I sent you?*

Bodhi: *I bookmarked it.*

Jaxon: *Mustangs are literally dying, and all you can think about is a couple of overpaid YouTubers?*

Bodhi: *That's not ALL I think about. There's Sydney too…*

Jaxon: *You're just proving my point.*

Bodhi: *And bull riding.*

Jaxon: *This is serious stuff.*

Bodhi: *If it were serious, don't you think more people would know about it? Seems kinda niche if you ask me.*

Jaxon snorted in disbelief. The problem wasn't that the information wasn't out there—it was that people were being constantly distracted by online influencers and big-name accounts like *Nuked*, who, ironically, were blowing up the Internet in all the wrong ways.

Jaxon: *I should go help my dad.*

Bodhi: *Cool. Let me know if you plan on gracing us with your presence on Saturday.*

Jaxon turned back to his research. He told himself that, in a way, he *was* helping Ray. The more he knew about the animals that lived around the ranch, the better prepared he'd be to take over its operation.

Ten

Hannah had always considered herself a strong, independent woman, especially after Ray's accident had forced her to take over the ranch's daily operation. In the months after he'd lost his leg, she'd not only been responsible for looking after the livestock and paying the bills, but had also found herself playing the role of family therapist: urging Ray to talk through his feelings about Bernard's abandonment, encouraging Bernard to face his fear of rejection, and helping his adult children navigate the unfamiliar landscape of reconciliation. Hannah had even managed to get through to Marcus about his drinking problem: for years, he'd struggled quietly with his addiction, masking his alcohol dependency with a free-spirited personality that made him the life of any party. He, in turn, had helped her to make peace with the past, instead of letting it tear her apart.

It was the kind of work Hannah had pictured herself making a career out of some day. If things had turned out a little differently, perhaps she would've had her own practice and the privilege of being called 'Doctor.' In an alternate universe where everything went exactly as planned, she imagined herself sitting in an office somewhere, her patient seated on the sofa across from her, a box of tissues positioned between them. By the time the hour was up, Hannah would feel like she'd done some good— taken someone's knot of despair and woven it into a blanket of hope.

But of course, that was just a fantasy. The reality was, she'd chosen Ray. She'd chosen early mornings and four hundred head of cattle. She'd chosen to break young horses instead of the glass ceiling, and she'd done it with a smile on her face because she knew that this lifestyle, though unforgiving at times, had given her a different kind of purpose.

At four A.M., Hannah got out of bed, dressed in a pair of old jeans and a sweater, and headed down to the kitchen to start the coffee. The other members of the household followed one by one. First came Ray, still fastening the cufflinks of his shirt as he came downstairs. He poured himself a cup of coffee and put two slices of bread in the toaster as the smell of breakfast filled the room.

"How'd you sleep?" Hannah asked as she stirred scrambled eggs.

"Well enough." Ray's expression was troubled as he turned to her. "I'm thinking of sending Josh into town to pick up the dewormer I ordered. I'd do it myself, but someone needs to oversee the fences and keep Jaxon in line."

"Why are you worried about Jaxon?"

"Because he's always on his phone."

"He's sixteen."

"Exactly. When I was sixteen, I wasn't always on my phone. I was working—" As two blackened slices of toast popped out of the ancient appliance, he stacked them on a plate and smeared peanut butter on each one. "I had no other choice."

As Hannah divvied up the eggs, she said, "Correct me if I'm wrong, but before Jaxon was born you and I agreed that we wanted our future children to have options, whether that was going to college, entering the workforce, or a combination of the two. But the way you're talking makes it seem like you resent Jaxon for not being more like you."

"I don't resent him. I'm glad he has it better than I did at his age. All I'm saying is, maybe getting him a phone was a mistake." Ray held out his plate so Hannah could scrape some eggs onto the side. "Thank you."

"You're welcome." As he carried the plate and his coffee over to the table and took a seat, Hannah posited, "You know, you and Bernard spend a lot of time together."

"Well, he has a lot to make up for," Ray said, biting into one of the toast slices.

"And he's not exactly accustomed to the conveniences of modern life," Hannah went on.

"What can I say? You can take the man out of the wilderness, but you can't take the wilderness out of the man."

"My point is, you never took issue with Jaxon having a cell phone until you and Bernard started working on the fences, which leads me to believe your father's gotten into your head again."

Ray nodded, looking resigned. "He always does. Even when he was out of my life for twenty years, he was always at the back of my mind— sometimes it was comforting, and other times it drove me crazy. Now, I have kids, and he thinks he's some kind of expert on how to raise them." He finished the first piece of toast and started in on the second. "He should stick to what he knows best, which is training horses."

Hannah glanced toward the stairs. To her surprise, Jaxon was already awake, dressed, and apparently ready to take on the day. He cut a beeline to the front door, then paused and stepped into the kitchen, his expectant gaze going straight to Ray.

"Hey, dad, can I borrow the Chevy this morning?" he asked.

"Why do you need the Chevy?"

"I have an errand to run. I won't be long."

Ray picked up his fork, loaded it with a generous bite of eggs, and told his son, "Sorry, bud, but no. Josh is going to need the Chevy to go pick up dewormer."

"He can't take his bike?"

"His bike isn't practical. Besides, how is he going to bring back ten bags of feed on the back of the Ducati?"

Hannah watched as Jaxon's paper-thin veneer of politeness began to deteriorate. He wasn't usually manipulative, but in this moment his demeanor was unrecognizable. Could Bernard actually have been right about something—were Jaxon's unpredictable moods the result of prolonged cell phone use, or just another growing pain they'd have to overcome?

"Well, then, maybe you should've hired someone with a truck," he spat out.

Ray looked up at him, his features hardening. "This is my ranch, and I will hire whoever I want, for whatever reasons I deem valid."

"If it's 'your' ranch, then I guess the fences are 'your' responsibility."

"Jaxon," Hannah snapped.

"What? All I'm saying is that it's a little unfair how dad expects me to work for him, but he doesn't take any of my feelings into consideration."

"And what feelings would those be?" Ray asked.

"You give Josh special treatment. And Kyle, too. Her, I get, because she's never worked on a ranch before and doesn't know what she's doing. But the only reason you're helping Josh is because you feel sorry that his dad died."

"Yes, I do feel sorry about his dad's passing. In case you've forgotten, his dad was a friend of mine. He's the one who convinced me to put myself out there and start hosting clinics, so that maybe you, me, and your mom could have a better life." Ray held Jaxon's gaze. "I'm helping Josh because I understand how hard it is to not have a father. But you *do* have a father, and while I may not be perfect, I do want the best for you. So no, you can't borrow the Chevy—not until you learn to appreciate this ranch and everything your mom and I have done to keep it running."

Jaxon shook his head. Admittedly, he hadn't thought his plan all the way through, but how hard could it be to find a herd of mustangs? If he could figure out where they were hiding, he could study their dynamics and hopefully raise awareness about the dangers they faced. Of course, all of this required having access to a vehicle—and he wasn't talking about the helicopters that had been circling their property for days.

As he threw open the door and stepped outside, the windchime's fluty notes drifted through the entryway. Hannah closed the door behind him and faced her husband, staring down at his plate with palpable disappointment.

"He's sixteen," she said again, gently, "he's just going through a phase."

"I'd like to believe that, but another part of me says there's more here than meets the eye. I mean, he's always been a good kid."

"You're right—and good kids have a way of being grounded." Hannah approached the table, picked up Ray's empty plate and mug, and placed both in the sink. "Whatever's bothering Jaxon, it won't last forever."

"I hope you're right." Ray stood up. As he made his way over to the door, footsteps sounded on the stairs again and Kyleigh appeared wearing a long-sleeved grey shirt and dark blue jeans—the closest her wardrobe came to being "ranch appropriate."

"Morning," she greeted, flicking her eyes between Ray and Hannah. "I smell coffee."

"Help yourself. There are eggs, too," Hannah said.

Kyleigh took down a mug from one of the cupboards. Like Hannah, she'd been up since four A.M. as well, but rather than heading downstairs immediately, Kyleigh had sat cross-legged on her bed and typed out an overdue update to Samantha and Terry. In it, she described some of the work she'd been doing around the ranch, her daily routine, and a few pertinent details about Hannah and Ray, but chose to leave out what she'd learned the night before about the Bionic Cowboy Tour. For reasons she didn't quite understand yet, this was something she wanted to keep to herself, at least until she'd gotten all the answers she needed.

"What's the plan for today?" Kyleigh asked, accepting the serving of eggs Hannah piled onto her plate.

Ray replied, "Same as always: barn chores, then fences, then everything else."

Kyleigh nodded and tucked into the eggs: hot, fluffy, and perfect for a chilly mountain morning. And yet, as she watched Ray don his hat and boots in the doorway, Kyleigh felt her appetite fade away. She'd been hoping to speak to Hannah alone, and now that it was just the two of them, all the words Kyleigh wanted to say got jumbled in her mouth like alphabet soup. She took another bite of her breakfast and washed it down with some coffee as Hannah busied herself at the kitchen sink.

"So, this is what Ray makes you do while he's down at the barn," Kyleigh began.

"Ray doesn't *make* me do anything. When you're married and you live in a place like this, you have to work together in order to keep things running smoothly." Hannah faced her daughter. "May I ask you something?"

"Sure."

"What made you want to come here?"

Kyleigh stared at her, unsure whether to feel surprised or offended. "I wanted to know where I come from. Is that so wrong?"

"Where you come from," Hannah repeated, turning the words over on her tongue. She furrowed her brows. "Technically, you're from Kamloops, BC—my hometown."

"That's what Terry said. I'm not talking about where I was born. I'm talking about…" Kyleigh searched Hannah's face, the small wrinkles at the corners of her mouth dancing as she chewed her bottom lip. "I don't know. I guess I've always wondered who I could've been, if I hadn't ended up in Toronto."

"I see." Hannah turned back to the sink, soggy toast crumbs and spongy remnants of egg swirling in the brackish water. She scooped up a handful of cutlery, then raised her gaze to the window. "Do you blame me?"

"Blame you?"

"I'm the one who put you up for adoption. Ray wanted to keep you, but I was convinced we were too young to be parents. I didn't want to give up my career." How ironic, Hannah thought, that she ended up doing precisely that. "I'm the reason you ended up in Toronto."

For a time, Kyleigh was quiet. Hannah watched Kyleigh's reflection in the glass as she cupped her hands around her coffee and gnawed on her bottom lip.

"Yes," Kyleigh whispered at last.

"In that case, I'm sorry."

"No, don't be. I mean, it used to bother me when I was younger, knowing I had another set of parents somewhere who wanted nothing to do with me. But now that I'm older, I realize people don't always behave the way you want them to."

"I've had to accept the same truth about Ray. I can't change him, no matter how much I want to some days."

"Speaking of Ray, Jaxon told me about the Bionic Cowboy Tour."

"What did he tell you, exactly?"

"He told me about how Ray lost his leg, and that he was on the road for a few months hosting his clinics." Kyleigh could feel her anger clearly now, like the bladed edge of a shard of broken glass. She cupped her hand gently around this emotion, trying to acknowledge its existence without letting the worst of it cut her to pieces. "You never told me any of this. Not once in all those conversations we had on Facebook or WhatsApp did Ray's amputation ever come up. I had to learn about his accident from my younger brother. Don't you think that's a little messed up?"

"It's not an easy thing to slip into casual conversation," Hannah said with a short laugh. "Don't you think it's a little hard for me to talk about it?"

"Still. You had plenty of opportunities."

"So did you, but you never asked," Hannah sighed and gestured to the dirty dishes. "I should get back to work here. Why don't you go find Ray? I'm sure he could use a hand out at the barn."

Kyleigh stood up and carried her mug and plate over to the sink.

"Women always have to choose," Hannah said, causing Kyleigh to shoot her a look of confusion. "That's what my mother used to say to me. She said even in the twenty-first century, women still have to choose between career and family. I always imagined I'd have a successful career as a family psychologist, but in the end, I chose Ray."

"Do you ever wish you'd chosen differently?"

"Sometimes," Hannah admitted in a small voice, "but if I'd chosen another path, I wouldn't have had Jaxon or this place. Happiness is about gratitude, not getting everything you want all the time."

Kyleigh didn't know what to say to this. Instead, she crossed to the front door, slipped on her boots, and stepped onto the veranda just as a whirring sputter broke through the susurrus of the trees.

Josh steered his bike toward the shed and cut the Ducati's engine, removed his helmet, and swung his right leg over the seat. Peeling off his leather jacket, he hung it on a nail just inside the shed door and began rolling up the sleeves of his red plaid shirt before greeting her with a nod.

"Morning," he said.

"Morning. Ray's at the barn." As Josh started in on his other sleeve, she asked, "This is going to sound like a strange question, but were your parents happy together?"

Josh shrugged, the plaid tightening on his elbow as he surveyed the paddocks in their vicinity. "Happy enough. Granted, my dad wasn't around that much when I was a kid, but they made it work. I guess that's all most people can hope for, right?"

"I don't know. Settling for functional instead of happy seems kind of sad."

"I agree. If I ever get married, I want it to be the best thing I've ever done. That way, I can set an example for my kids and grandkids to follow."

"You want a family?"

"I always have. What about you?"

"I think I'd like to get married one day, but I'm still on the fence about having kids."

"Well," Josh said, a sunny smile spreading across his face as Ray approached them. "At least you have the freedom to choose, right?"

Kyleigh nodded, thinking about her conversation with Hannah from a few minutes ago. *Women always have to choose.* And what if she chose wrong? As Ray filled Josh in on the day's agenda, Kyleigh wandered down to the paddock, where a brown-and-white gelding stood with his head over the top rail. She smoothed a hand down the horse's neck, the warm velvet of his coat calming her worries.

She heard Ray say to Josh, "You can take the Chevy that's in the shed. Keys are on the rearview. Bernard and I will be in the field when you come back." Sending Josh on his way, Ray turned and made his way over to the paddock.

"I heard you get up early this morning," he said.

"This is a working ranch, isn't it?" Kyleigh replied.

He chuckled. "If only Jaxon understood that too."

"Where is he? I haven't seen him since I got up."

"He's putting down hay for the horses." Ray indicated the barn. The door to the loft stood open, allowing Kyleigh to see Jaxon tossing bales of forage down through the ceiling hatch. "Fair warning: he's in a bit of a mood this morning. I told him he couldn't borrow the truck, and he got mad and stormed out."

"Why does he want to borrow the truck?"

"Apparently, he has an errand to run." Ray shrugged. "He's sixteen. He doesn't need a good reason to hate me."

"Why would he hate you?" Kyleigh asked as she fell into step with Ray, their shadows overlapping on the ground as they made their way into the barn. Another bale plummeted down from the ceiling, bounced off the pile on the floor, and landed against the side of one of the stalls. Ray wrapped his hands around the twine and lifted, the pendulous weight of the hay pulling at his forearms and shoulders.

"Maybe hate wasn't the right word," he replied, carrying the bale to an empty stall at the end of the aisle. As Kyleigh came to stand in the doorway, he turned to her again, and for a moment he wondered what she'd been like at sixteen—if she'd given Samantha and Terry as much trouble as Jaxon gave him. "He's a teenager. He thinks I give him too much responsibility and not enough freedom. And I *do* expect him to take responsibility for things, but only because that's what was expected of me at his age."

"What were you like at sixteen?" Kyleigh asked as Ray exited the stall to retrieve another bale.

"Average, I suspect. I had a driver's license and hung out with my friends when I wasn't working."

"What about your home life? Your family?"

He bent down to pick up another bale. "Ours looked a little different than most, as I'm sure you're already aware."

Kyleigh nodded. "Why did Bernard leave?"

Ray carried on with his task, ferrying bale after bale to the vacant stall without comment. Not only did stashing the hay at the horses' level save him a trip up to the loft, but it also provided an extra layer of insulation on those chilly nights when the doors alone couldn't keep the wind out. He'd seen a lot of chilly nights in his lifetime: after Bernard had left, there'd been countless times when Ray and his brothers had been forced to sleep in front of the fireplace because they couldn't afford the heating bill that month. Now, as an adult, Ray couldn't imagine leaving Hannah and Jaxon in such an uncomfortable position.

"If I had to guess, I'd say it was because he was afraid. He didn't know how to run this place without your grandmother, who took her own life when I was very young." Ray looked at Kyleigh, surprised when she stiffened at his words. If there was one thing he did know about his daughter, it was that nothing seemed to faze her. She wasn't indifferent, exactly, but guarded with her emotions like Victor tended to be. "Bernard knows what he did was wrong—that's why he stayed after Jaxon was born. But it doesn't magically fix the damage he caused when I was a kid." Ray's expression softened. "I'm not sure if I'll ever fully forgive him. Or myself."

"Because of your accident, you mean."

He glanced down at his right leg, his prosthesis hidden from view beneath his jeans.

"I know how you lost your leg," Kyleigh said, uncrossing her arms and tucking her hands in her back pockets. "What I don't understand is why no one told *me*."

"The fact that you were eight years old when this happened might've had something to do with it," Ray admitted. "I guess there was never a good time to bring it up. I mean, we didn't know until just a few days prior to your arrival that you were even planning to come for a visit. Hannah and I had agreed that we would interfere with your life as little as possible, and if you decided that you wanted to communicate with us, we'd reciprocate in kind. But the way you're saying it makes it sound like we conspired to keep family secrets from you, which couldn't be further from the truth."

"Still, you could've reached out. So, why didn't you?"

"It's not that I didn't want to—"

"You were scared."

"Yeah, I guess I was."

"Why?"

"Because I've made a lot of mistakes in my life and I didn't want you to think less of me. You may be my daughter biologically, but Terry's your dad, and I'd never want to get between you two." Ray spread his arms. "I'm sorry if you feel like I've abandoned you in some way. Or that I let you down."

Kyleigh stared right into those eyes that were the same shade as hers, and willed him to see what he'd been missing. Maybe a traditional adoption would've been better: Hannah and Ray could've closed that door and been done with it altogether instead of orbiting her life at a distance that made seeing anything clearly impossible. But did she feel abandoned, as Ray obviously did with Bernard?

Jaxon climbed down the ladder, his boots scuffing the wooden rungs. Picking a stitch of hay off his shirt, he walked straight past Ray and Kyleigh, sidestepping the mountain of hay on his way out of the barn.

"Where do you think you're going?" Ray asked.

Jaxon turned back to him with a scowl.

Ray indicated the hay bales. "This all needs to be put away."

"You told me to bring the hay down from the loft. You didn't say anything about putting it away."

"The second part was implied."

Jaxon flicked his eyes at Kyleigh. The rule around here was that everyone was expected to pitch in—and yet, she seemed to be the exception. Frankly, it pissed him off.

As Ray approached him, Jaxon retreated. He stalked up the laneway to the house, determined to put some distance between himself and Ray.

"Hey," Ray snapped, "don't walk away from me."

"Why? Does it trigger you?" Jaxon stopped and faced him. Even under his cowboy hat, Ray's face was an ornery shade of red.

Ray cocked a finger at him in warning. "I don't like your tone."

"Well, I don't like your double standard," Jaxon bit back. He waved a hand at the barn. "Why doesn't *she* have to do anything? Is it because she's a girl?"

"Kyle helps when she can. I'm not going to force her to do anything because it's not her job."

"What about Josh? He's only been here for a few days and you let him drive the Chevy."

"I let you drive the Chevy all the time," Ray argued, his brows pulling together. "Is that what this is about? You're mad because I wouldn't let you take the truck?"

"It's about a lot of things. Not that you ever ask."

Ray shook his head. "What's that supposed to mean?"

"Forget it," Jaxon said, sticking his hands in his pockets as he turned away, "you wouldn't understand."

"You're not done with the hay yet," Ray said, but Jaxon just kept walking. "Jaxon!"

Stepping out from the shade of the barn, Kyleigh walked over to where Ray stood as her brother disappeared into the house, slamming the door hard enough to be heard across the yard. "I'll help with the hay," she said.

He sighed, looking down at her, then back at the house. "I know you will." Ray led the way back to the barn. "You'll want to wear gloves for this. And since it looks like we're going to be here a while, maybe now's a good time for us to catch up on some things."

*

It took Josh forty-five minutes to locate the feed store, a sprawling green building with a pitched metal roof and a pair of rain barrels to mark the entrance. The sign above the door said *Lloyd and Sons Ltd.* in plain white lettering, with a slightly smaller line of text beneath it that read *Livestock and Farming Supplies*. Several pickup trucks were parked outside: most of them were newer-model Tundras, Rangers, and aptly-named Super Duties that were built for hauling trailers or stacking forty bales of hay in the bed. Josh steered the Chevy into a space, removed the keys from the ignition, and got out of the truck.

Josh stepped through the dusty glass door and headed toward the counter on his left. The bespectacled clerk manning the register wore a plaid shirt, black jeans, and a broad silver belt buckle depicting a Texas Longhorn. A pall of thick, white hair covered the shopkeeper's head, but his sharp chin and chiseled nose seemed better suited to a man half his age. He lifted his gaze as Josh approached and pulled a slip of paper from his back pocket.

"Hi, there. I'm picking up an order," Josh said, unfolding the page and laying it on the counter.

Furrowing his brows, the man picked up the receipt and skimmed it quickly. "Ah, yes. We got the Ivermectin in yesterday. Now, where did I put it…?"

He scanned the space behind the counter. After a little rummaging, he uncovered a cardboard box with its flaps torn open. Inside were a dozen doses of apple-flavoured equine dewormer, which Ray had ordered last week to prevent a parasitic outbreak in his herd. The clerk slid the medication across the counter before turning toward a door behind the register, which Josh could see led to a storeroom of some sort. "I've never seen you around here before. You new in town?"

"Kind of. I'm really just here for the summer."

"Gareth!" the clerk called, his voice ringing out across the adjacent warehouse. "You got that order ready for Ray Fisher?"

Josh glanced around at his surroundings as the clerk and Gareth exchanged words. Several clothing racks in the middle of the floor displayed plaid shirts, shearling jackets, and oilskins in a variety of sizes and styles. Brand-new Levi's and crisp, blue Wranglers sat neatly folded on a series of shelves along the backwall, directly beneath a row of ball caps ranging from plain black to flamingo pink. And that was just the part of the store Josh could see. Beyond this bounty of outerwear and branded apparel was a seemingly endless assortment of farm and ranch supplies that included everything from lead ropes to calving chains, all of it organized by function and stickered with small green price tags. Josh turned back to the counter as the clerk emerged from the store room and nodded perfunctorily.

"Here's your receipt," he said as he handed it back. "Now, you just drive your truck around back and the boys will load up the feed for you."

"Thanks." Josh turned to leave, but before he could take a step toward the exit, a man approached the counter and clapped a hand on his shoulder.

"I know you," the stranger said cheerfully.

A spark of recognition lit up Josh's face. "Waylon, right?"

"You've got a good memory. So, Ray's got you running errands for him, I see." Waylon nodded at the Ivermectin. "We had a bad bout of ringworm in our herd last year. But Ray always stays on top of these things."

"Sure seems like he knows what he's doing," Josh agreed.

"He does. Good guy, too. How'd you meet each other?"

"He used to be friends with my dad, Mickey Hammond." Josh braced himself for Waylon's reaction. In the state of Montana, where it seemed like every other person he met was a cowboy or a ranch hand or a rodeo clown, Josh had found that most people's opinion of his dad fell one of two ways: admiration or disgust, and both sides were all too willing to argue why the other was wrong.

Waylon cocked a brow. "Hammond? Doesn't ring a bell, I'm afraid." Josh let out a breath as Ray's neighbour engaged the clerk in conversation. "You got any more flax bedding, Marty?"

"I'll go have a look," Marty said, and disappeared into the storeroom to call upon Gareth once more.

"Anyway, you can tell Ray I said hi," Waylon said, bracing his hands on the counter as Josh lingered halfway between the door and a spinner rack bursting with brochures. "If he needs a hand with the fences, my offer stands."

"Will do. By the way, how's it going with the mustangs?"

"The mustangs? Oh, right." Waylon waved his hand. "They're taken care of—the BLM was able to round them up and move them to the Biffman Stockyard. One less thing to worry about if you ask me."

As he said this, Marty sauntered up to the till and asked Waylon, "How many bales do you need?"

"I'll take whatever you got," Waylon replied, and slapped his credit card down on the scratched-up counter separating salesman from customer.

Josh tucked the box under his arm and shouldered through the door. Placing the Ivermectin on the Chevy's passenger seat, he climbed behind the wheel and drove around the far side of the parking lot. There, he located a wide door that opened onto a warehouse, which was stacked to the rafters with everything from chicken feed to shrink-wrapped bales of pine shavings. Several men in t-shirts and steel toe boots wandered amid the pallets of ruminant supplements, filling orders for local ranchers. As Josh backed the Chevy up to the door, a man he presumed to be Gareth walked up to the truck and lowered the tailgate, then proceeded to toss in the forage as if each bag weighed no more than a pack of cigarettes.

"You need a hand?" Josh offered as he got out.

Gareth hoisted the last bag of roughage onto his shoulder and scowled. "Nope. I got two that work just fine, thanks." As the paper sack landed in the Chevy's bed, he closed the tailgate, brushed his perfectly-capable hands together, and retreated to his shadowy labyrinth of fodder once again.

Josh continued to stand there, feeling useless as the warehouse door closed and the sound of traffic came rushing back into his ears. This wasn't the first time he'd questioned whether he was in the right place, but it was too late to do anything about it now. Ray was counting on him to do whatever was asked, no matter how trivial the task might've been.

He ducked behind the wheel, put the Chevy in gear, and circled around to the exit. The road back to the ranch was a winding line that led up through the mountains into the high country, and as he drove, he allowed himself to believe he was going home.

Eleven

Later that evening, after the Chevy had been unloaded and another hundred feet of barbed wire strung along the pasture's east side, Josh sat down to his first homecooked meal in nearly two weeks. Up until now, he'd been surviving on a diet of McDonald's cheeseburgers, microwave lasagna, and soggy egg salad sandwiches from the gas station near his Airbnb. He was sick of living like a college kid, couch-surfing his way through his twenties while the rest of his friends celebrated engagements and promotions. At least for tonight, he could forget about his failings and surround himself with people who didn't care about his past.

"It all looks so good," he enthused, taking a seat across from Kyleigh at the patio table. They were having meatloaf tonight, its top crust thick and steaming. Mashed potatoes, steamed green beans, and a party-sized Caesar salad from Costco rounded out the meal, leaving just enough room on the table for plates, cutlery, and the leftover floral-print napkins from Easter.

Hannah smiled and set the butter dish on the pebbled glass tabletop. "I'm glad you could join us. The more, the merrier, as Laney used to say."

"Laney was my late wife's best friend," Bernard explained as Josh glanced over at him. "After Ray's mother passed away, Laney helped me take care of the kids. The woman was a force to be reckoned with—and her artichoke dip was divine."

Hannah smiled tightly. Bernard wasn't exaggerating about the artichoke dip, but now wasn't the time to set the record straight about the extent of Laney's involvement in Ray's upbringing.

Just then, Ray strode through the patio door carrying two beer bottles in each hand. He passed one to Josh, another to Bernard, and offered the third to Kyleigh before setting the fourth bottle down next to his plate and prying off the metal cap. "What are we talking about?" he asked.

"Laney," Jaxon answered without looking up from his phone.

"Wasn't she your godmother?" Kyleigh asked Ray.

"She was," he replied, meeting Bernard's gaze. "Laney and her husband, Jim, became our legal guardians when I was eight years old. They basically raised me and my two older brothers."

Kyleigh's focus drifted back over to her grandfather, whose face had turned noticeably pinker at this new information. "I thought you said she helped you," she recalled, narrowing her eyes.

"She did," Bernard answered awkwardly. He reached for his beer and looked back at his son. "More than I could've ever imagined."

Jaxon turned his phone over and nodded at the bottle in Ray's hand. "Can I have a beer too, dad?"

Ray's expression hardened. "Are you kidding me?"

"What? At least I asked you first."

"Ask me again in five years." Ray shook his head, which was heavy with exhaustion and throbbing from prolonged exposure to the sun.

Hannah sat down beside him and surveyed the faces gathered around the table. Laney had had a knack for bringing people together in ways that made them forget about their differences, but now that she was gone, all that was left to show for her legacy was a house that reeked of whiskey and a grieving widower who shunned any form of human contact. As the food made its rounds, Hannah made a mental note to talk to Ray about the next steps in managing Jim's estate.

"I hope Marty didn't give you any trouble today," Ray said after several minutes. He pricked a crouton with his fork and added, "He can be a bit cold toward outsiders."

"He was fine. It was Gareth I had to worry about," Josh replied.

Ray nodded understandingly.

"By the way," Josh said, carving a hunk of meatloaf with his fork, "I ran into Waylon."

At this, Jaxon perked up. "You mean, from next door?"

"Yes."

"What did he say?"

"Nothing, really." Josh shrugged. "We only talked for a few minutes. I told him about my dad. He bought some bedding and I went on my way." He brought his fork to his mouth and eagerly took another bite of meatloaf. After weeks of choking down greasy bread and burnt pasta, he had to make a conscious effort to eat like a civilized human and not a caveman crouched over a slain mammoth. "Oh, I asked about the mustangs too."

Jaxon was practically levitating above his seat. He wasn't sure what it was about these animals that fascinated him so much. All he knew was that he had to know more. Know everything. "Yeah?"

"Jaxon, let the man eat," Hannah chided.

Josh swallowed hastily. "It's okay. I don't mind the conversation."

"What did he say?" Jaxon pressed.

"Jaxon," Ray cut in. He indicated his son's phone, which had started making a series of obnoxious noises as notifications from various apps came pouring in. "I thought we agreed no phones at the dinner table."

"You have *your* phone," Jaxon argued with a nod at Ray's front pocket.

"Mine's on silent."

"Fine. Then I'll put mine on silent, too." Jaxon picked up the device to toggle the volume button.

"I'd prefer if you put it in the kitchen. Just until we finish eating."

"But what if—"

"Bodhi won't call you. Trust me."

"How do you know that?"

Ray chortled, "I may be old, but I'm not blind. No one your age ever uses a cell phone to talk to another human being."

Jaxon's shoulders slumped, clearly exasperated with his dad's know-it-all tone and haughty smirk. Here he was trying to talk about something important, something that *mattered*, and all Ray cared about was making his generation look bad. Well, two could play at that game. "You're telling me you never sent a single text when you were my age?"

"Oh, I sent plenty. But I also called people—namely, your mother."

"It's true: we used to talk on the phone all the time when we were dating," Hannah recalled. "I think our record was four and a half hours. Ray fell asleep first."

"Did I?"

She flicked a smile in his direction. "It took me a full five minutes to realize you weren't listening anymore, but I was exhausted too, so I didn't care."

"I used to call Ray's mother every Friday night," Bernard said with a twinkle in his eyes. He looked at his son first, then at Jaxon, before pointing a calloused finger at the house. "We used to have an old push-button phone on the end table in the living room there. An ugly yellow thing, with a long, curly cord that always got tangled. Anyway, I'd sit in that chair and I'd call your mother at seven P.M. every Friday night, and we'd talk a little. I'd tell her about work and she'd tell me about her college classes. I didn't realize it at the time, but that was the high point of my week. There's not a day I don't wish things could be simple like that again." Bernard sobered as he turned his gaze on his grandson. "You kids are always in such a hurry to grow up that you miss the best parts of being young. Your dad's right—whatever's on that phone doesn't matter nearly as much as what's directly in front of you."

Jaxon furrowed his brows, thinking of the articles he'd been reading and the countless websites devoted to educating the public on America's history. What he'd learned was that, along with the plains bison and the mustangs, countless Indigenous tribes had been wiped out as a result of the colonists' westward expansion. The United States had been built on a foundation of famine, genocide, and strategically-deployed diseases like smallpox, all so that a few key resources like land, water, and minerals could be controlled and exploited by the wealthy. *That* was the kind of stuff currently on Jaxon's phone: not choreographed dance routines or videos of guys blowing up everyday objects, but cold, hard facts about his country's roots.

He smiled indulgently. He couldn't change the past, but maybe there was still hope for the future. "Yeah, I guess he has a point."

After dinner, everyone assisted with the cleanup before going their separate ways. For Ray and Bernard, this meant heading down to the barn to continue their earlier work in the feed room. Hannah and Kyleigh had started going on walks together in the evening, exploring the trails around the ranch and discussing both sides of the family's history. Rather than helping his dad and grandfather, Jaxon crossed the front yard to where Josh was standing over his bike, wiping a smudge from the visor of his helmet.

"Hey, Josh, wait up."

Josh turned around and smiled. "How's it hanging?"

Jaxon cocked a brow. "How's what hanging?"

"It's just a saying. You know what, never mind. So. Got any big plans for the summer?"

"My best friend invited me to a party on Saturday, but I doubt my dad will let me go."

"Why not?"

"He expects me to help him with the fences and such. I'm supposed to take over the ranch in a couple of years... It's a family tradition." Jaxon shrugged, trying not to sound annoyed. "I mean, I guess it's a good backup plan."

"You don't want to be a rancher?"

"I don't know what I want to be," Jaxon admitted. He glanced at the Ducati, imagining all the places he'd go if he had wheels like these. What was it like, having that kind of freedom? "I'll probably end up going to the local community college. Problem is, I'm not sure what to study." He met Josh's gaze. "Did you go to college?"

"Virginia Tech, game development. I lived up to all the usual nerd stereotypes."

"So you make, like, video games in your free time? That's pretty cool."

"Well, that was the plan," Josh chuckled. "I did create a few games while I was in school. If you want, I can send them to you and you can give me some feedback."

"Sweet. Maybe you can send your game to some of the big gaming accounts on YouTube and reach a bigger audience that way."

Josh indulged him with a smile. While the exposure would certainly help grow his career (assuming he still wanted to pursue it), he knew too well the power of public opinion to destroy everything he'd worked for. If his dad were still alive, he'd urge him to take the risk nonetheless: in a world dominated by content creators and online influencers, the only thing worse than bad press was total obscurity.

"So, um, I kind of came out here to ask you something," Jaxon hedged.

"Okay."

"Did Waylon say what happened to the mustangs? Were they rounded up or anything like that?"

"I think he said something about them being transported to a stockyard. Birdman or…"

"Biffman," Jaxon exclaimed.

"Yeah, that sounds right. Anyway, I should be going. See you tomorrow, Jaxon."

Josh lifted his helmet and slipped it over his head. As he did so, Jaxon caught a glimpse of his reflection in the visor: his eyes, the same marshy green as Hannah's, were narrowed against the incarnadine glow of the setting sun. Josh keyed up the Ducati's ignition and pushed off with one foot, riding slowly at first to minimize the dust that plumed out behind him. As the rumble of the bike's engine dissipated, Jaxon started back toward the house feeling electric with purpose. Tonight, he'd take everything he'd learned over the past several days and put that knowledge to good use.

Tonight, he'd find the courage to do the right thing.

Twelve

Jaxon had never snuck out of the house after dark... until now. He waited until he was sure everyone was asleep, then climbed out of bed, pulled on the blue hoodie draped over the back of his chair, and slowly turned the doorknob so as not to make a sound.

At the end of the hallway, Hannah and Ray's door was tightly sealed. Directly ahead of Jaxon was the guest bedroom: Kyleigh was lying on her back in the middle of the bed, her hair fanning in dark reams across the pillowcase. Her window was wide open, and through it Jaxon saw nothing but the shadows of the mountains and the flickering grey eyes of the aspens' papery leaves. He shuddered at the chill seeping from his sister's bedroom, then headed toward the stairs, sticking close to the edge where he knew the floorboards wouldn't expose him.

Once he was outside, Jaxon hunched his shoulders against the wind. The sky was boundless and clear above him, where the white disc of the moon bled its silvery light across the scudding clouds and treetops. Slipping through the barn door, Jaxon rolled up his sleeves, pulled his phone out of his pocket, and turned on the flashlight.

As he approached a stall halfway down the aisle, the pinto raised its head and focused a sleepy eye on the flashlight's glow. Jaxon lowered his phone and slid open the door.

"Hey, Barbell," he whispered, "you wanna go for a ride?"

Jaxon hauled his tack into Barbell's stall. He tried to keep his hands steady as he slung the fleece pad over the gelding's back and heaved the heavy leather saddle on top of it. Once his cinch was tight, Jaxon fed the metal bit into Barbell's mouth and pulled the bridle over his ears. The pinto gave a brisk shake of his head as the leather contraption settled over the various pressure points on his face. Jaxon collected the reins, slipped his phone back into his pocket, and led his horse out of the stall, where the half-moons of his hooves left faint impressions on the dirt floor.

"We'll be home before they even notice we're gone," Jaxon promised as he lifted his cowboy hat from a peg on the wall and pressed it onto his head. He slid open the barn door as Barbell followed him outside.

Jaxon placed his left foot in the stirrup and pulled himself into the saddle. Gathering the reins, he turned the pinto toward the grassy trail leading to the north pasture. From there, he would ride along the edge of the Hoyts' field until he reached the main road, where it was only a three mile ride to the stockyard.

Jaxon tapped his heels against Barbell's flanks. "Walk on."

The pinto launched into a lively trot, the sway of his great, warm body fording the night like a ship gliding along the surface of a black sea.

*

Jaxon could smell the stockyard long before he saw it: the effluvium of cattle, the cloying fragrance of hay, and the ammonic fetor of manure mingled in the cool nighttime air. As they rode toward the silhouette of the sale barn, Barbell lifted his head and flared his nostrils with nervous curiosity. Thankfully, their journey had been uneventful: they'd stuck to the ditch along the road, where the trees had concealed them from passing cars. Now, here they were, and although Jaxon wasn't exactly sure what he'd find when he got inside, he had a feeling he wasn't going to like it.

He reined the pinto to a stop and dismounted. Pulling his phone out of his pocket, he checked the time again—2:39 A.M.—then tied Barbell to the trunk of a slender grey tree before making his way across the dew-dampened grass toward the man door at the sale barn's rear.

During the day, the stockyard was a hive of activity, the movement of cowboys and livestock incessant. As a kid, Jaxon had trailed Ray around the dusty pens as he chatted with the yardmen about feed prices and finishing lots, or craned for a glimpse of the inventory as the auctioneer's chant echoed around the arena. Like the rangeland and the rodeo grounds, the stockyard was a vital part of Jaxon's history—but tonight, armed with the knowledge of what really went on behind closed doors, he couldn't see it as anything other than a prison.

Jaxon tried the door, surprised when it swung open unresistingly. He glanced over his shoulder, saw Barbell grazing at the edge of the woods, then drew a breath and stepped into the barn.

The sour warmth of the animals weighed on the air as he closed the door behind him. He stood perfectly still in the darkness, feeling the cattle's movement as they shuffled and snorted in their pens. He'd more than likely stood in this exact same spot countless times during the day, but in this moment, he was as lost as a sailor on a cloudy night.

Jaxon felt for his phone, switched on his flashlight again, and panned it from side to side. Trapped behind the rusty metal bars of the pens were hundreds of shining green eyes and moist black muzzles. He made his way down the aisle, passing the wall of brown and black bodies pressed against the sides of the enclosures. Cows, cows, and more cows. Just like he remembered it.

Clumps of manure lay scattered on the floor. He dodged the larger droppings as best he could, then headed down the next aisle as several steers shied away from the glare of his flashlight.

He paused next to one of the pens and scanned his surroundings once more. If he were in the business of selling wild horses, where would he keep them? In the main sale barn with all the other livestock, where the unfamiliar animals were guaranteed to get the cows riled up? One thing Ray had taught him was that the best way to manage a herd was to think like its members—to anticipate what might startle them before they got a chance to start running. And since fleeing wasn't an option in here, Jaxon had to look for other signs of restlessness.

He turned to the nearest pen. The cattle inside were mostly asleep, although a couple shook their heads as Jaxon walked past, trying to read their body language in the dark.

After checking four or five pens, he turned down another aisle. Here, the cows were younger, their black ears adorned with bright yellow tags. He peered between the metal bars as one of the steers flattened its neck and let out a long bellow of distress.

Jaxon cocked his head. Cows bellowed for all kinds of reasons, but the most common ones were pain or fear. He swiveled to look around him as an orchestra of bellows rose from the shadows: dozens of cows calling out to and answering one another.

Maybe they were afraid of *him*, Jaxon thought. After all, what was scarier to a prey animal than a creature that prowled around at night, and that could see in the dark better than they could?

Then, somewhere amid the ruckus, he heard a squeal. The cattle on either side of him jostled and grunted as he made his way to the rear corner of the sale barn, where eight or nine horses were crammed into a small corral.

Jaxon looked them over quickly. The horses were small, and had no brands as far as he could tell. Their manes were long and tangled with burrs. As he took a small step forward, one of the mustangs pinned its ears and charged the gate, the crash of muscle on metal echoing around the darkened barn.

He lowered his flashlight. The mare was lying on her side, her eyes dull and lifeless. His hands were shaking as he stuck his fingers between the bars to dab at the blood oozing from her nose.

Tears welled in Jaxon's eyes. He laid his hand against the dead mare's neck and stroked gently, but the warmth was long gone from her coat. Her windpipe was still beneath his touch, her ears limp and bristled with tufts of reddish-grey hair. A life taken for the convenience of humans.

The world needed to see this. Jaxon clicked on his phone's camera, turned the device sideways, and pushed the red button to start recording.

First, he shot the mare, panning the camera along the length of her body from tip to tail. Then he captured the mustangs closest to her: a lame yearling, a roan with a bitten shoulder, another mare who pinned her ears and kicked the side of the pen so hard, Jaxon could feel the vibrations of the metal bars between his teeth. While they were certainly smaller than the horses he was used to riding back home, he knew enough to keep his distance. Like his dad always said: a scared horse was a dangerous horse… and a feral horse that had never known captivity was as fearful as they came.

And now, Jaxon would have proof that these mustangs needed their help. It would have been irresponsible for Ray *not* to get involved, regardless of his dealings with the BLM. At the very least, perhaps he could convince whoever was in charge here to give the mustangs the veterinary care they desperately needed. A little hay and water would've been nice, too.

From across the sale barn, he heard a man's voice say, "They're over in the corner. The rendering truck will be here in the morning."

Shit. Jaxon turned off his camera and scanned his surroundings for a place to hide. Half-crouched, he scrambled over to a stack of straw bales near one of the cattle pens and flattened himself against the wall, the sour taste of panic filling his mouth.

Two men appeared. They could've been mirror images of each other, with their old jeans and scruffy denim jackets that gave off the faint aroma of livestock wherever they went. Their boots scraped along the floor as they approached the mustangs' pen and stood by the gate with their hands in their pockets, surveying the damage as if they were browsing the deli counter at the supermarket.

The one on the right cocked his head, stuck the toe of his boot under the fence, and kicked at the dead mare's shoulder. Jaxon watched, helpless, his stomach turning in on itself as her body jostled against the floor. He thought about recording this, but his hands were suddenly frozen stiff—a reaction that didn't quite match the sweat that sprang up along his backbone and armpits.

"How long do you think she's been dead?" the kicker asked.

His companion shrugged. "Couple hours, maybe."

"You want to get her out now, or wait until the truck comes?"

"What difference does it make? She'll still end up in the same place." He added, "We've only half the herd here. The rest of them are up near the old mines. Merle thinks we should be able to round them up within a few days if we can get the chopper up and running again."

Jaxon fumbled for his phone. As he was about to open the camera again, a notification popped up on the screen. He tried to swipe it away, but instead, pressed on the link. It took him straight to the latest *Nuked* video—*WE BLEW UP A FRIDGE!*—and without fail, Cory, in his trademark Australian accent, began narrating their latest shenanigans.

"Welcome back to *Nuked*, where we make science exciting *and* educational! Today we're going to be doing something that's going to totally blow your mind!"

"Shit," Jaxon hissed, frantically toggling the volume.

The first man turned around, staring out into the dusty darkness of the barn with half-squinted eyes. "Did you hear that?"

Jaxon turned off the phone and peeked over the bale. Through the horizontal shadows of the livestock pens, he saw the man walking in his direction, his hands still in his pockets and the outline of his cowboy hat sitting like a mountain on top of his head.

"Probably rats," the other man said.

"It wasn't rats," the first man replied, "it sounded like a person."

As the sound of footsteps drew closer, Jaxon darted over to the nearest pen. He dropped down on his belly and slithered beneath the bottom rail, then lay perfectly still in the reeking yellow straw with his heart bucking in his chest. A steer with a long black broom of a tail nuzzled his shoulder. If he kept quiet—and if the men out there didn't make any sudden moves—maybe, just maybe, he could avoid being trampled to death.

The footsteps ceased. The cowboy looked around as the usual sounds of the sale barn rose and fell in waves, the mustangs having settled into a state of resigned silence behind him.

"Come on, Rhett," his partner said, turning away from the mustangs. "You're hearing things now."

"Maybe." Rhett glanced between the pens again. Just when Jaxon thought he couldn't hold his breath another second, Rhett's shoulders relaxed and he circled back toward the aisle. "Get Casey on the phone. He'll know what to do with the deadstock."

Jaxon waited until he could no longer hear the men's footsteps before exhaling a sigh of relief. Still on his belly, he shimmied out of the pen, leaving the steers to their cud-chewing. His clothes were filthy, his shirt was torn, and he was pretty sure he smelled like cow shit. But none of that mattered. What mattered was finding the rest of the mustangs and moving them far enough away that the BLM would never threaten their herd again.

Jaxon slipped out the backdoor and crossed to the trees. He untied the reins, lifted his hat off the saddle, and led Barbell back toward the road, where he swung a leg over the pinto's broad back and rode off in the direction of the ranch.

Daylight was breaking on the horizon when he arrived. In the north pasture, swirls of mist eddied on the surface of the pond. The fence line was dark and indistinct, each row of barbed wire hanging against the pale scrap of sky like the ruled pages of a notebook. Barbell trotted briskly through the long grass at the edge of the field, down the footpath, and into the barnyard, where the rest of the horses were already fanning out across the paddock in search of sweet morning grass.

As they rounded the corner of the barn, Bernard came through the door. He sized up his grandson, who swung down from the saddle and gathered Barbell's reins in his hand.

Bernard raised his gaze from Jaxon's shirt and said in a low, level tone, "You better go inside."

Jaxon handed him the reins, saying nothing as he headed toward the house. There, he pushed open the front door to find his family waiting for him.

"Oh, thank god," Hannah breathed, taking Jaxon into her arms.

He looked over her shoulder at Ray, who stood up, slow and calculated, and crossed the floor to his son.

"Do you mind telling me," Ray began, "just where the hell you've been?"

Thirteen

"I can explain," Jaxon started.

"You'd better. Do you have any idea what you put your mother through?" Ray gave a half-nod in Hannah's direction, in case Jaxon hadn't noticed her pale, queasy expression.

As Jaxon's gaze shifted back toward his father, Ray took another step forward. Unlike Hannah and Kyleigh, he was already fully dressed: his days started at four A.M., long before everyone else woke up. When questioned about his tendency to rise before the sun, he always claimed he wanted to get a head-start on chores and checking his business emails, but now that Jaxon was older, he knew the reason had as much to do with Ray's chronic pain as it did with maximizing productivity. And since one of the biggest aggravators of pain was stress, he could only imagine how much his dad's leg was bothering him. "I'm sorry," Jaxon whispered.

"Sorry? That's all you have to say for yourself?"

"Can I explain?" Jaxon asked. "Please?"

Ray pointed to the sofa. "Sit down."

"But I'm filthy."

"I said sit down."

Jaxon raised his hands. "You don't have to tear my head off about it."

He moved to sit on the old leather couch, perching as lightly as he could on the edge of the middle cushion. He knew he stank, and he also knew he'd be better off burning his clothes instead of trying to wash them, but in this moment, nothing mattered more than making his family aware of the situation he'd witnessed tonight. As he kneaded his fingers together, trying to decide where to begin, Kyleigh drifted toward the armchair and took a seat, pretzeling her legs beneath her body as she watched. Hannah continued to hover in the kitchen doorway with her housecoat drawn tightly around her waist.

Jaxon began, "I wasn't trying to scare you—or mom. Remember those mustangs Mr. Hoyt was telling us about?"

"I remember you promising me you wouldn't meddle," Ray replied, folding his arms. "By the way, I called Waylon this morning and asked him to keep an eye out for you. Mr. Hoyt is a good neighbour, but he doesn't suffer fools lightly. Just keep that in mind the next time you feel like trespassing."

"You're not even letting me tell my side of the story!" Jaxon blurted.

"Fine. Go on."

Jaxon let out a breath. "I went to the stockyard—"

"Which one?"

"I'm getting to it."

"Ray, just listen," Hannah said firmly.

He raised his eyes to hers, set his jaw, and looked back down at his son with a small nod of encouragement.

"I went to the Biffman Stockyard," Jaxon continued. "I've been doing a lot of research lately, about the mustangs and the BLM, and it made me realize we're all complicit. And I started to wonder: what if grandpa was right and the off-range facilities are actually killing the mustangs instead of trying to help them?"

"We're not complicit in anything, we're just running a business. This is a working ranch, and we have a duty to look out for our livestock."

"But why does running a business always seem to mean that someone else gets hurt? Why can't we look out for our livestock and be stewards for the mustangs?"

"You *have* been reading a lot," Kyleigh put in, and Jaxon wasn't sure if she was trying to be supportive or sarcastic. Maybe a little of both.

"Exactly," he replied, turning his focus back to Ray. "So, I came up with a plan to… well, I was going to sneak onto Mr. Hoyt's property and see if I could see the mustangs—"

"You cannot trespass on private property and expect me to defend you. You're not a child anymore."

"Just listen," Jaxon growled.

"Is that why you wanted to borrow the Chevy?"

"Yes. But I never went through with it, did I?"

"You thought about going through with it, and that's bad enough."

"Okay, fine—I'm a bad kid. That's what you want me to say, isn't it?"

"I want you to realize that the path you're on isn't going anywhere you need to be. And if you can't recognize right from wrong at your age, then we have a much bigger problem on our hands than whatever is happening to a herd of wild horses."

Jaxon closed his eyes, clenched his fists. If he were a bottle of soda, he would've blown his lid clean off by now. For someone who was apparently so good at listening to horses, Ray was practically deaf when it came to hearing what his own son had to say.

Nevertheless, Jaxon told him, "I was right, dad: they're killing them."

"Who's killing them? And who's 'them'? The mustangs?"

Jaxon pulled his phone out of his pocket. "Maybe I should just show you instead."

"Wait, is this true?" Kyleigh sat forward. "When I came to talk to you the other night, you showed me all those articles and pictures. But they were old, weren't they?"

"They were, but that doesn't mean it's not still happening." Jaxon clicked on the video and turned his phone around to show Ray. He took the device from his son's hand and squinted at the shaky, poorly-lit footage. The microphone had picked up on Jaxon's laboured breathing in the background. Ray watched as the camera panned over the dead mare's body, her coat a washed-out shade of copper and her legs lying limp in the bed of saturated straw. The video jumped to the next horse, and the next one, and the next, painting a gruesome scene that the public would never get a chance to see.

"There were two yardmen on duty. I hid behind some bales as soon as I heard them coming, but they were talking about the mustangs and then one of them said as soon as the chopper's up and running again, they were going to round up the rest of the herd. They're up near the old mines." He paused. The video had ended, but Ray had yet to relinquish his phone. "I bet we can find them."

Ray looked at him fully now, his eyes wide, disbelieving. "*We?*"

"Oh, come on. You can't possibly watch that video and *not* feel something unless you're like, a sociopath."

"Believe me, I feel just as sickened and angry as you do. I mean that. I've seen some horrific things in this business and it never gets easier."

"Then you know we have to do something. You and me."

"Jax—"

"We can go to the old mines. We can go at night when no one's around and we can drive them a few miles in any direction. Somewhere they'll be safe. Please, dad."

"We're not risking our safety or the mustangs' safety by chasing them around in the dark. I know it doesn't seem fair what the BLM is doing, but managing feral horses is their job. We may not agree with their methods, but we can't interfere or this place could be shut down. Do you understand what I'm saying?"

Jaxon jumped to his feet, his face scarlet with rage.

"When did you become such a coward? The old you would've done something, not sat around and waited for a miracle!" he roared.

For a long moment, Ray was silent, his gaze never wavering from Jaxon's face. They stared each other down, Jaxon's shoulders heaving as his breathing grew heavy before slowly returning to a normal rhythm. Eventually, Ray glanced away, letting his attention rest on his feet.

"Go to your room," he said in a small voice.

Jaxon's brows arched. "Really? After all that, you're telling me to *go to my room*—?"

"I said go to your room!"

Kyleigh flinched. Hannah straightened. Jaxon grimaced, then stormed over to the stairs and pounded up to his room in a fury.

His door slammed. Everyone was quiet.

Then Hannah spoke. "Ray, he didn't mean it…"

Ray turned toward the front door, stepped outside, and headed for the barn.

She looked at her daughter. Kyleigh had both feet flat on the floor, Ray's explosive reaction having triggered some fight-or-flight instinct she knew was buried deep in her bones. He was not a yeller, Hannah had told her: even in a crowd, his voice rarely rose above what most people would consider shouting. Even then, it was clear it didn't come naturally to him. He spoke with his hands and his eyes and his posture: only when the circumstances demanded all of his passion or all of his fear did he give himself over to the primal power woven into his male DNA. A voice that, for centuries, men had reserved for battle cries and fallen kingdoms—or simply reasoning with their teenaged sons.

"Now what?" Kyleigh asked.

Hannah sighed. "Now, we give them both a chance to cool down."

"That might take a while."

"It will."

Kyleigh stood up. "Maybe we could go for a walk?"

Hannah nodded and angled toward the stairs. "I'll get dressed."

*

By midday, Jaxon had still not left his room. When Hannah came in to collect the soiled clothes scattered across the floor, she found him in bed with the covers pulled over his head. His laptop sat open on the desk, and on the screen was a Word document titled *Colleges Near Aspen*, with Aspen Mountain College being the first, and only, entry on the list. The rest of the page was blank. Clearly, Jaxon's mind was too preoccupied with the mustangs and the fight with his dad to care about something as frivolous as his future career. Hannah shut the laptop, tucked the ball of clothes under her arm, and pulled the door shut.

She carried the clothes into the laundry room. There, she separated each article and examined it for rips and stains. As she fingered the tear in his shirt, Kyleigh appeared in the doorway behind her.

"How is he?" Kyleigh asked.

Without turning around, Hannah replied, "He's sleeping." She lowered the shirt and picked up the sweater, covered in dirt and bits of straw. Glancing over her shoulder at Kyleigh, she said, "This isn't the first time they've had a big fight. I doubt it'll be the last."

"Do you agree with him?"

"Who?"

"Jaxon."

Hannah turned around and immediately averted her eyes. "Are you asking me if I agree with my sixteen-year-old son wanting to rescue some wild horses? Because if you are, my answer is yes."

Kyleigh's eyes widened. "File that under things I never expected to hear you say."

Hannah smiled mildly. "I know I sound like a bad mom, but I know my son—and I know my husband. Those two are like peas in a pod. I'm not saying I want them to go out there, but Ray has such a hard time turning a blind eye to things he knows are wrong."

"So, if they decided to go all Batman and Robin on these BLM guys, you'd be cool with it?"

"Well, no, but Batman and Robin wouldn't be Batman and Robin if they let the criminals take over Gotham City, would they?" Hannah went back to worrying about Jaxon's laundry. "I'm going to talk to Ray when I bring him his lunch. You should come."

"Sure. I'm always down for a hike."

"We're not hiking this time. You've been here for about a week… I think it's time you learned how to ride a horse."

Kyleigh felt her whole body stiffen at the prospect, her hands instantly clammy. "Is this a bad time to mention that I don't like farm animals?"

"You'll be fine. And yes, it is."

"I'm not a horsey girl though. I mean, horses are cool, but I don't think I'm ready to ride one."

"I know it's a little scary," Hannah said as the washing machine began to fill, "but I promise everything will be okay. This is a working ranch. No one gets away with not being able to ride."

"That's a heck of a slogan. 'Welcome to our ranch: you either ride or die trying.'"

Hannah laughed. "You have no idea how true that is."

"You're really not selling me on this lifestyle, you know."

"You chose to come here—I never forced you to get on that plane. So, maybe a part of you is ready to try something new. To be one of us."

Kyleigh chewed her bottom lip. It was true: she had come here alone, and she did want to fit in with her biological family, but that was only because she hadn't yet seen what was involved in keeping the ranch running. Perhaps if she had, she would've made up with Derek and gone back to his apartment. The devil she knew was a long-haired, cheating bastard, but it beat whatever devils were lurking in the shadows here, pitting fathers against sons and killing wild horses.

"In that case, what's for lunch?" Kyleigh asked.

*

In Jaxon's absence, Ray had called Waylon for help and was surprised when he brought his two oldest sons, Roman and Cal, to assist with the fences. For the next several hours, the group worked tirelessly to dig holes for new posts and unspool the wire that would eventually keep the cattle contained. Conversation came and went, but Ray was in no mood for chatter. Instead, he stayed several sections ahead of his crew, ensuring the fenceposts went in straight, and tried not to think of the video Jaxon had taken. Christ, of all the places in the world he could've chosen to sneak around, why did it have to be the Biffman Stockyard? Why did it have to be the one place where the only thing more recognizable than Ray's face was the American flag hanging above the auction stage?

Waylon approached him. As Ray looked up from his work, he asked, "Is there a problem?"

"The fence is coming along nicely," Waylon replied, standing back to get a better look at their progress.

Ray nodded. "I appreciate you dropping by on such short notice."

"Don't mention it. I figured I'd be hearing from you one way or another." Waylon indicated Roman, a natural redhead who had a tendency to slouch, and added, "If you want, I can let you have him for the rest of the summer. Not Cal, though—I need him to help me inoculate my cattle once the calves start dropping."

"Thanks, but I'm really hoping this is a temporary arrangement."

His neighbour nodded gravely. "Of course. But, you know, maybe it's time to consider that it isn't."

"What do you mean?"

"I don't want to sound like I'm questioning your parenting," Waylon said, raising his hands in an innocent gesture, "but if Jaxon were my kid, he'd be packed and waiting for the bus to military school right about now."

"I agree," Bernard said. He was squatting down in the shade at the edge of the woods, munching on a pepperoni stick sheathed in a long plastic tube. "That's what my father would've done if I'd acted out. Young horses got the whip, my brothers and I got the belt."

"I'll tell you something else," Waylon continued, "we live in a world without order. We saw it during the pandemic, when people were fighting in the stores. And you know what triggered that?"

"The fact that there was a deadly virus going around that no one had immunity to?" Ray drawled.

"That's what the media wanted you to think. They had an agenda, you know, with the vaccines and such. New world order."

"I remember the conspiracy theories. What does any of this have to do with Jaxon and the mustangs?"

"My point is, a strong society is built on traditional family values. Kids these days have all this freedom and no discipline. You hand them a phone, and suddenly they think they know everything, and they're gonna educate the rest of us on how to behave. Can't say this, can't say that. They haven't been around long enough to know they're being controlled by these apps the way the media tries to control us." Waylon gestured to Ray, Bernard, and the rest of the team. "I know your boy's got a phone. So do mine. But I wonder sometimes if that was really the best idea."

"It's not the phones that are the problem, it's how they're being used," Ray insisted.

"How they're used depends on how they're designed. Every year the brains behind these gadgets get smarter, and we all get dumber. That's why you gotta be on top of what Jaxon has access to. And more importantly, you gotta teach him to see *you* as a figure of authority. I'll tell you this: when my boys were little, I got down on my knee, looked them in the eyes, and said, 'I'm your father. I don't do love—I do tough love.' And look how well it worked. Roman's managing my herd, Cal's learning to be a veterinarian, Dwight's got himself a swanky apprenticeship in town, and by this time next year, Bellamy's gonna be an HVAC tech. Do you think they would've done as well if I'd told them their feelings were important?"

"I guess it depends on what feelings we're talking about," Ray answered. "My whole life, I was expected to man up. They told me cowboys don't cry, and I believed it. I thought that was a good thing because it meant I was tough. Then I met Hannah, and I realized I couldn't fool the people who cared about me." He shrugged. "I understand where you're coming from, but I'm speaking as someone who saw his mother die a slow death at the hands of mental illness. The way I've chosen to raise my son, I want him to know that he's allowed to be upset about things."

"How's that working for you?" Waylon asked.

"Jaxon's not a bad kid," Ray said, turning back to the fence, "he just did a bad thing."

"You can excuse his actions all you want, but the law won't be so lenient if it catches up to him."

Ray grimaced. His eyes flickered toward the trees as Hannah appeared riding one of their geldings, Kyleigh following on her own horse a few paces behind.

"Now, there's a sight for sore eyes," Waylon said, a grin breaking across his face. "Two lovely ladies on horseback, and I'd be willing to bet they brought us lunch."

Ray shot him a sidelong look. "I value tradition as much as anyone around here, but my wife can do more than make a sandwich."

"I know she can. Doesn't mean I'm not hungry."

Ray shook his head as Hannah dismounted and left her horse ground-tied in the shade.

"The fence looks great," she said. "Good to see you again, Waylon."

He tipped his hat at her. "Pleasure's mine."

In the background, Josh approached Kyleigh. Despite Hannah's assurances that her horse wouldn't bolt, Kyleigh had spent the entire ride with her hand wrapped around the saddle horn. Now, as the gelding dropped his head to nibble on the grass at his feet, Kyleigh reluctantly let go of the pommel and flexed her fingers to loosen the joints.

She glanced down at Josh, who patted her horse's neck. "How am I doing?" she asked.

"You look like a natural."

"Really? Because I feel like I'm never going to be able to walk properly again." Josh laughed.

"I'm sure you'll get used to it. It's in your blood, after all." He turned to look at the fence, the barbed wire glistening in the sun.

"It's really coming along," Kyleigh offered.

"It is." Josh faced her again, his smile lingering. "You want to stick around for a while and give us a hand?"

"I would, but I already agreed to help Hannah with a few things."

Josh's disappointment was subtle, but Kyleigh noticed it all the same. In fact, up here, her senses seemed to be in overdrive, leading her to notice things she normally wouldn't, from the way the ground felt under her horse's hooves to the pattern of shadows on Josh's face.

"Well, if you change your mind, we'll be here all day," Josh told her, his voice hopeful.

"I know." Kyleigh glanced down at the grime on her hands from where she'd been clutching the reins and asked, "Hey, quick question: why have I not seen you ride a horse yet?"

"I guess it's because I'm here to work, not ride."

"Hmm. I don't buy it. The rule around here is you either ride or die trying."

"That goes for just about every ranch. Unfortunately, I nearly died trying when I was three, so now I don't ride at all."

"You ride a motorcycle," Kyleigh pointed out.

"You're right. It's safer. At least my bike can't buck me off." Josh patted her horse's neck again before returning to his section of the fence.

As Waylon headed over to check in with Roman and Cal, Hannah turned to Ray. "Could we go talk in your truck for a minute?" she asked.

He turned to address his crew. "Do you guys want to take five?" The team set down their supplies as Ray led Hannah over to his truck, parked under a large maple tree. As soon as they were inside, Ray let out a breath.

She glanced over at him. "Are you okay? You seemed kind of upset when we arrived."

He shook his head, watching Waylon strut around as his sons sprawled out in the shade. "Waylon's just getting on my nerves. Don't get me wrong, I appreciate the help, but the man has no business questioning my parenting."

"You know you're a good father, so it doesn't matter what anyone else thinks."

"Am I? I mean, Jaxon's never acted out like this." Ray's attention drifted over to Kyleigh, who was receiving an impromptu riding lesson from Bernard.

Hannah followed Ray's gaze. "This isn't because of Kyle," she said before he could come to any baseless conclusions. "Has it been strange having two kids in the house instead of just one? Sure, but that doesn't mean she's responsible for Jaxon's behaviour. He's sixteen, Ray, not six—he's not going to be jealous that we're giving her attention."

"Then I don't know what's going on." He propped his elbow on the driver's door and ran a hand through his hair. "Maybe Waylon's right. Jaxon doesn't see me as a figure of authority in his life. All he cares about is that damn phone—and if he's not careful, he's going to end up in a situation far worse than the one he's in now." Ray sighed, dropping his hand. "I knew things would change as I got older, but I didn't think they'd change this much."

"Have you completely forgotten what you were like when you were younger?" Hannah asked. She turned slightly in the passenger seat so that she was more or less facing him. But Ray, as she suspected, wasn't interested in confronting the truth head-on. "You were just as stubborn as Jaxon, if not more so. You didn't listen to anyone. Even when Marc and I tried to tell you something was dangerous, you just had to go and do it anyway."

Ray met her gaze, his expression wounded. "Why do you think I'm trying so hard to keep Jaxon on the straight and narrow? I did a lot of stupid things when I was younger, but nothing this bad."

"No, it was worse. Jaxon's gambling with the law, but you were gambling with your life." Hannah sat back, exasperated. "God, Ray, if only you knew the stress you've put on me over the years. You want there to be an easy solution, but I don't think it exists. If you want to get through to Jaxon, you're going to have to make peace with yourself."

Hannah reached for the door and threw it open. As she exited the truck, Waylon and Bernard turned around, their banter briefly interrupted by the hope that she'd brought enough food for the whole group.

As she removed the cooler bag strapped to her horse's saddle, Ray walked over and said, "What do you want me to say? I can't go back in time and stop myself from getting shot or falling into that ravine."

"I know that."

"So, what do you expect me to do?"

"Honestly, I just want you and Jaxon to get along. I don't really care how you achieve it." She passed him the bag and gathered her reins. "Seeing those mustangs really affected him. I know it affected you."

"It did."

"And Jaxon's right: you've always spoken out against cruelty."

"But this is different. I'm not saying what happened to those mustangs isn't terrible, but I'm certainly not going to put our family at risk for the sake of some animals that were probably not going to survive another winter out here. Nature takes care of her own, and so should we." Starting today, Ray resolved to be more like Waylon and Bernard: this meant no more attitude, no more excuses, and no more sneaking out after dark. If Jaxon wanted to indulge his heroic impulses, then he could start by saving the backtalk.

"You're right." Hannah sighed and climbed onto Bullet's back before giving the horse's flanks a gentle squeeze with both heels. "I'll be at the house if you need me."

Ray watched Hannah and Kyleigh ride off, his stomach aching with guilt. Was it truly wise, he wondered, to alienate his wife in front of his team? Hannah had done far more for him than most people who set foot on the ranch, and while they may have disagreed on how to raise their son, she was the only person Ray could count on to share the burden of Jaxon's upbringing.

As Ray set his focus back to his work, Bernard said, "I told you to take away his phone, didn't I?"

"Don't start," Ray warned.

"Everything Waylon said is true—and it's exactly what I've been saying for weeks. But you won't listen to a word that comes out of my mouth because you think I'm a failure."

"Are you finished?"

"No. It's your job as Jaxon's father to teach him right from wrong. And if you won't do it, then someone else will. Maybe it'll be someone from the BLM, in which case you won't be able to save him without putting everything you care about on the line." Bernard slapped his hat against his thigh. As he placed it back on his head, he told Ray, "I'm taking a break."

"You already had a break," Ray reminded him. "Twenty years, to be exact."

Bernard turned back and stuck out his finger. "You watch your mouth. Just because you're a grown man doesn't mean I won't tan your hide in front of everyone here."

Ray fought the urge to laugh. "Did you just threaten to tan my hide?"

"Is this funny to you?"

Ray's demeanor changed. "No, it's not. It's not funny that my son has been trespassing on private property, and here you are blaming me for it. I've been a part of Jaxon's life every single day for the past sixteen years, and I've done everything in my power to prove that I have what it takes to be a decent father… I've wanted to walk away about a hundred times, but you know why I'm still here?" Ray paused, all too aware of how his team was looking at him. Bernard raised his chin, urging Ray to continue. "Because I'll do anything to make sure I never end up like you."

Bernard spread his arms as he panned his gaze over the field. "If this is what a bad life looks like, I'd hate to see anyone do any real damage." He pinned his focus on Ray again. "You know, I used to think Marcus could hold a grudge, but he's clearly moved on. The longer you hold that anger inside, the more poisonous it becomes. It ain't going to kill me, son, but over time, it will kill you."

Ray ground his teeth. He didn't have it in him to concede his side of the argument: letting go of his anger would mean opening himself up to the possibility of getting hurt again, and perhaps the next time would be worse.

"You're dismissed," Ray told Bernard as he turned back to the fence, "don't bother me again for the rest of the day."

Bernard grunted, "With pleasure," and trudged noisily through the woods toward the bunkhouse.

Fourteen

When Bernard hadn't appeared at dinnertime, Ray had told Hannah about their dispute in the field, which led to an hourlong fight and Ray retreating to the barn to cool down. He was still in possession of Jaxon's phone, which sat in the corner of his desk, a haze of fingerprints covering the black screen. Ray hadn't decided when he would give it back; the end of the week seemed reasonable, although it probably felt like a lifetime to wait for a teenager. Had he been this addicted to technology when he was Jaxon's age? He couldn't remember. His youth seemed so far behind him now, like the glowing specks of human civilization to an astronaut floating high above the surface of the earth.

He picked up Jaxon's phone. With just a few taps, Ray had access to his son's whole life: pictures he'd taken, memes he'd saved, phone numbers for the revolving door of cute girls, games he played when he was bored in class, messages from Bodhi, emails about college open houses, Google search results for his history paper, a scientific calculator for math class, YouTube, WhatsApp, TikTok. Everything a sixteen-year-old boy could possibly need to navigate the messy, complicated world of high school, plus a few other things he never expected to encounter.

Ray clicked on Jaxon's photo album; thousands of tiny thumbnails filled the screen. Near the bottom of it was the video clip Jaxon had captured hours before. Steeling himself against the feeling that he was trespassing, Ray pressed play and turned the phone sideways so that the footage filled the screen.

The dead mustang looked young: he could tell by her teeth, visible through the once prehensile white lips. He heard a rustle, then a whisper, as Jaxon circled the outside of the pen with quick, shuffling steps.

Ray turned up the volume and replayed the clip. He held the phone up to his ear and focused on the noises in the background.

It was Jaxon, speaking to the horses. "I'm sorry. I'm so sorry I let them do this to you."

Ray stared at the last frame of the video, which featured a shot of a weanling colt leaning against the side of the pen, too weak to even stand on his own. His eyes were dull and distant, almost as if he knew exactly what his fate held and saw no point in fighting it.

He switched off the phone's screen and returned it to the corner of his desk. Too late to do anything about the mustangs now: they'd likely already been sold to kill buyers at a steep discount. As for the ones near the mines, well, they'd probably moved on in search of water or better grazing land, or so he hoped.

Josh stepped into the storage room, his blue and white plaid shirt smeared with dirt and his sleeves rolled up to his elbows.

He hooked a thumb over his shoulder. "Just thought I'd let you know the stalls are done."

"Thank you," Ray replied. "Are you heading home?"

"Yes—unless you need me to do anything else."

Ray couldn't get his thoughts to focus. All he could think about in this moment was the desperation in Jaxon's eyes as he recounted the horrifying details of his visit to the stockyard. Since he hadn't come down for dinner, Hannah had taken a plate up to his room. Ray imagined it was still sitting on his nightstand, the food cold and semi-congealed from neglect.

"No, I think we're okay for tonight," Ray said at last.

Josh nodded. "How's Jaxon?"

"He's still up in his room. Hannah's been checking in on him every couple of hours." Ray leaned back in the chair. "He said there are more mustangs up near the old mines. Of course, who knows if that's actually true. The problem is, he wants to go on a rescue mission before the BLM decides to cull them."

"I thought the BLM's job was to protect the wild horses, not exterminate them."

Ray lifted a shoulder. "Technically, their job is to limit the number of mustangs in a given area so they don't overgraze the land and make it unusable for livestock. The governor of Colorado has been pushing for more humane methods of population control, but a sterilization program can be costly and time-consuming to implement. So, they choose the helicopters instead."

"My dad used to have friends who worked for the BLM. As far as I know, the Pryor Mountain range is the only herd management area in the state of Montana." Josh smiled to himself and looked away. "Dad loved all horses, but he had a particularly soft spot for the wild ones. Said once you got past their natural defenses, they were the best partners a cowboy could ask for."

"He tried to talk me into adopting a mustang once," Ray recalled. "It was just a couple of weeks after Jaxon was born. I was worried having a wild horse on the ranch would be too dangerous, but your dad thought it would put me back on everyone's radar after my yearlong hiatus."

"Is that what inspired you to go on tour?"

"Partially. Your dad pulled a few strings, making sure I booked the right arenas and such. I owe a lot of my success to him…" Ray glimpsed Jaxon's phone, thinking of the mustangs in their cramped corral. "Mickey was a true horseman. Everything he did was an expression of his love for those animals. And you."

Josh folded his arms and leaned in the doorway, his gaze dropping to the floor. This was the most he'd talked about his dad since his death: most people, including his own mother, were too afraid to even bring the subject up, as if the mere mention of the Horse God's greatness would cause Josh to fall into a riptide of grief and be swept away forever.

"About a month after dad was diagnosed, we got into a huge fight over something stupid. At the time, I felt justified in being angry, but looking back on it, I wish I'd been kinder to him. I could've let it go, you know, but I just had to have the last word." Josh shook his head. "I know he loved me. When I was sitting by his bed in those final days, I kept thinking about how, every time he came home from being on tour, he'd take me to Dairy Queen for a Blizzard. It became our tradition." A smile flashed across his face and vanished just as quickly. "I haven't had a Blizzard since he passed. Doesn't feel right to eat one on my own."

"Maybe one day when you have a son, you can carry on the tradition with him," Ray suggested. "Jaxon wants me to go to the mines with him, but I said it was too dangerous. Plus, if the Bureau finds out we've been interfering in their operations, we might be denied grazing permits in the future. That means our main source of income—the cattle—will dry up, and I don't know if I can keep the roof over our heads on my horse training business alone." Realizing he was rambling, Ray faced his desk again and told Josh, "Thanks for all your help today."

"Anytime." Josh turned away and headed for the barn door. But as the cool evening air grazed his sunburned cheeks, he stopped and circled back toward the storage room again.

"Look, I know this is none of my business," he said, prompting Ray to glance up from his computer, "but if I had the chance to spend even one more night with my dad, I'd take it in a heartbeat."

Ray thought of his own father, about all the missed opportunities and untold stories that defined their rocky relationship. One day, when Jaxon had children of his own, maybe he'd finally understand that Ray's unwillingness to save the mustangs was rooted not in cowardice, but in the love he had for the family he'd worked so hard to create.

"Goodnight, Josh," he said quietly. With a nod, Josh turned and vanished through the door.

Ray lingered in his office. When he felt he'd made a sizeable dent in his emails, he shut the laptop, slipped Jaxon's phone into his pocket, and stepped out into the aisle. The stalls were immaculately clean, each wooden box giving off the distinct perfume of fresh pine shavings and alfalfa hay.

Ray touched his fingers to the brass nameplate on Barbell's halter, hung on a metal peg beside the gelding's stall. A hundred things could've gone wrong last night: someone could've spotted Jaxon sneaking into the sale barn, his horse could've been spooked by a passing car, he could've been thrown from the saddle and broken his neck. Even just filming the mustangs could've had disastrous consequences, had the animals not been so weak from dehydration.

Lost in thought, he didn't notice when Hannah stepped through the door. She tucked her hands into the pockets of her windbreaker and watched the storm pass over her husband's face.

"How much longer are you planning to stall?" she asked.

Ray let the halter slip from his grasp and tried to act like he'd simply lost track of time, though he knew he had no hope of fooling her even on the best of days.

"How's Jaxon?" he asked instead.

"You'd know if you came inside."

"I've been catching up on work. It's not my fault our son chose such an inconvenient time to become an activist."

Hannah knotted her brows. "Do you know why I came out here?"

"I'm guessing it probably wasn't to admire Josh's work."

"Once upon a time, I knew a young cowboy who believed he could save everyone and everything," Hannah began. "People said he had a gift, and that gift led him to become one of the leading horse trainers in Colorado. Eventually, that cowboy had a son, and from that day on, all he wanted was for his son to be exactly like him: a horse whisperer."

"Technically, I wanted him to be a commercial rancher," Ray replied. "And he's still a long way off from *that*, judging by his attitude toward everything the job entails... Look, I know what you're trying to do here, and it's not going to work. Whatever it was that made me believe I was some kind of hero back then is long, long gone."

He sighed and hobbled over to the bench. As he lowered himself onto the wooden seat, Ray pointed to the barn door and said, "What Jaxon needs is more discipline. He has to learn that what he did is not okay— it doesn't matter what his intentions were."

"Oh, really? And what do you propose—boarding school?"

Ray faltered. "I was thinking military, but that could work, too."

"We're not sending him anywhere. We're his parents. He may not want to believe it, but deep down, he knows he still needs us. And I would think you of all people would be against breaking up our family, especially with how much Bernard's leaving affected you."

"What do you want me to say? I don't know what to do here."

"For one thing, you can stop avoiding the conversation you know you need to have with your son. Jaxon knows he can sneak out now, so I wouldn't be surprised if he tried to do it again. He was lucky no one got hurt this time, but maybe the next time will be different."

"You know, I seem to recall you used to be an optimist. If there was a silver lining, you always found it."

"What can I say, Ray? Things change." Hannah took a breath and glanced away. "I'd be lying if I said I wasn't worried about what Jaxon's going to do next. He knows where the mustangs are, he knows how to get there, and he knows what the BLM will do if he doesn't take action. I'm not saying I want him to go to the mines, but I'd feel a lot better knowing you were with him."

Ray stood up. This was ridiculous. Insane. Absurd. The fact that Hannah was even condoning Jaxon's whims made him wonder if they were truly fit to be parents, and he'd always viewed her as the sensible one.

"We could get into a lot of trouble for this," he told her, "and I'm not just referring to Jaxon and myself. If we get caught, it will put the whole ranch in jeopardy. Is that what you want?"

"Of course not. But since when does everyone get what they want out of life?"

For the second time that day, Hannah walked away from the conversation. As Ray stared after her, he pictured Jaxon holed up in his room and wondered how he'd managed to pass the time without his phone. But mostly, Ray thought about what he would've done if he were thirty years younger and came across a herd of wild horses in need of protection. And it didn't take much wondering to arrive at an answer.

Ray took one final look around at the stalls before making his way down the aisle. Upon reaching the door, he flipped off the light and stepped out onto the gravel driveway beneath the milky glow of a gibbous moon and its posse of twinkling silver stars. There was enough light to see the ground beneath his feet, the clean lines of the paddock fence, and the eyes on the trunks of the aspen trees huddled around the tractor shed. Ray turned his hand out in front of him to gauge the level of detail in his palm. As poor as his vision was, he could make out the fork of his lifeline and the shadowy creases between his callous-thickened fingers. Maybe it would be enough, he thought. Ray sighed, then climbed the porch steps and went into the house.

Jaxon couldn't remember how old he'd been the first time he'd picked up a pencil and started drawing. All he knew was that sometimes, it was easier to talk to the blank page than it was to talk to other people. Sitting on his bed with his back against the wall and his sketchbook propped against his knees, Jaxon let his mind wander back to his conversation with Ray from earlier that day. Now that he'd had some time to process everything, Jaxon didn't feel quite so furious—only disappointed that the one person in the world who should have cared about the mustangs, didn't. Maybe growing up meant learning that his parents, whom he'd always admired for their wisdom and kindness, weren't as perfect as he believed them to be.

His hand rested lightly on the page, the tip of his pencil skating back and forth until lines and shapes appeared. He started with a large circle for the jaw, a smaller one for the muzzle, and a rectangle for the nose. Two triangles marked the location of the ears, slightly above the dark oval of the eye. By changing the amount of pressure he applied to the paper, he could simulate light and shadow, or add texture like hair and whiskers. He'd just started in on the horse's mane when he heard a knock at his bedroom door and looked up to see Ray sticking his head into the room.

"Mind if I come in?" Ray asked.

Jaxon shrugged. "I guess." His gaze dropped to his sketchbook as Ray crossed to his desk, pulled out the chair, and turned it toward the bed. As Ray took a seat, Jaxon hoped this wasn't the beginning of some lecture about how he should've known better, and how his actions would have negative consequences for the future of the ranch. All of that might've been true, but Jaxon didn't feel the least bit guilty. If he didn't advocate for the mustangs, who would?

Ray indicated the sketchbook. "You're going to need a new one pretty soon."

"What does it matter? It's just a bunch of drawings."

"That's what your grandma used to say about her paintings. She thought their value came from what people were willing to pay for them, not from how much joy they brought her." Ray paused, sawing his jaw. "I wish we'd kept her pieces. Sometimes you don't realize how important something is until you lose it forever."

Jaxon closed his pencil inside his sketchbook and set both on his nightstand. The plate of food from dinner had been scraped clean. He sat up, his disappointment morphing back into frustration as he let his legs hang over the side of the bed.

"You say that, but then you pass up every opportunity to do the right thing," he said, sweeping his hair back with his hand.

"That's not true. I've always tried to do the right thing, even if it meant putting my life at risk."

Jaxon looked up, a shadow of regret drifting over his face.

Ray went on, "I know you feel strongly about the way the BLM has been treating the mustangs. And that's a good thing."

"So why are you making it seem like I'm just trying to cause trouble?"

"I'm not. This is a very complicated situation. I can't take sides without potentially hurting the people I care about most."

Ray looked around the room again until he spotted the basket of clean laundry next to the dresser. Hannah had mended the tear in Jaxon's shirt and placed it neatly on top of the pile of folded clothes. When Ray was Jaxon's age, he was already doing his own laundry, preparing his own meals, and taking care of more animals than most of his classmates could ever dream of owning. How could so much have changed in only one generation?

"You really should put those away. It would help your mom out," Ray said.

"What difference does it make if they're in the basket or in the dresser? At least they're clean."

"It's about the principle, Jax. The dresser is for clean clothes. The basket is for dirty clothes. You should be old enough to understand this by now."

Jaxon glanced at Ray's face. His dad looked exhausted, and the endless debate about chores, both household and barn-related, probably wasn't helping. Jaxon nodded slowly and turned his attention back to his sketchbook. "I understand. I'll put them away before I go to bed."

"You can put them away in the morning."

"Why not tonight?"

"Because," Ray said as he stood up, "you're going to need something to wear. It'll be cold outside, so you'll want to layer up. Make sure you pick something that's dark blue or black, so you don't draw too much attention to yourself."

Jaxon's eyes widened. "Wait, where are we going?"

Ray turned back to his son.

"To the mines," he replied. "We're going to go save your mustangs."

Fifteen

It wasn't the father-son bonding exercise Ray had hoped for, but at least they were finally doing something together other than fighting.

In the barn, they cross-tied their horses in the aisle, flicked the dust and debris from their coats with a brush, and scraped the hard-packed dirt from their hooves. They saddled their mounts and gradually tightened their cinches, ensuring the horses' skin didn't get pinched or irritated. As midnight approached, Ray hoped Jaxon might have a change of heart about the mustangs, but instead he continued to work in a quiet, straightforward manner, his face pale but resolute as he slipped on Barbell's bridle and secured the throat latch. When it was all said and done, he picked up the extra clothes he'd left on the bench and stuffed them into his saddle bag. A nylon sleeping bag was already rolled up under the back of the saddle's seat, with a pair of leather strings attached to each end to keep it firmly in place. Jaxon lifted the reins over his gelding's head and turned to look at Ray.

"Okay, let's go," he said.

"You have everything you need?" Ray asked.

"I think so."

"All right. In that case, you can open the door."

Jaxon hauled open the barn door. Although he'd never been to the mines, he knew what to expect out there in the rugged, stone-scabbed hills. Their plan was to locate the mustangs, drive them toward the wooded area near the mountains, and ride back along the river early tomorrow morning. With any luck, they'd never see another wild horse on their land again, and neither would the BLM.

"I hope we can find them," Jaxon said, leading Barbell outside. "It's pitch black out here."

Ray glanced at the scrim of moonlight reflecting off the smoky blue clouds before closing the barn door and checking his cinch one last time.

His horse, a stocky roan gelding with exquisitely long ears, merely sighed, as if riding into the high country in the dead of night were a regular occurrence.

"When we get up near the mines, stick close to me. The land can be unpredictable, so I'm going to need you to do whatever I say, when I say it. If at any point the situation becomes too dangerous or the horses start acting up, we turn around and go home, and I don't want to hear any whining. Okay?"

"Okay."

Ray placed his left foot in the stirrup and swung his right leg over the saddle. He shifted sideways until he was comfortably seated, then picked up the reins and directed his horse toward the trail.

Jaxon followed at a brisk pace, his body bouncing with each of Barbell's choppy steps. He owed it to the mustangs at the stockyard to do the right thing, no matter how scared he was. After all, it was the middle of the night, and even though saving the mustangs was the right thing to do *morally*, it wouldn't make a lick of difference to a judge if he and Ray got caught sneaking around. On top of that, there were plenty of animals that came out after dark to hunt, and two cowboys and their horses were easy pickings. He dug his heels into Barbell's sides and closed the gap separating him from Ray, who slowed his gelding as the trail narrowed before them.

"This isn't the trail to the north pasture," Jaxon said as Barbell picked his way over the tree roots, his hooves striking the gnarled wood with a dull resonance.

Ray glanced over his shoulder. "No. It's a different trail—this one goes northwest, then cuts along the riverbank for about two and a half miles. It's the only route I could think of that doesn't cross any other ranches between here and the mines."

Jaxon loosened his hold on the reins, allowing Barbell to use his head and neck for balance. Every so often, the pinto would stumble over the obstacles in their path, and Jaxon would lurch forward onto the saddle horn with a soft curse of pain or surprise. A few feet ahead of him, Ray leaned his body this way and that to avoid the low-hanging branches.

The air tingled with the smell of peat moss, horse sweat, and saddle leather, creaking volubly under Ray's weight. He took his right hand off the reins and lifted a pine bough away from his face, saying, "Heads up— or down, I suppose."

Jaxon hunched over his horse's neck. Barbell was an old, experienced ranch horse and had been ridden along trails just as narrow and treacherous as this one, but that didn't make Jaxon feel any better about the prospect of losing an eye. The spiny branches slapped at his neck, face, and shoulders as Barbell tried to keep pace with Ray's horse. Eventually, the trail sloped upward again, the tree cover grew sparse, and when Jaxon gained the courage to raise his head, he heard the thunderous torrent of the river rolling and crashing against the rocks.

They rode toward the bank at a walk, careful to maintain a safe distance from the fast-moving current. Even in the summer, the water was ice-cold, most of it comprised of runoff from the snowy mountain peaks. But for the past several years, the level of snowmelt had been steadily decreasing as the general temperature of the state—and the planet—rose higher and higher. Wherever human beings went, their impact on the natural environment was undeniably negative. Jaxon wondered if there would be any wild animals left by the time he was his grandfather's age, and how the world would deal with the lack of food once all the ranches and farmland disappeared.

"I've never seen this part of the river," Jaxon commented, keeping several feet behind Ray as he led them upstream.

"That's because we never cross the cattle here. The current's so strong we'd lose the entire herd."

"Makes sense. So, what did you used to do at the mines?"

"Just hung out with people from school. I know it seems hard to believe, but I was pretty popular back in the day. You might even say I was cool."

Jaxon scoffed. "Sure, dad. Whatever you say."

Ray slowed his horse so Jaxon could ride beside him. "One day, when your son's old enough, you can tell him about the time you came to the mines to rescue a herd of wild horses. Let's see if he believes *you*."

"He will. I'll have proof."

"Proof?"

Jaxon patted his coat pocket. "You really think I'd leave home without my phone?"

"Of course not. I doubt you'll get much of a signal all the way out here, but I'm sure a phone will come in handy at some point." Ray adjusted his grip on the reins, trying not to let his apprehension get the better of him. The nearest ranch—the Andersons'—was roughly six miles south of the mines, so he wasn't terribly concerned that anyone would see them. What worried him was the thought of being separated from Jaxon if one of them had to go for help, especially after he'd promised Hannah he wouldn't let anything happen to their son.

They rode in silence for a while, the moon crouched above a chain of mountains to the east. Far from the hum of traffic and the roar of the river, the world seemed like an infinite and untouched space. Some of Ray's fondest memories involved camping out in the high country during cattle drives, safe in the company of six or seven other cowboys who'd agreed to tag along. Once they got a fire going, Ray was sure he'd feel differently about being out here after dark, but right now all he knew was that he had to stay alert.

As they rounded the side of a hill, Jaxon looked up. "What's that?"

Ray followed his gaze. A tall, wooden structure jutted from the hillside: its shape resembled that of a barn, with an opening near the angle of the roof through which light and fresh air could pass. Even in the dark, it was clear the mine had been abandoned for years, with boards dangling by rusty nails and the pungent aroma of rotted timber hanging heavy in the air.

"It's an old mine shaft," Ray explained as they rode around the side of the structure. "Doesn't look like it's changed much since the last time I came here."

"That's good though, isn't it?"

"Yes and no. Abandoned buildings may look safe from the outside, but over time they slowly break down, making them more dangerous to explore." Ray pointed out the slightly smaller building hidden behind the headframe they'd initially spotted. "That's the hoist house. It's how they used to raise and lower heavy equipment down to the mining tunnels."

"Did you ever go inside, when you used to come here with your friends?"

"Once," Ray admitted, his tone becoming stern as he looked over at his son, "and it was a really idiotic idea. Of course, we didn't think so at the time, but you'd do well to stay out of the hoist house, no matter what time of day it is or how many people are with you. You never know when something might go wrong."

"And yet, here we are in the middle of the night, looking for mustangs." Jaxon smirked.

Ray gave him a long, hard look. "Do you think I want to be out here?"

"Uh, no?"

"Exactly."

"So, why'd you come?"

"Because your mom was worried you'd go off and do something reckless. For some reason, you've decided that these horses need your help, and I know you won't quit until you get what you want. I know that because you're just like me." Ray paused, glancing up at the shadowy frame of the mineshaft before continuing. "For a long time, I thought losing my leg was the worst thing that could have happened to us, but it wasn't. The absolute worst thing would be losing you."

"You're not going to lose me," Jaxon said, but his voice came out gravelly and raw, and his eyes started to water. He blinked hard a couple of times, blaming the irritation on the dust blowing through the cracks in the timber and not his own stupid emotions.

"But I am," Ray whispered, "every day, I lose you a little bit more. And I get it, you know—you have school and your friends. You want to be out *there*, not stuck on the ranch working fences. I get it," he said again, "but it doesn't make it easier."

Jaxon cleared his throat. He was afraid this would happen. Of course his dad would want to talk now that they were alone. But they were wasting time. The mustangs were still out there somewhere, and if they didn't find them before the BLM did, then it was all too clear how this story would end. As if Jaxon needed any more reason to feel guilty right now.

"We should keep going," he announced, jerking Barbell's reins. The pinto lifted his head and clopped across the dry plateau as the grass swayed and bowed in the wind. Soon, Jaxon heard Ray ride up from behind, his gelding snorting at the injustice of no longer being the lead horse.

"Are you sure you heard the guys right?" Ray asked after a few minutes of scouring the field. There appeared to be no sign of any horses anywhere: no hoofprints, no droppings, not even a patch of tamped-down grass where a mustang might've seen fit to roll and stretch her back.

"They clearly said they were up by the old mine," Jaxon argued, growing frustrated, "where else could they be?"

Ray hung back as Jaxon forged ahead. There were countless mines scattered across Colorado, from Castle Rock to Grand Junction. To presume the yardmen had been referring to the one closest to the Fishers' ranch only proved that Ray was no better at seeing the big picture than his son was. If that was the case, how was he supposed to help Jaxon navigate the unforgiving world of adulthood?

Barbell threw back his head. As Jaxon fought to get him under control, Ray trotted over and grabbed Barbell's reins near the bit. A flash of pain coursed through Ray's shoulder as the pinto attempted to yank his head free, his nostrils flaring as his agitation grew.

"Easy," Jaxon urged his horse, who gradually conceded his side of the fight. He glanced at Ray. "What the hell was that all about?"

"Something must've spooked him."

"It didn't spook Monty." Jaxon indicated Ray's horse, staring out into the blackness of the foothills with both ears pricked forward. Every fibre of his being was tuned in to his surroundings: even if Jaxon couldn't see it, Ray felt the ripples of fear radiating across Monty's back like static from an old TV.

Ray scanned the field. There were mountains on both sides of the valley and a tangle of trees straight ahead. From somewhere off in the darkness he heard the low, grinding noise of running water and the breathy sound of an animal moving steadily toward it.

He held out his hand. "Give me your phone, please." Jaxon rummaged in his pocket and surrendered the device.

Ray switched on the flashlight and raised it slowly. First, he saw the animal's legs, followed by the jade glow of its eyes and the triangular tips of its ears. Another set of eyes, another long snout. White clouds of warm breath billowed around their muzzles as they gazed in stunned confusion at the bright spot that had suddenly and inexplicably descended on their hideout.

"Mustangs," Jaxon whispered.

Ray lowered the phone. One look at these creatures was enough to tell him they didn't belong to anyone: they were short, stocky, and unbranded. Lifting the phone again, he did a quick count of the animals he could see. Heads popped up from behind the writhing mass of necks and backs, but the mustangs didn't make any move to flee.

"I didn't know feral herds got this big," Jaxon said, stroking Barbell's shoulder until he calmed down. "Do you think this is all of them?"

Ray switched off the light and handed back Jaxon's phone. "I don't know, but I counted over thirty. They look to be in good shape, too."

"They won't be once the BLM shows up." Jaxon scowled.

Ray considered what to do next. Moving a herd in the dark was risky business, but if they waited until daybreak, it might be too late. Their best bet was to approach the mustangs slowly, and drive them deeper into the trees in hopes they'd eventually find their way to safety.

"Okay, here's the plan: we'll drive them north toward those mountains over there. There's a valley on the other side that has water and plenty of room to graze. Once morning comes, we can continue pushing them into the foothills and, hopefully, under the BLM's radar," Ray explained.

Jaxon nodded. "I think it might work."

"Don't follow the herd too close, and try not to cause a stampede. We've got at least four hours until the sun comes up—that should be enough time to do what we need to do without anyone seeing us." Ray lifted the reins. "I'll take the right flank. You go left."

"Got it."

Squeezing Monty's sides, Ray said, "Walk on." The gelding heeded his command and started forward at a willing pace. The mustangs on the fringes of the herd raised their heads as the unfamiliar horse approached. Then, all at once, they turned inward and began to run.

As soon as Ray got within a few feet of the herd, several mares and their foals disappeared into the bushes for safety. Jaxon and Barbell shadowed them at a trot, the white blotches on Barbell's coat making him easily visible in the moonlight. As the trees closed in, Ray quickly amended his original plan. The mustangs would have little trouble navigating the roots and branches that lay ahead. But for Monty and Barbell, who'd been bred for life on the range, one small slip could lead to lameness and stall rest—and that was the *best* case scenario.

"Jaxon," Ray called over to his son, "I don't think we'll be able to get through here. Not at night, anyway."

"What are we going to do then?"

"It's risky, but I think we should try and go back the way we came. Past the mines."

He couldn't see Jaxon's face, only the silhouette of his arm as he raised a hand to adjust his hat. "We'll be out in the open though."

"I know, that's why I said it's risky. But I'm not sure it's any worse than trying to get past all these trees in the dark."

Jaxon considered this logic. They had to act quickly if they wanted to keep the herd together. "I say we do it."

"Good. Try and get ahead of them if you can. Once we gather the herd, we'll pick up the pace."

Jaxon pricked Barbell's sides with his spurs, causing the pinto to launch into a lope. He kept a firm hold on the reins as he rode past a cluster of mares and their foals before circling around them in a gentle arc. Startled, the mustangs broke into a chaotic sprint, bumping and jostling against each other as they fled. As the herd reassembled, the pinto surged ahead, trying to keep pace with the mustangs now storming across the valley.

"Not so fast," Ray yelled as he caught up.

"I'm not driving them. I'm following." The wind stung Jaxon's eyes as Barbell galloped across the plateau, caught up in the excitement all horses felt when they ran as a group.

Jaxon grinned. All the stress of the last few weeks seemed to blow away as the pungent, earthy aroma of the mustangs surrounded him in a gritty cloud of dust. Peering out from under the brim of his hat, he saw the outline of the mine shaft jutting into the starry sky. While it may have posed some danger to a group of overly-curious teenagers, the old building was just another fixture on the horizon to the horses.

Before long, the herd slowed to a more manageable pace. Jaxon loosened his hold on the reins as Ray rode up on his left. The mustangs moved steadily ahead of them, treading carefully now over the rocks and other debris that littered their path. One horse in particular caught Jaxon's interest: she was lagging slightly behind the others, her bulbous body swaying from side to side with each step. Slipping his hand into his pocket, Jaxon pulled out his phone again and turned on his flashlight in order to see her more clearly.

"I think that one's pregnant," he said.

Ray squinted. "She's bagged up, all right," referring to the mare's swollen udder. "I wouldn't be surprised if she dropped the foal within the next couple of days."

"It's a good thing we found her. Imagine if she had to have her foal in a stockyard."

"It wouldn't be any more dangerous than having her foal out here," Ray stated. He nodded at Jaxon's phone. "Better put that away before you lose it."

"Right." Jaxon switched off his flashlight, plunging the valley back into darkness.

Ray studied his son. "We really shouldn't interfere," he began to say as Jaxon patted Barbell's neck. "I know it's hard to see things you don't agree with and not want to get involved, but nature abides by its own rules. Sometimes things work out, and sometimes they don't."

"Yeah, I know. But I kind of feel like we owe it to them, you know? I mean, we moved into their habitat, we built ranches on their land, and now we're telling these animals they don't have a right to exist?" Jaxon shook his head. "People suck."

"Maybe, but my point stands: we do only as much as we need to in order to ensure the mustangs are out of harm's way, and then we go home. After that, we let nature take its course."

Jaxon remained silent.

"Jaxon, tell me you understand," Ray urged.

"I understand," Jaxon mumbled.

"Good. Think of it as putting a baby bird back in its nest. It's a small thing, but it makes a difference."

"Do you really think that's the same thing, dad? Birds fall out of their nests all the time. Remember that swallow chick we found in the barn when I was a kid? You said the mom might've pushed it out because she knew it would never be big enough to fly. Nature makes decisions based on survival—it doesn't go around blowing baby birds out of nests for the fun of it."

Jaxon spurred Barbell into a trot. As they rode ahead, Ray thought of the little boy Jaxon used to be, the one who'd scooped that featherless chick off the dusty barn floor and begged Ray to revive its tiny, lifeless form. After explaining as best he could why some animals didn't make it to adulthood, Ray had helped Jaxon bury the baby bird behind the barn. They'd even gone so far as to lay a rock on top of its grave, although Ray knew it wouldn't deter predators from digging up a midnight snack. Despite his own feelings about being a rancher, deep down, Ray realized Jaxon was right: nature always had her reasons, but greed wasn't one of them.

"I think we can get through here," he heard Jaxon say. As Ray lifted his gaze from between Monty's ears and scanned the horizon for Barbell's milky white hide, he saw Jaxon pointing toward the top of the ridge. The incline wasn't all that steep, but who knew what lay on the other side of it?

"You think it goes to the valley?" Ray asked.

"I think there's only one way to find out."

"We can keep going, Jax. I'm sure we'll find another spot to cross closer to the river."

"You don't trust me, do you?"

"It's not about trust. It's dark and we don't know what the terrain is like. We have to be sensible about this."

"Look, the herd is already moving in that direction," Jaxon said. "Do you trust *them*?"

"What did I just say about trust?"

"Oh, my god. You just said we have to let nature take its course." Jaxon gestured to the mustangs. "This is *their* land. *They* know what they're doing out here. We're just tagging along to make sure they get there safely."

Ray sighed and reined in his frustration.

"You want me to take over the ranch, but you can't give up even a smidge of control," Jaxon went on, his voice sharp like glass in the night, "all you do is order me around, and when I try to talk to you about things that matter, you shut me down. You're doing exactly what grandpa used to do to you."

"I don't want to hear you say that ever again. I'm nothing like Bernard. I've given you everything you could possibly ask for."

"Well, I'm asking you for one more thing. I'm asking you to trust me."

Ray tried to rub away the stabbing pain in his left eye that signaled the onset of another headache. Every minute they spent arguing pushed the mustangs closer to capture, and with the moon slipping further west, they couldn't afford any more delays.

"All right," he said at last. "Let's take them over."

Jaxon lifted the reins, dug his heels into Barbell's sides, and set off toward the stony incline.

The mustangs circled tightly, following his lead. As the ground began to slope upward, Jaxon leaned forward in the saddle and rode hard toward the top of the ridge, each powerful thrust of Barbell's body sending a jolt through his legs and back. He could smell the dust rising as the herd converged on the narrow path, each horse pushing and shoving to get ahead, then fighting to maintain a foothold on the loose dirt and stones. Nervous squeals and grunts of exertion pierced the murky darkness, but still Jaxon rode on, his horse clambering over the hazardous terrain. Far behind him, somewhere in the unendingness of the night, Ray's voice urged the stragglers on. In situations like these, momentum was key: they couldn't stop until they reached the other side, or gravity would drag the entire herd down in a landslide of broken bones.

As the ground evened out, Jaxon stepped aside and allowed the mustang herd to regroup. He'd been right—there was a valley on the other side, surrounded by hills and trees that cut sharply into the night sky.

Ray crested the ridge and rode over to stand beside Jaxon at the edge of the field. Together, they watched the wild horses disappear into the shadows of their new home, seeking refuge among the sagebrush and long grasses that danced and quivered in the wind.

"We did it," Jaxon said. His voice was thin, wonderstruck, and a little out of breath.

Ray glimpsed the outline of his face and smiled. "We did."

"Do you think they'll be safe here?"

"For now. We'll stick close for a bit, just to make sure they settle in."

Glancing around, Jaxon pointed to a small copse of trees standing about thirty feet to their right. "We can tie the horses there. Maybe we can make a fire?"

"Yes, but a small one. I think we could all use some rest after tonight."

After securing Barbell and Monty to the trees and stripping the heavy saddles from their backs, Ray cleared a spot in the dirt for a campfire. He gathered several fist-sized rocks and arranged them in a ring around the fire pit, lined the dugout with dry leaves and twigs, and struck a match to ignite the kindling. Jaxon had untied his sleeping bag from his saddle and spread it on the ground a few feet from the inferno, where he sat and watched the leaves curl and blacken in the heat.

"I can't believe we actually found them," Jaxon remarked as Ray brought over a bottle of water and a sleeve of saltine crackers from his saddlebag.

"You found them, mainly." Ray handed Jaxon the refreshments before easing himself down onto the saddle blanket that served as his bed for the night. He stretched out his right leg and massaged the area around his prosthesis. He'd never worn his leg for this long: the pain was bearable, but persistent. He hoped that by taking some weight off of it for a few hours, he'd be able to ride home in the morning without any complications.

Jaxon observed him uneasily. "How's your leg?"

"It's all right. Just a bit sore." Ray shifted into a more comfortable position and nodded at the crackers. "You should eat."

Setting the water aside, Jaxon peeled back the plastic and pulled out one of the crackers. He should've been ravenous, like he usually was after a long ride, but all he could focus on was the sound of horses in the valley and the aching in his muscles from trying to control Barbell. Plus, he was exhausted, and with how the smoke was swirling around, he thought it might not be a bad idea to close his eyes for a while.

Shoving the last bite in his mouth, Jaxon stood up and headed toward the shadows at the edge of their campsite.

"Where are you going?" Ray asked.

"Relax, I'm just going to the bathroom."

The sky to the east was beginning to lighten as dawn approached. As Jaxon made his way back to camp, he stopped and squinted into the bowl of the valley below, trying to discern the faint movement of animals wandering around in the dark. The pregnant mare was somewhere among them—possibly even searching for a place to deliver her foal. That baby was going to survive because of *him*, he thought. Sure, he might get in trouble for trespassing at the stockyard, but standing here under a sky full of stars while a herd of wild horses roamed freely beneath it, he didn't honestly care. He'd done the right thing tonight, and that was enough for him.

Ray glanced up as Jaxon settled down on the sleeping bag and wrapped his arms around his legs.

"Mom's probably worried about us," Jaxon said idly.

"Not too worried, I hope. After all, this was her idea."

"Really?"

"She knows you better than you think. And she knows me pretty well, too. That being said, you're still grounded until you're thirty-five."

"Jeez. That's practically a slap on the wrist." Ray's eyes crinkled as he laughed. "Hey, dad?"

"Yeah?"

Jaxon smiled. "Thanks for coming with me."

After a few minutes, Ray glanced sideways to find Jaxon's eyes glazing over as he stared into the fire.

"It's been a long night," Ray said as Jaxon tried to pretend he hadn't been drifting off. "Why don't you try and get some sleep?"

"But what about the mustangs?"

"Don't worry. I'll look out for them."

Jaxon nodded and lay down on his side. He closed his eyes and was asleep within seconds.

Ray put a hand to the back of his son's head, feeling the warmth of his hair against his fingers and palms. Even now, sixteen years after the doctor had handed Jaxon over, Ray still felt that blinding wave of first love wash through him with unimaginable force. What a wonderful, caring, courageous person he and Hannah had created together. What a gift it was to be his father.

Sixteen

Ray awoke a couple of hours later to a charred pile of firewood and clear blue skies in all directions. He sat up, his breath condensing in a silvery cloud as he blinked away the dregs of sleep. For all the times he'd slept on the ground, he'd never been this sore the following day. Even just turning his head to scope out the valley was agony.

Ray glimpsed the sleeping bag near his feet. At one point in the night, Jaxon had crawled sleepily into the nylon cocoon and buried himself deep in its warmth. Now, though, the sack lay partially open, the corner thrown back to reveal the red and black checkered lining inside. Aside from his hat, there was no sign of Jaxon anywhere. Ray glimpsed the trees where Monty and Barbell had been tied; both horses were still standing in the shade, their saddles resting on the ground. Ray climbed to his feet, wincing at the pain in his right leg as he turned a slow circle, scanning the landscape for his son.

What he saw was a valley covered in wildflowers and short, scraggly trees that quivered in the wind. He saw the mountains he'd grown up with, dark green giants casting their shadows on the hills below. Ray raised a hand to block the sun's light, and that was when he noticed the pond, half-hidden behind a screen of cattails. Where there was water, there were wild horses. Where there were wild horses, he was bound to find Jaxon.

Jaxon had awoken at dawn. As the sun had risen in a glaring red disc over the mountains, he'd crawled out of his sleeping bag, pulled on his jacket, and started down the hill toward the trees hoping for a glimpse of the elusive creatures.

He'd located the herd down by the pond, then sat on the bank observing their dynamics as the sky brightened and widened above him. Like their domestic counterparts, wild horses were bound by a strict set of duties. The lead mare was responsible for ensuring the herd remained safe and well-fed, a role she typically shared with the lead stallion. When rival mustangs or predators threatened the herd's safety, it was the stallion's job to defend it, just as it was his job to mitigate any conflict that arose within the herd. Rounding out these feral bands were several younger mares, their foals, and a handful of juvenile stallions who, upon reaching maturity, were expelled from the herd and forced to create their own. It amazed Jaxon just how similar mustangs were to human families: he thought of his dad, fighting every day to protect his land from external forces; his mom, fixing his meals and washing his clothes; his grandpa, lower in the pecking order but still a key part of the family's success; and now his sister, whose role was still largely undefined. If he could somehow get people to see the wild horses as a reflection of themselves rather than a threat to their way of life, would it be enough to change the course of history?

At the sound of footsteps, Jaxon turned to find Ray picking his way down the side of the hill.

"Dad, look," Jaxon said. He pointed to the pregnant mare he'd seen last night—and, beside her, the knobby shape of her newborn foal. "He was already walking around when I found them. I'd say he's about two hours old."

Ray glanced down at his son, then back at the mustangs. "That's the thing about prey animals: they have to be ready to run as soon as they're born."

Jaxon turned back to the herd. That might've been the only real difference between humans and horses, he thought. But the rest of it— the family dynamics, the reliance on the land for survival, not to mention the fact that so many horses were forced to spend their lives working for evil people the way human beings worked for evil corporations—only proved why the two species needed each other now more than ever.

"I counted thirty-three mustangs," he went on, his arms wrapped around his knees. "I took a video of them too, just like I did with the mustangs at the stockyard. I thought maybe…"

Ray crouched down beside him and caught a glimpse of his reflection in the murky water. "You thought maybe, what?"

"We could make a video and upload it to your channel. I could narrate over it and talk about some of the things I've been reading. I'd do my research, of course. And all the editing."

Ray shook his head slowly, his mouth drawn into a fine line that matched the wrinkles forming around his eyes. "I don't know if that's the best idea, bud. While I have no doubt you've done your research, I can't be using my channel to campaign against the BLM."

"I know, but you have over a hundred thousand subscribers. Don't you feel obligated to use your platform for good?"

"I *am* using it for good. I'm using it to generate business leads to keep our family fed and housed. I'm sorry if that's not the answer you were hoping for."

He was expecting Jaxon to argue, like he'd done a thousand times before. Instead, he turned back to the herd as it fanned out across the strip of grass between the pond and the woods, where pockets of wildflowers shivered in the tenacious breeze. "It's okay. It was just an idea."

Ray arched his brows. "Really?"

"Yeah. I've been sitting here for a while, and I've had a lot of time to think. I know lately I haven't been acting the way I should, and I think it's because everyone expects something from me without asking me what *I* want. What's important to me. Even you—sometimes you treat me like I'm still a little kid, and it makes me feel like you don't take anything I say seriously."

"You're right," Ray said, bowing his head slightly, "and I'm sorry if you feel like I don't take you seriously. The truth is, I'm just scared. I know how hard it was for me to grow up on the ranch, and I don't want you to struggle the way my brothers and I did. I wish I could protect you from everything, but maybe I don't need to." He indicated the mustangs. "Clearly you can take care of yourself, just like these guys can."

Jaxon's smile widened, his eyes scrunched nearly shut against the blinding sun. "I'm going to take really good care of the ranch," he promised.

"I know you will. And take good care of the fences, unless you want to be putting in a brand new one when you're forty-five."

Jaxon stood up, the slightly soggy ground yielding under his boots as he walked around the edge of the pond. When he was within twenty feet of her, the mare raised her head and pricked her ears toward him, her eyes wide and assessing. For the next month or so, her foal would be fully dependent on her for feeding and protection. Back at the ranch, Jaxon knew to keep a safe distance from their lactating mares, although it was sometimes necessary to get between mother and baby. If for some reason a foal had to be separated from its dam, the mare would pace the paddock fence until she was reunited with her offspring once again.

He knew all this, and yet Jaxon's feet continued to carry him forward.

Ray climbed to his feet, panic ringing in his voice. "Jaxon, don't get too close to the foal."

"Dad, it's okay." Jaxon faced the baby again. At just under a hundred pounds, he looked about as stable as the abandoned mine shaft they'd passed last night. The velvety slits of his nostrils opened to receive the bevy of mingled scents.

Jaxon extended his hand and held his breath. He'd stand here all morning if that's what it took to earn the foal's trust. The thought that he'd be the first, and possibly only, person to ever make physical contact with this mustang sent goosebumps up his arms. It was the feeling he imagined people who went to church experienced when the choir sang *Amazing Grace*—like he was a part of something much bigger, touched by the invisible hand of the Holy Spirit.

The foal took a faltering step toward him. Jaxon stood perfectly still, refusing to breathe as the colt inched closer and closer. Meanwhile, Ray considered the quickest route to the Andersons' ranch in case his worst fear—that Jaxon would be trampled by a wild horse acting on instinct—came true.

Thirty breathless seconds later, the foal stuck out its neck to sniff Jaxon's hand. Its muzzle was warm and soft like the sun kissed skin of a peach, the short, smooth hairs around its mouth tinged with golden sunlight. Jaxon couldn't believe it—he was actually petting a wild horse.

A wild horse that he'd saved, and that would one day run free in the mountains like God intended.

Jaxon turned back to Ray and grinned. As he faced the foal again, the mare lowered her head and pinned her ears. Heeding her warning, Jaxon took several steps back until his heels sank into the muck at the edge of the pond.

"Did you see that?" Jaxon asked as Ray moved to stand next to him.

"I saw. You're lucky the mare didn't attack you."

"Why would she attack me? She's had hours to get accustomed to my scent." He tipped his head back and scanned the watery swath of sky. "Do you hear that?"

"Hear what?"

Jaxon shielded his eyes with his hand and searched the horizon again, his heart booming in his chest. "A helicopter."

The craft flew in from the south, the glass dome of its cockpit glinting in the sun. Jaxon couldn't hear anything above the stutter of its rotors whipping the treetops around in a frenzy. The helicopter veered toward the hills, vanishing from sight for a few seconds before reappearing at the far end of the valley like a large, buzzing insect seeking purchase on a brightly-coloured flower. Soon, having found a relatively flat area between the woods and the pond, the craft levelled out and landed gently in a patch of grass.

As Ray and Jaxon made their way across the field, the pilot ducked out of the cockpit. He was an abundant man, broad-shouldered with plenty of neck to spare. He wore a windbreaker made from a thin blue material, beige khaki pants, and dull black shoes, as well as a headset with a microphone so he could communicate with his copilot. He removed the headset as his partner exited the chopper and hunched his shoulders against the wind.

"Howdy," the pilot called out. "We didn't realize anyone was camping in this area."

"Last I checked, it isn't illegal to camp on public land," Ray replied. "Are you with the Bureau of Land Management?"

"Yes, sir. My name's Jed Thompson. That's my partner and copilot, Ron McGrath."

Ray smiled inscrutably. Jed and Ron both looked like the kind of men who spent their days behind a desk, approving or denying grazing permits while Ray and his fellow ranchers tried to work within the confines of their zoning requirements. "It's nice to meet you," he said.

Jed flicked his eyes at Jaxon, standing a few feet to Ray's right and scowling like a Doberman that had just scented an intruder. If the noise from the helicopter was hurting *his* ears, he could only imagine what it was doing to the mustangs.

"So," Jed said, switching his focus back to Ray, "mind if I ask what you gentlemen are doing all the way out here?"

"I wanted to show my son the old mine," Ray explained, pointing to the ridge. "Our campsite's over there. We're on horseback."

"I see. Well, the mines sure hold a lot of history—and I'm not just talking about the silver boom."

Ray noted the streaks of grey in Jed's hair. For all he knew, perhaps they'd crossed paths at a tailgate party years ago: the mines had attracted plenty of older kids too, nipping at bottles of Tennessee Whiskey they'd pilfered from their parents' liquor cabinet. Who knew they'd one day find themselves back here, separated not by a roaring campfire but by an opposing set of values?

"I seem to recall this being a hot spot back in the day. Seems pretty quiet now though," Ray said.

"No kidding. When I was your son's age, my friends and I used to love poking around the hoist house—we knew it was dangerous, but that was part of the fun." Jed laughed, a high-pitched, wheezing noise that grated on Jaxon's nerves. As he sobered, he looked at Ray again and furrowed his brows. "Sorry, do I know you?"

"I don't think so."

"Hmm. Just thought you looked familiar."

Ron, who'd been silent up to now, waved his hand at the bushes flanking the meadow. "Did you happen to see any wild horses?"

"We did."

"They're quite something, aren't they?"

Ray only nodded. He could feel the anger radiating off Jaxon like a heatwave, and he was sure Jed and Ron could feel it too.

Suddenly, Jaxon said, "There's a newborn foal in that herd. He's too young to keep up with the other mustangs, so you shouldn't be chasing them around in a helicopter."

Jed humored him by saying, "Trust me, I don't like the chopper any more than you do, but it's the quickest way to get the job done. Besides, the chopper doesn't hurt them."

"That's not what Amanda Bowman said," Jaxon argued.

"Who's Amanda Bowman?"

"She's an animal rights activist. She's been trying to raise awareness about the plight of the mustangs in Colorado. She requested to observe one of the BLM's roundups, but the BLM barred her from the area. When she showed up anyway, she was told to leave or she'd be arrested and charged."

"Amanda Bowman," Jed muttered, reaching back through his memories for a face that matched the name. "Can't say as I've ever met her, but I'll tell you this: the BLM conducts roundups on both public and private land. It's very possible she was attempting to trespass on private property, which would've surely warranted legal action."

"It wasn't private property—it was a field just like this one." Jaxon spread his arms in an encompassing motion. "Like my dad said, it's not illegal to camp on BLM land. If that's the case, why threaten to arrest her unless the BLM knew they were doing something wrong?"

"What makes you think the BLM was doing anything wrong? If you ask me, it sounds like whoever Ms. Bowman was in contact with didn't want her to get in the middle of a potential stampede," Ron volunteered.

He had sad-looking eyes like a Bloodhound, but something in his tone made Jaxon think his bite was deadly. "Mustangs aren't pets—they're wild animals, and they need to be controlled."

"They need to be protected," Jaxon fired back, "they were here long before we showed up, and they're going to be here long after we're gone."

Suddenly, Jed raised his brows and wagged a thick finger at Ray. "I *do* know you. Bionic Cowboy Tour—you did a bit at the rodeo in Tulsa, Oklahoma."

Ray felt all the air leave his lungs. Gone was any hope he had of maintaining his anonymity, of disappearing under the BLM's radar. Fame, it seemed, was a double-edged sword—something Mickey had proven over and over again. "That's me."

"My son couldn't stop talking about you—said he wants to be a cowboy when he grows up." Jed chuckled. "Boys, am I right?"

"I think we should be going," Ray said with a nod at his son. "It's been good chatting with you fellas."

Jaxon eyed him hotly. "You're not just going to walk away, are you? And let them kill the mustangs?"

Jed furrowed his brows. "What's he talking about?"

"Nothing, just something he read online," Ray replied, curling his fingers around Jaxon's arm to lead him away.

"You shouldn't believe everything you read. Most of it's just rumours," Ron put in.

"It's not a rumour. I have proof." Jaxon dug his hand into his pocket and pulled out his phone. He clicked on the video and showed it to the pilots. "Recognize these? They're the mustangs you rounded up a few days ago. Notice the one on the ground isn't moving."

"Jaxon, we're leaving," Ray gritted.

"I went to the stockyard," Jaxon continued. "I saw for myself what the BLM is involved in, and it's definitely not protecting the mustangs."

"You watch yourself," Ron warned, taking a noticeable step toward Jaxon.

"Or what? If you go through with this roundup, I'll post the video online and tell everyone what *really* happens out here."

"You do that," Jed chimed in, "and you'll have a lawsuit on your hands, young man."

Ray couldn't move. If Jaxon were anyone else's son, Jed's threat would have been enough to put an end to this foolish behaviour. Hell, if he were Waylon's son, Ray was certain Jaxon wouldn't still be standing here. But Jaxon was *his* son, and that meant he was going to stand his ground whether Ray liked it or not.

Jed's congenial façade crumbled. He inclined his head forward, his gaze hardening as they fixated on the obstinate boy. "I'm going to give you and your dad one last chance to do the right thing and walk away."

"What happens if we don't?" Jaxon asked.

"Well, that's a problem, you see. Now that we know your names—" Jed cast his eyes at Ray "—we can suspend all future grazing permits. With just one phone call, I can take away everything your family has worked so hard for. If you truly believe that having a roof over your head means less than those wild horses you love so much, then you're no smarter than they are."

Jaxon's innards twisted into a burning ball of rage. As the heat surfaced on his face, he lunged toward Jed intending to teach him a lesson. But the pilot was quicker, and before Jaxon could react, Jed reached for his jacket and shoved him to the ground.

A searing pain exploded across Jaxon's face. He blinked several times to clear his vision and raised a shaky hand to his cheek. His fingers came away slick with blood.

He turned his unfocused gaze back to Jed, but instead saw the faded brown material of Ray's jacket.

"Touch my son again and I swear to God, I'll kill you with my bare hands," Ray said.

Jed had the audacity to look bewildered.

"Your son charged *me*," he argued, "and I acted in self-defense."

Jaxon rose unsteadily, his heart racing and his face throbbing in pain. He might as well have been trying to navigate a pitch-black room: out here, in a place he once thought he knew so well, he found himself moving with exaggerated caution and a heightened awareness of his own vulnerability. He clenched his teeth, determined not to cry in front of these strange men as fear and anger mingled in his gut.

"Self-defense," Ray repeated, his voice strained. "What's to stop me from pressing charges?"

"You won't. You think I believe you came all the way out here to investigate some old mine?"

"You're miles from any mines," Ron chimed in with another hooded glance in Jaxon's direction.

"If you press charges," Jed went on, "I'll make sure you never graze another animal anywhere in the state of Colorado. But feel free to call my bluff."

"Dad, don't," Jaxon whispered.

Ray reached behind him for Jaxon's arm. Protecting his family was the most important job he'd ever have, but raising cattle was a close second. He swallowed the bitter taste of panic and nodded at the men.

"That's what I thought." Jed looked at Ron as he angled back to the chopper. "Round 'em up."

"Dad, I'm sorry," Jaxon quivered.

Ray faced him. His expression was a bizarre mix of terror and relief. When he realized the extent of Jaxon's injuries, he drew his son against his chest and covered the back of his head with his hand. The chopper lifted into the air behind him, its rotors purring as it careened away. "No. *I'm* sorry. I never should've brought you out here," Ray said.

"Where are they going?" Jaxon wrestled free of Ray's embrace and tracked the helicopter's movements across the sky. "Where are the mustangs?"

But he knew. Somewhere in the jagged shadows of the mountainside, thirty-three wild horses were about to meet an awful fate. They'd undertaken a perilous journey just to wind up in a metal corral at a stockyard. This land was theirs, but it wasn't. At the end of the day, weren't they all—cowboys and mustangs alike—just pawns in the BLM's game?

"This isn't fair," Jaxon heard himself say over the buzzing in his right ear. He turned back to Ray. "We found them first. Why do they get to decide what happens next?"

"Because that's the way life is," Ray explained. "You can do everything right and still fail." He examined the cut on Jaxon's face as he flinched and tried to pull away. "Does it hurt?"

"It's not that bad. I know I shouldn't have charged him."

"That's no excuse for what he did. No one lays a hand on my son and gets away with it."

Jaxon nodded. His face was sore, but it was no match for the gut-wrenching agony he felt when he thought of the newborn foal. Its life was just beginning, and already it was over. How was any of this even remotely okay?

Tears spilled down Jaxon's cheeks. It was like being hit by a bus, the way the pain ripped him apart.

We have to let nature take its course. Those were the words Ray had uttered last night, knowing that humans, in their perpetual foolishness, always hoped nature would take their side. But the hardest part about being a parent—and the part no one had warned Ray about—was how telling his son the truth felt like he was letting him down. So, he lied and told him everything would be okay, when he knew damn well it wouldn't.

Seventeen

Ray knew he was in trouble. It wasn't the first time he'd crossed a line, but this particular instance carried more weight simply because Jaxon was involved. Add to that the fact that Hannah was expecting her son to be returned to her unharmed, and Ray could already feel the shift in his marriage the way animals could intuit forest fires. The difference was, they had the good sense to run away from danger, while he was headed directly into the wall of suffocating black smoke.

They rode back to the ranch in near total silence. Monty, as usual, assumed the lead, traversing the wide dirt path while meadowlarks sang their distinctive, two-note song. As daylight surged into full brightness, the air became almost uncomfortably warm—a far cry from the nippy conditions that had behooved them to dress in layers the night before. But that was how it seemed to be out here, Ray mused, glancing over his shoulder to ensure Jaxon was keeping up: just when he thought he knew what to expect, life proved to be full of surprises. He faced the trail again, trying to ignore the pulsating ache at the junction of his real leg and his artificial one, but with every step Monty took, the small, scattered vibrations rocked Ray to his core. He longed to stop and rest, but doing so would only delay their return, thus heightening Hannah's anxiety. So, they rode on, their pace slow but unfaltering beneath the dim shadow of the clouds.

After another thirty minutes of riding, the sound of rushing water drowned out the volley of birdcall. Ray figured this would be a good time to water the horses, whose laboured breathing suggested they were not tolerating the heat any better than their riders.

As the riverbank came into view, Ray nudged Monty toward a stand of evergreen trees. Their bark was slick with moisture from the tumbling current. As it surged past the bank in a tumultuous clamor, Ray swung his leg over Monty's back and eased himself to the ground, cussing softly at the pain that flared halfway up his thigh. He hobbled over to the river's edge and stared down at the churning rapids, where the metallic fetor of the mountainside rose up to greet him. The current was too strong to do anything here: they'd have to walk half a mile downstream if they had any hope of quenching the horses' thirst, but for a time he merely stood on the flat pedestal of rock and admired the power of the natural world as if this vast, untamed place hadn't tried to kill him on multiple occasions.

Jaxon pulled on Barbell's reins and dismounted. He let the left rein slip to the ground and walked over to stand beside Ray, his feet spread slightly apart for balance.

"This all came from the mountain?" Jaxon asked, admiring the river's unbridled force.

"Most of it." Fear squeezed in Ray's chest as he looked over at his son. *One slip, and I'd lose him forever.* Ray quelled the urge to pull him back by saying, "The level's lower this year. Every year it goes down a couple of inches thanks to the shorter winters and declining snowmelt. Not that you can tell just from looking at it that anything's different."

Jaxon retreated, calming some of Ray's worry. "There's got to be a point where it slows down, right?" he asked.

Ray considered his answer. *Was* there a point where everything slowed down and allowed him to catch his breath? For years he'd watched his life go by in a blur, his days taken up by work and raising his family. The further he ventured into his forties, the faster time seemed to accelerate. One day, this moment would be nothing but a faint memory he reached for in the darkness of old age. Even as he was learning to let Jaxon go, another part of him yearned to cling to him for eternity.

"Dad? There's a point where it slows down, right?"

"There is," Ray replied, turning back to Monty and Barbell. "We'll walk the horses downstream. Give them a break from carrying us."

They followed the river's course, never able to match its pace. As it curved around a large boulder, the frothing waves lost some of their momentum. Another hundred feet down, the river twisted in the opposite direction, and in doing so, lost some of its strength.

Jaxon tied his horse to the trunk of a tree and approached the water's edge. He was desperately thirsty, and even hungrier for some relief from the oppressive heat. Kneeling in the grass, he scooped a handful of icy water into his cupped palm and drank until his fingers became numb and pale from the runoff. Soon, Ray walked over and offered him one of the empty bottles from his saddlebag.

Ray squatted down and dipped the open end of the second bottle into the river. As it filled, he looked over at Jaxon and asked, "How's your eye?"

"It's okay." Jaxon put the lid on the bottle and set it aside. He could see his reflection in the small, eddying pools that filled the gaps between the rocks. His right cheek was puffy and dark; the cut, approximately an inch in length, stung each time he blinked. He leaned close to the surface of the river and splashed water over the right side of his face, cleansing the dried blood and residual dirt from his skin.

Jaxon sat back on his heels, his cheek shimmering with dampness. "I'm in a lot of trouble, aren't I?" he asked as Ray lifted the bottle out of the current.

"No. I am."

"But I stood up to the BLM."

"I took you out there, and I actively threatened them. As the adult in this situation, I should have taken the necessary steps to reduce the risk of you getting hurt. But now I realize I'm not capable of making good judgment calls." Ray paused. He felt Jaxon watching him, but couldn't meet his son's gaze. The river babbled incessantly, keeping the uncomfortable silence at bay.

At last, Ray said, "I'm not saying anything will happen, but it's important for you to have all the information you need in order to run the ranch."

"What do you mean?"

"The password for my computer is July2015. On it, you'll find a folder called 'Emma.' It contains everything related to the family business— breeding records, expense sheets, you name it. There's also a separate folder for industry contacts, in case you don't have the hay guy's number, for instance."

Jaxon had gone pale, making the cut on his face more noticeable. "Can't you just show me all this stuff once I turn eighteen?"

"I will. But in case I don't get the chance—"

Jaxon stood up, anger flashing in his eyes. He took a step back from the riverbank as Ray stared at his wedding ring, pushing the gold band close to the knuckle in case, after two decades of marriage, it should suddenly slide off.

"Stop it," Jaxon scolded, "stop talking crazy! Nothing's going to happen."

"Jaxon, I'm just trying to prepare you—"

"I don't want to hear it. I don't want to be prepared."

Ray looked up at him and sighed. "I know you're scared. But it's going to be okay." He rose to a standing position. To think that only a few weeks ago, he'd been questioning whether Jaxon would ever be ready to take over the ranch. Now, it seemed imperative to share as much knowledge as he could before the consequences of his actions caught up to them.

Jaxon cleared his throat. His eyes were red and glistening with moisture, but he lifted his chin anyway, defiant in the face of his own emotions.

Ray continued, "Bernard knows this business—and this land—like the back of his hand. Don't be afraid to ask him for help. And your mom…" At this, Ray's voice softened, fear closing like a vice around his neck. "She knows as much as I do, if not more. You take care of her and she'll take care of you."

"Dad, nothing's going to happen," Jaxon insisted. "I mean, I'm glad you're finally treating me like an equal and everything, but I don't want to do this without you."

Ray's throat was on fire. He used to think love was something light, like a warm breeze batting at the pearly blooms of a bearberry bush, but this time it felt heavy, crushing. He detested the idea of not being there for Jaxon's high school graduation the way Bernard had been absent from his. There was still so much to teach his son, but for now, this would have to do.

"I don't like this," Jaxon murmured, "and I wish I'd never tried to save those mustangs."

"You did what you thought was right."

"If I'd known it would lead to this, I wouldn't have gotten involved in the first place!"

Ray's expression softened. "Yes, you would have. You're my son, and that means you're always going to look out for the horses." He flicked his eyes at their mounts. "Speaking of horses, those guys need water."

They untied Monty and Barbell from the trees and led them to the river to drink. Jaxon was staring off into the trees when Ray glanced over the saddle at him. Was he thinking about the wild horses again? About the foal that had gone against its deepest instincts? Or was he thinking about the weeks, months, and years ahead, about who he wanted to be versus who he truly was? At a time when everything was shifting, was anything meant to remain unchanged?

Monty lifted his head, water running off his whiskered muzzle in dazzling streams. Jaxon had already climbed onto Barbell's back and was reining him toward the trees, where a narrow path littered with leaves and fungi would eventually lead them to the ranch. "We should get going. I'll bet mom's worried sick."

Ray mounted Monty and circled toward the trail, happy to let Jaxon take the lead for a change.

Eighteen

"Since when do you take naps?" Hannah asked as she carried two bags of groceries into the kitchen.

Ray brought a hand up to his face, stars swirling behind his eyelids as he rubbed away the dregs of sleep. He seldom slept during the day, but he couldn't deny the toll last night's ride had taken on his body. His leg had gotten the worst of it, followed by his neck, shoulders, and back. With Jaxon in bed, Hannah running errands in town, and Kyleigh and Josh assisting Bernard in the fields, Ray had slipped away for a couple hours of much-needed rest, hoping that when he woke up, his headache would be gone and life would be somewhat normal again.

Hannah walked around the coffee table and took a seat on the hearth. Early afternoon light filtered through the living room window, highlighting the small imperfections in the hardwood floors and the worn edges of the area rug spread beneath the furniture. The warm, rich smell of leather hung in the air, along with the smoky fragrance of the fireplace and its gaping mouth full of ash and soot. Ray sat up slowly, pressing the heels of his palms against his eyes as pain sizzled and shifted throughout his body.

Hannah sighed. "I hate seeing you like this. The worst part is, I'm afraid it won't be the last time."

"I'm afraid you might be right. If Jaxon keeps going down this path, I'm going to have no choice but to follow him." Ray lowered his hands but avoided meeting her gaze.

"I always hoped Jaxon would turn out like me," he confessed, turning his head to look out at the endless sway of the trees and horses against the stillness of the mountains and sky. "And he did, but not in the way he should have. I know it's my fault. I should've set a better example, not tried to be the hero at every opportunity."

Hannah furrowed her brows. "You're saying you don't want your son to be brave?"

"I'm saying I don't want him to be careless." Ray shook his head and, at last, found the courage to look Hannah in the eyes. "How have you put up with me for this long?"

"I've put up with you for this long because, despite all your perceived shortcomings and failures, you're a wonderful husband and father. Sure, you've made mistakes, but so have I. We've grown stronger together, and this, like everything else we've faced, will inevitably pass." Hannah smiled, the rose pink of her lips fading into the soft creases that bracketed her mouth. She stood up, touching a hand to Ray's shoulder as she passed, and walked back into the kitchen to finish unloading the groceries. "You must be hungry."

"Starving, actually." Ray rose to his feet, but before he could stretch the kinks out of his muscles, a flash of sunlight caught his eye. A pickup truck with a silver grille and unnaturally bright headlights came barrelling toward the house in a cloud of dust. Turning away from the fridge, Hannah squinted at their uninvited guest at the same time that Ray was reaching for the door.

He'd just stepped out onto the porch when the driver's door opened and Saul Biffman exited his vehicle. Saul was in his mid-fifties, with thick salt and pepper hair and a year-round fondness for black turtleneck sweaters. He closed the door, a smile rising like smoke on his clean-shaven face as Ray walked over to greet him.

"Saul, what a surprise," he said.

"Are you really surprised, though?" Saul asked, his eyes narrowed against the brightness of the day.

Ray feigned ignorance. "Should I be?"

"Look, we've known each other a long time," Saul went on in a clipped tone, "and I don't do house calls. So, I think it would be better for both of us if I cut right to the chase here. A couple nights ago, two of my guys were checking up on the cattle when they swore they heard a voice. So, I checked my security cameras, and who should I happen to see sneaking into my sale barn but your son?" Saul held Ray's gaze. "Where I come from, that's trespassing. Now, I don't know what the hell he was planning to do in my stockyard, and frankly I don't care. But if I catch him sneaking around again, you can expect to hear from my lawyer."

"I understand you're upset, and I promise I'll talk to Jaxon about what he did. But is legal action really necessary?"

"Oh, I'm sorry—is that what you're teaching your kid? That he can break the law and get away with it? Because as far as I'm concerned," Saul added, nodding pointedly at Ray's right leg, "you haven't had the best luck with trespassers."

Every inch of Ray's body blazed with the urge to dislocate Saul's jaw and hogtie him to the front of his overpriced Ford Super Duty; to drag him facedown through the freshly spread horse shit in the main paddock and brand his sorry ass with the hottest iron he could find. Saul may have been a decent businessman, but thanks to Jaxon's amateur camerawork, Ray knew exactly what the yardmen had been checking up on, and it wasn't the cattle.

Saul cocked a finger at Ray, his expression steely. "Do me a favour—stay the hell off my property."

"Same to you," Ray intoned.

Saul retreated to his vehicle. As the truck pulled away, Hannah took her place, as always, at Ray's side. Over the years, she'd grown accustomed to people they knew (and a few they didn't) dropping by to sort out unfinished business. But few of those interactions had left Ray so visibly shaken. No self-respecting cattle rancher wanted to be in Saul Biffman's bad books if they intended to stay in business. The man was both the spider and its web, ready to devour anything that buzzed too close.

"Dad?" At the sound of Jaxon's voice, Ray turned to find him standing in the doorway, his sleep-tousled hair shading his eyes. The wind rippled his white t-shirt and plastered his green-and-black checkered pajama pants to his legs. "Was that Mr. Biffman?"

"Yes."

"What did he want?"

"I think you know." As Jaxon continued to stare at him, Ray added, "Saul is under the impression that you snuck into his sale barn with the intention of causing trouble, but I think he's banking on nobody finding out about the mustangs. Do you still have that video on your phone?"

Jaxon nodded. "Are we going to tell someone?"

"We're not going to do anything right now. The only reason I mentioned the video is because if he decides to take any sort of legal action against us, we'll have a plausible defense. It doesn't excuse what you did, but you have to be prepared for anything these days…"

Again, Jaxon bobbed his chin. He recalled their conversation down by the river—the water rushing and clattering over the rocks, the icy fear crystallizing in Ray's voice. Up until now, Jaxon had always believed the ranching community was basically one giant, happy family: during the branding season, everyone pitched in, then got together afterwards to celebrate with burgers, ribs, and lemonade. But beneath that warm, welcoming façade was the same crumbling foundation on which this country was built, where the fight for the land was bloody and alliances rose and fell like the sun. Ray sawed a hand over his mouth, trying to smooth away the tension in his jaw, then started down the path to the barn—his retreat from a world fraught with conundrums.

Hannah faced the house. "Did you sleep okay?" she asked as she climbed the steps.

"More or less."

She made her way back into the kitchen, Jaxon trailing behind. A cloth bag gaped open on the counter, revealing a handful of cans and produce she'd picked up at the store. Jaxon set to work on putting the food away.

"What did dad mean about being prepared for anything?" he asked.

Hannah placed a jug of milk on the top shelf and closed the fridge. "It means you need to know who your friends are. Who you can count on if things suddenly go south."

"Who can we count on?"

"We can always count on each other. That's the purpose of being a family." Hannah looked at him and smiled thinly. "If you need to take your mind off all this, I could use a hand tomorrow out at Fitzgerald Farms. There are lots of broken branches that need picking up and weeds that need pulling. Or, if you'd rather, you can help me try and make headway inside the house. Jim has decided that nothing should be thrown out, so it's up to us to figure out what's garbage and what isn't. Expect resistance."

"What about dad?"

"Your dad will be fine," Hannah promised, lifting the second bag of groceries onto the counter and emptying its contents. "I know you're worried about him. I'm worried, too. But if there's one thing I know, it's that he always fights back. He's not going to let anyone take his ranch from him."

Jaxon took what little comfort he could from her reassurance. After a bit more digging, he uncovered the Pop Tarts buried near the bottom of the bag. He tore into the cardboard box, the chemical sweetness of the icing wafting out as he peeled off the foil and stood by the sink nibbling on the brittle crust and sticky, fruit-flavoured filling. Jim didn't want to let go of the past, and Jaxon couldn't blame him: life had been so much easier when he was a kid. His parents' problems might as well have existed in a totally separate universe for how far away and inconsequential they seemed, but with each passing day, Jaxon could feel the gravitational pull of their choices more than ever. In two years, Ray would sign the ranch over to him, and Jaxon would have to deal with people like Saul on his own—would have to know just what to say to keep this land under his feet, to keep his world spinning exactly as it was.

"Okay, I'll come," he mumbled, starting in on his second Pop Tart.

Once the last of the groceries had been put away, Hannah gathered up the bags and ferried them into the mudroom. Jaxon heard her rummaging around in the closet, trying to find space for them among the chapped leather boots and musty coats, the ones that were too tattered to hang by the front door with all the others. Apparently, Jim wasn't the only one who had a hard time letting things go.

*

After two weeks on the ranch, Kyleigh knew it was time to go home. Samantha and Terry had already prepared the spare bedroom and purchased extra groceries in anticipation of her stay. All Kyleigh had to do was pack her bags, and soon she'd be back in Toronto, surrounded by the ineluctable drone of traffic and people, the perfectly uniform shape of skyscrapers bending against the flat blue of the sky.

She hauled her suitcase onto the foot of the bed, slid the zipper around the sides, and opened the lid. A handful of clothes lined the bottom. Pushing them into a corner of the suitcase, Kyleigh turned to the armoire first and began removing her clothes from its musty shell three or four hangers at a time. As she laid the shirts on the comforter to be folded, Jaxon came upstairs and stopped in the doorway.

"What are you doing?" he asked.

Kyleigh glanced back at him. "What does it look like?" She grabbed another handful of hangers and tossed it on top of the pile before closing the armoire and moving on to the dresser.

Jaxon flicked his eyes over the suitcase. "Nice underwear," he said, a smirk hedging his lips.

More annoyed than embarrassed, Kyleigh slammed the lid down on the suitcase to shield the pink thong from view. "What do you want?"

"I don't know. Just passing by, I guess."

"Well, keep moving then."

He watched her rifle through the dresser. Spare pillow shams and decorative baskets of potpourri occupied the bottom row of drawers; the middle row was virtually empty save for an antique silver mirror and matching hairbrush. In the top row, Kyleigh had placed several of her travel essentials and a scattering of hair accessories, including the black

166

clip she normally wore to keep her hair out of her face. For a city girl, she sure seemed at home out here. She seemed to like Josh a lot too, although Jaxon knew better than to say anything about *that*, given the current state of Kyleigh's dating life.

When he remained where he was, Kyleigh gave up her search for her other sock and sighed. "Sorry. I'm not normally so…"

"Bitchy?"

"Exactly."

He shrugged and slipped his hands into his pockets. "It's okay. I know you probably think we're pretty messed up… I wouldn't blame you for not coming back."

"I don't think you're messed up," she replied.

"You don't?"

"I mean, this family's not normal, I'll give you that." Kyleigh met Jaxon's gaze, his eyes wide and overflowing with curiosity. "But… I think it's kind of nice how you guys always come through for each other. How you stick together, even when you disagree on things."

"We have to be able to count on each other. It's why we're a family." He asked, "What about your family? Your adopted family, I mean."

"We're not *close*, close, but Sam and Terry have always been there for me. I'm going to be moving back in with them for a while, at least until I figure out what comes next."

Kyleigh looked down at the lone sock in her hands, thinking about Derek. A few nights ago, she'd caved and sent him a message, asking if he'd be willing to meet up for coffee and to talk about their relationship. Derek had been effusively accommodating, saying he'd take the day off work: they could go out for lunch, if she wanted, and maybe later she could come back to his place for dinner. Short of collecting the rest of her belongings, Kyleigh knew she had no reason to go home with him— and yet, a part of her longed for the familiarity of their routine, the Downy scent of his bedsheets, and the rich, herbaceous fragrance of his kitchen. But no, she couldn't. She wouldn't. If she'd learned anything from coming here, it was that doing the right thing often meant being uncomfortable, and it almost always meant doing it alone.

Sensing a shift in her mood, Jaxon entered the room and walked over to the dresser. "You know, we call this one the Houdini drawer. Sometimes we put stuff in there and it just kind of disappears."

Kyleigh arched her brows. "Are you telling me there's a portal to another dimension back there?"

He laughed. "Probably." Pulling the drawer all the way out, he slipped his hand inside and felt along the dark recesses for any gaps or crevices where the missing sock might've fallen through. After a few moments, he withdrew his hand and presented her with the dusty sock. "*Ta-da.*"

"Gross, but thanks." Kyleigh tossed both socks onto the pile of shirts and hangers before reaching into her back pocket for her phone. She clicked on one of the icons and handed the device over to him. "Here, put your number in my WhatsApp."

Kyleigh gazed around the room. Despite her initial reservations, the space had grown on her, the outdated décor a charming contrast to the whitewashed minimalism of Sam and Terry's condo. Downstairs, the TV was on and some newscaster was droning on about the war overseas. In the laundry room next to the stairs, the washing machine hummed and sloshed. The white noise was constant around here, but not quite so jagged as the soundtrack Kyleigh had grown up with in the city.

"Here," Jaxon said as he returned her phone.

"Great. I'm just going to make one little, tiny adjustment." Kyleigh tapped the small screen, then nodded in satisfaction. "Perfect."

"What did you do?"

"I changed your name to 'Annoying Little Brother.' It has a nice ring to it, don't you think?"

"I'm not annoying. I found your sock."

"And made an inappropriate quip about my undergarments. The name stays."

"Whatever. By the way, mom and I are going over to Fitzgerald Farms tomorrow to help Jim clean up his house. You should come."

"Nah, I have to pack."

"Fair enough. I'll leave you to it then."

Jaxon crossed the hall to his room, where a basket of clean laundry sat on the floor next to his dresser. Hannah had changed his bedsheets earlier in the day and opened the windows to air out the room. Now, as he stood in the doorway breathing in the freshness, Jaxon found himself thinking of the mustangs in the valley and the parallels between human families and horse herds. How their members needed each other in order to survive. In all this madness, Hannah had never wavered in her role: instead, she'd been a paragon of maternal dependability, giving all of herself and expecting nothing in return.

From down the hall, Jaxon heard the creak of mattress springs. He headed toward his parents' room, where the eggshell glow of a lamp spilled through the gap in the door. Jaxon hesitated for a moment before raising a hand to the door and tapping it lightly.

"Come in," Ray replied.

Jaxon found him sitting on the bed. He'd removed his prosthesis and was in the middle of doffing the sleeves and liners designed to cushion the residual limb when Jaxon took a seat beside him.

"Why did you take your leg off?" Jaxon asked.

Ray worked a thumb under the edge of the protective sheath. "Doctor's orders. She said I'm supposed to let the leg breathe now and then to prevent skin breakdown."

As the final layer was removed, Jaxon stared at the tapered end of Ray's thigh, thinking about how, as a kid, he'd told all his classmates that his dad had only one leg. *Like a pirate?* they'd asked, their cherubic faces registering shock and amazement at this factoid. God, how could he have been so stupid? Even now, knowing what he did about chronic pain and the taxing life of a full-time rancher, he couldn't resist dragging Ray into this mess with the mustangs. Jaxon felt he ought to apologize, but he had no idea where to begin.

Ray massaged the stump, working his hands down the length of his thigh and circling the scar with his fingers to loosen the skin. "Mom's taking you to Fitzgerald Farms tomorrow?"

"Yeah. At first I wasn't going to go, but then I thought it might help me clear my head." He looked at Ray and asked, "When I take over the ranch, am I allowed to change anything?"

"What were you thinking of changing?"

"In five generations, the ranch has never been passed to a girl," Jaxon pointed out, "it always goes to the oldest son. I mean, your grandpa had two older sisters, but neither of them inherited the ranch."

"I know. You have to understand things were different back then. Daughters married out of the family, whereas sons kept their last names. I'm not saying I agree with it, but most people don't like to mess with tradition."

"Maybe they should. What if you and mom hadn't had me? Who'd get the ranch then?"

Ray continued kneading his leg, muscle and sinew softening under his touch. The skin was warm and pink, but not burning, like it had been a few nights ago. "I don't honestly know. It wouldn't have made sense to leave it to Kyle, with her living in Canada and having no notion of how to run a ranch. If we hadn't had you, I guess we would've had to sell."

Jaxon's eyes widened. "Yeah, right. Like you'd ever let *that* happen."

"You asked me a hypothetical question, and I gave you a hypothetical answer," Ray replied. "Thankfully, we did have you, so we don't have to consider the alternative. Now, what did you want to change?"

"I think Kyle should co-own the ranch with me. She can keep living in Canada if she wants, but I want it to be her ranch too. That means she gets equal say in all business decisions, right?"

By now, Ray had all but forgotten about his leg. While he'd been surprised to see how naturally Kyleigh took to the work around here, there was a world of difference between doing what one was told and taking charge of the operation. And with Jaxon at the helm… well, it would certainly be an interesting experiment, if nothing else.

Jaxon said, "I'm asking you a hypothetical question. That means you have to give me a hypothetical answer."

"Hypothetically," Ray sighed, "yes, she would have equal say. But just because you're family doesn't mean you two are going to agree on how things should be done. I ran this ranch with Uncle Marc for years, and there were plenty of times we wanted to kill each other."

"But you didn't," Jaxon pointed out. He looked down at Ray's leg again. "He took care of you. He did it because he knew it was the right thing to do."

Ray nodded.

"So, can I add Kyle's name to the papers?" Jaxon asked.

"We'll see. The choice is really up to her, and if she says no, then you have to respect her decision."

"That would mean I'd be running the ranch alone."

The thing no one had told Ray was that Jaxon would always be learning how to walk—from those unsteady first steps he'd taken in the kitchen as a baby, to the slightly bigger steps he was taking to try and save the mustangs. The only thing that hadn't changed was Ray's instinct to swoop in before Jaxon lost his balance, even if he knew that sometimes, it was necessary to let him fall.

"You're not going to be alone," Ray promised. "I'll still be here to guide you for as long as I can. And one day, when you have a son—or a daughter—you're going to pass this knowledge on to them and hope that whatever they plan on changing about this place, changes it for the better."

Jaxon rose from the bed. In the doorway, he stopped and turned back to Ray, saying, "I hope she decides to stay."

"Who, Kyle?"

"Yeah. It's been nice having her around."

"I agree." As Jaxon disappeared, Ray looked down at his prosthesis. For something he hadn't expected to need, he couldn't imagine living without it.

Nineteen

Jaxon couldn't believe what had become of Fitzgerald Farms. When he was a kid, his parents would leave him with Jim whenever they had business in town or needed a night to themselves: during these visits, Jim would make popcorn on the stove—a great, huge batch of fluffy white kernels practically swimming in melted butter—and the two of them would sit in front of the living room TV and watch the kind of movies Jaxon wasn't allowed to watch at home. Sometimes, Jim would teach Jaxon how to play cards or backgammon; other times, he'd regale him with stories from the past, most of them centred around Ray and his brothers when they were kids. Eventually, as Jaxon became old enough to stay home alone, these trips to Fitzgerald Farms had grown more infrequent until, as with so many things in life, he couldn't recall the last time he'd set foot in Jim's house.

Jaxon ferried another garbage bag to the front door. Shortly after arriving, Hannah had put him to work cleaning out the fridge. Most of the groceries she'd purchased a couple of weeks ago, including several bags of fresh produce, had rotted away behind multiple takeout containers of Chinese food and clamshell boxes of half-eaten Big Macs. Kneeling in front of the fridge, Jaxon had emptied the drawers, cleared the shelves, and organized the handful of condiments on the door. Once the liquified vegetables, sour milk, and moldy cheese had been disposed of, he'd sprayed every inch of the fridge's guts with an all-natural cleaning solution and scrubbed at the stuck-on food rings until his eyes watered and his fingers trembled. It wasn't much, but at least he could take solace in knowing Jim wouldn't get food poisoning from eating expired chicken.

As Jaxon added the garbage bag to the pile on the front lawn, he spotted Hannah crouched among the raised planters in the garden. Several gardening tools were scattered around the dirt, but even Jaxon could tell it would take more than a trowel to repair the damage caused by years of neglect.

He crossed the lawn, unlatched the gate on the white picket fence enclosing Laney's former oasis, and stepped inside. Hannah glimpsed his silhouette, pale shafts of sunlight spilling around the edges of Jaxon's shoulders. As he crouched beside her, she turned back to the planter and dug the tip of the trowel into the jigsaw of dry soil. The garden was overrun with weeds, to say nothing of the lawn or the flower planters under the windows, which at one time had been a hotspot for pollinators like hummingbirds, butterflies, and bees. Grasping the thistle near the root, Hannah gave a firm tug on the invasive plant. At first, it was determined to remain where it was, proving that even Mother Nature struggled to part with things sometimes.

"This used to be a beautiful garden," Hannah stated, tossing the uprooted thistle aside. "Laney took great pride in her vegetables."

"What kind of vegetables did she grow?" Jaxon asked.

"Just about every kind you can think of: cabbages, peas, zucchini, squash, peppers. In fact, she grew so much produce that she often ended up giving at least half of it away to neighbours and the local soup kitchen. It's a shame you never got to see the results of her green thumb."

Laney had moved to a nursing home called Alpine Terrace before Jaxon was born, but had often talked about her beloved garden as if it were a friend from long ago. A series of uniform holes lined the rectangular planter before him, where burgeoning tomato plants had once twined their delicate green stems around wooden stakes. "Do you think anything will ever grow here again? If we get rid of all the weeds and turn the soil, do you think it could go back to the way it was?"

Hannah combed her gloved fingers through the crumbling dirt, freeing nuggets of rock and the flaky remnants of dead leaves from the layers of once prolific topsoil.

"To tell you the truth, I don't think it'll ever be the way it was. Not without Laney. But I think if we keep coming out here, little by little it'll start to transform into something resembling a home again. Of course, there's the minor issue of Jim still occupying the house…"

"He's moving out too, isn't he? That's what dad told me."

"I think it would be best if Jim didn't live alone anymore. Even though he swears he can take care of himself, it's pretty obvious he can't. I've called a few places in town to inquire about cost and some of the services they offer. Basically, he'd be living in an apartment, and an aide would come in a few times per day to check up on him and do some light housekeeping."

"Would we still be able to go and visit him?"

"Of course. In fact, one of the places I called is just down the street from your school. You could even drop by after class, if you wanted. Maybe you don't remember this, but you used to have so much fun with Jim when you were younger. Some nights, we could barely drag you home."

Jaxon smiled. "I remember. He said even though he wasn't my real grandpa, I was always welcome in his home." His smile faded as he pictured the kitchen, buried under a mountain of dirty dishes and expired food. "I don't get it. How does a house go from normal to this?"

"Grief can destroy a person's life," Hannah answered simply. "It starts off as sadness and snowballs into something so much worse. Without Laney, I don't think Jim sees much point in looking after Fitzgerald Farms." She brushed the dirt from the creases of her pants and glanced at the growing pile of trash on the lawn. "I saw you brought out another bag."

"I cleaned out the fridge. Most of the food was bad, so I threw it out. If it's okay with you, I thought I'd take a break from the kitchen and try one of the other rooms. Just until I get my sense of smell back."

"Fine by me. Oh, you could try the guest bedroom. Jim's been using it for storage, so it's bound to be a mess, but I'm reasonably confident you won't find any sour milk under the bed."

"Let's hope."

Jaxon rose to his feet and followed the stone pavers through the garden and up to the house. Earlier in the day, they'd cleared a semi-circle of space around the front door so they could come and go without tripping over mismatched shoes and boxes of old magazines. Jim, as usual, had yelled at them for interfering before slipping off to the back porch with a tumbler of whiskey. Since then, he'd only ventured back into the dingy abode two or three times to refill his glass or grumble about not being able to find anything.

Jaxon walked down the hall toward the bedrooms. The door to the guest room was closed, so he braced himself for what he'd find on the other side. Wrapping his fingers around the handle, he took a deep breath and pushed open the door, revealing the room's secrets inch by careful inch.

Hannah had been right: the space was more closet than bedroom. Pushed into the corner just to the right of the door was a twin bed draped in a light blue quilt, with a single pillow resting against a wrought iron headboard. Directly across from it was a dresser, a wooden chair with a faded seat, and a standing mirror with a crack in the upper left-hand corner. Jaxon eased the door the rest of the way open. Towers of cardboard boxes and durable plastic totes surrounded him like strangers in an elevator, each of them silent and indifferent to his arrival.

Jaxon approached the bed first. Numerous small appliances, including a salad spinner and brand-new, still-in-the-box Keurig coffee machine, sat at the foot of it. Over the years, his parents, aunts, and uncles had bought all kinds of things to make Jim's life easier or more comfortable, but like those weeds in the garden, he'd let his grief spread and consume him. No amount of love or charity could fill a hole the size of the one Laney had left, or dig a person out of a rut carved by daily substance abuse. Jaxon picked up the Keurig and examined the packaging for signs of damage, then set in aside and reached for the next item.

He spent the next thirty minutes creating two piles: things to discard, and things to donate. Afternoon light slanted through the window and illuminated the tumbleweeds of dust rolling and spinning across the hardwood floor. With every step Jaxon took, every box he opened, and every item he picked up, the air shimmered with silvery specks of debris. He waved the motes away from his face as he set another box in the pile of things destined for the trash. The label on the outside of it said *Clothes – Laney* in neat, uppercase letters. There were plenty of things worth saving in this world, but moth-eaten sweaters and crusty fringe jackets weren't among them.

Jaxon glanced up as Jim appeared in the doorway, his eyes dark and glassy. His gaze dropped to the box of clothes at his feet. Gripping the doorframe for support, his focus went back to Jaxon again.

"What are you doing in here?" Jim demanded.

"Mom told me this room needed cleaning," Jaxon replied with a shrug.

A wounded look feathered over Jim's face. Taking a couple of steps into the room, he bent down and pulled Laney's prized fringe jacket from the box, shook it out, and sent another wave of dust particles flying toward Jaxon's face.

"This is Laney's jacket," Jim said, looking the garment over. He lowered it to glare at Jaxon. "You're not throwing this away."

"Come on, Jim. No one's going to want to buy this. Look—" Jaxon reached for the sleeve to show him the tattered leather strings sewn along the underside. The jacket itself, once pearly white, had turned yellow and dull with time. "The lining's practically falling out, and it stinks. I know her clothes mean a lot to you, but you can't—"

"Don't tell me what I can't do," Jim barked. The whiskey had gone to his head, making him unsteady on his feet. Jaxon watched as he swayed and grimaced, the jacket folded over his right arm for protection. Furious at the intrusion, Jim began pawing through the box like an animal, pulling out each item and tucking it into the hinge of his elbow until he could hold no more. Still, the clothes kept coming.

"These," he huffed, "are Laney's clothes. Who do you think you are, coming in here and opening everything? I had it all neatly sorted! And now look at what you've done." Jim picked up a blouse and threw it over his shoulder, covering himself with whatever remained of his wife. "You've ruined everything!"

"Jim, I'm just trying to help."

"You know, you're just like your father," Jim continued, his tone sharpening as he clutched the bundle of clothes. "You think you know what's best. Well, let me tell you something about your dad—if he knew everything, he'd still have his leg. Man's a goddamn fool some days."

"Don't talk about my dad like that," Jaxon scrapped out.

"I raised him. I'll talk about him if I damn well please."

Jaxon didn't know what to do. He knew this was mainly the whiskey talking, and he knew that somewhere in there, buried beneath the pain of Laney's death and her heap of musty clothes, was the man who'd babysat him and treated him like a biological grandson. Jaxon drew in a breath, his anger ebbing somewhat as sadness and regret took over.

"Maybe we can keep a few things," he hedged, "but the rest of it has to go in the trash. If you hold onto it, it'll make you sick."

Jim's face, reddened by drink and fury, crumpled and hardened at the suggestion. "Oh, don't go lecturing me about my health. Between your mom and your dad and you…"

"What's going on in here?" Hannah asked as she stepped into the room.

Relief flooded Jaxon's veins. He sighed and indicated Jim. "Ask him."

"I'd thank your son to mind his manners," Jim said, turning to his goddaughter-in-law. "Can you believe he was willing to throw all this away? I tell you, this new generation—"

Hannah calmly raised both hands as Jim fell silent. "I think maybe now's a good time for us to step outside," she said.

"I was just outside!" Jim scanned the room for somewhere to set the clothes. He'd had the place so well organized. Now, with all this dust floating around and Laney's memories laid out on the floor, it looked downright sepulchral. "Oh, hell. This is a goddamn disaster."

As his frustration rose up and washed over him, Jim threw the armful of clothes down, like a toddler pitching a tantrum, and hastily exited the room. When Hannah attempted to place a hand on his back, he shied away from her touch, the very suggestion of comfort an insult to his

178

desire to carry the pain alone. In the kitchen, he clattered around in the cupboards in search of his favourite anesthetic. "It's all gone, Jim," Jaxon heard Hannah say as she trailed a few paces behind.

"Gone?" he growled. A door slammed.

"You drank it all," she explained. Jaxon was amazed by the way she held her composure in the face of Jim's belligerence. Like Ray, she knew how to fight back. "We're going to get you into a program, okay? For right now, though, I want you to sit down and try to relax."

"I can't relax. Not with you and your son here, not with everyone trying to tell me what to do all the fucking time."

Jaxon was leaning into the hall. He couldn't see Jim anymore, but he could hear the thump of his recliner opening up and the sharp, noisy way he moved things around to make himself more comfortable. Hannah reached into one of the cupboards, filled a glass with water from the sink, and carried it into the living room.

"I don't want it," Jim grumbled.

"I don't care," Hannah returned.

Jim eventually relented and took the glass from her hand. Moments later, Hannah crossed back into the kitchen and set the empty vessel on the counter before continuing where Jaxon had left off in the sink, the clinking of dirty dishes drowning out whatever silence the TV couldn't.

Jaxon retreated to the guest room once again. He stared at the clothes on the floor, the geometric eyes of the rhinestones winking up at him in the waning light. He scooped the garments into his arms and set them down precariously on top of a tote brimming with cowboy boots, blue jeans, and the glossy silver plates of hand-crafted belt buckles. What was life but an accumulation of stuff? Even his parents had way more clothes and knickknacks than room to store them, and Jaxon figured that when he was their age, he'd have to sort through their belongings the way Hannah and Ray were sorting through Jim's. While every generation had its troubles, some things never changed.

Putting aside the clothes for now, Jaxon concentrated his efforts on some of the smaller boxes wedged between the dresser and the wall. He picked the first one up, set it on the chair, and threaded his finger under the strip of brown packing tape holding the flaps closed. There was nothing written on the outside to indicate what the carton contained. He would just have to take his chances and hope it wasn't full of rotten food.

A plume of dust wafted into the air as Jaxon lifted the cardboard flaps. Balls of crumpled-up newspaper greeted his curious gaze. Reaching into the box for the first item, he carefully unwrapped a teacup with a slender handle and pink flowers painted around the outside. He set the cup aside and uncovered three more, each of them wrapped in newsprint with extra padding on the handles to prevent them from breaking.

He lined the cups up on the dresser. Their saucers, if they had any, were probably buried in this box as well. If they were intact, they could easily be donated to a family in need. Jaxon found the first two stacked beneath a sheet of classified ads; the third was tucked along one of the box's inner walls. He'd just uncovered the fourth and final plate when one of the newspaper balls fell to the floor and landed between his feet.

Jaxon set the saucer back in the box and picked up the broadsheet. Printed near the top of the page were the letters *ARD*. He sat down on the edge of the bed and smoothed the page over his lap, revealing the rest of the headline: *FIRE DESTROYS BIFFMAN STOCKYARD.*

The photo beneath the headline showed several cows silhouetted by a wall of fire, its jagged yellow teeth spitting black smoke into the night sky. According to the article, the inferno had started with a cigarette butt and ended with hundreds of thousands of dollars in damage—to say nothing of the loss of animal life.

"We could smell it in the air as we pulled up," one of the firefighters who responded to the 911 call, said. "When a barn catches fire, and there's livestock inside, the smoke is different. It smells like death."

Jaxon had never seen a barn burn down. But he'd helped Ray brand thousands of cattle, and he knew too well what burning flesh smelled like.

At the bottom of the page was another picture, a headshot of a woman with a blonde ponytail and black cocktail dress beaming into the camera. The caption read: *The remains of Yolanda Biffman, 31, were recovered from the scene of the fire. Investigators have ruled her death an accident.*

As footsteps sounded down the hall, Jaxon hastily folded up the article and tucked it into the back pocket of his jeans. Hannah appeared in the doorway, her sleeves rolled up to her elbows and splotches of water staining the front of her shirt.

"Is Jim okay?" Jaxon asked. His heart was making a racket in his chest; a cold sweat greased his armpits. Yolanda Biffman, if she were still alive, would've been around Saul's age. Her death certainly didn't strike Jaxon as accidental, not after everything he'd witnessed with the mustangs.

"No, not really." Hannah's gaze wandered over the room, bathed now in the thin pewter light of early evening. She reached down to switch on the lamp next to the bed before saying, "I just have a few more things to do here, then we can head home."

"Cool. I'm almost done too."

She smiled. "I really appreciate you coming with me. Cleaning this house has been such a nightmare... as much as I'm going to miss Fitzgerald Farms, I can't say as I'll miss the smell of it."

Jaxon pictured the blackened structure of the sale barn, the flames purling over the support beams and rafters—and somewhere inside, Yolanda's young and beautiful face turning black too.

As Hannah disappeared down the hall, Jaxon repacked the cups and saucers, folded down the flaps, and pressed the tape back on top. The clothes he left in a pile on the bed for Jim to sort through once he sobered up. When it was all said and done, Jaxon switched out the lamp and closed the bedroom door before heading to the kitchen to find Hannah wiping the counters and Jim passed out in the armchair.

"How long's he been like that?" Jaxon asked.

"Fifteen minutes or so. I managed to find a can of tuna in the pantry, so I made a couple of sandwiches and left them in the fridge in case Jim gets hungry later."

Hannah rinsed the cloth and draped it over the faucet. When she lifted her gaze to the window, her eyes went automatically to the gazebo. She hoped the next family who lived here would take similar comfort in the property's features and restore the overgrown backyard to its former glory.

"Can we go home now?" Jaxon asked.

"Yes. I'll finish putting everything away here if you want to wait for me in the truck."

They drove the backroads in silence, each lost in their own thoughts. Just once, Jaxon wished for the kind of summer his friends were having: warm evenings filled with bonfires and non-existent curfews, the ability to sleep in or stay up as long as he pleased, and the freedom to follow the wind wherever it blew him. Plenty of his classmates had gotten jobs in town, but those jobs were merely a way to make money, not a lifestyle they were inextricably bound to.

Jaxon felt the land rise up and into him as Hannah steered the truck into the driveway. When they arrived at the house, Bernard was in the kitchen making dinner, Josh was in the living room talking to Kyle, and Ray, who rarely ended his workday before sunset, was sitting on the bench swing waiting for his wife and son.

Ray stood up and approached the truck, where half a dozen garbage bags, several pieces of broken furniture, and a handful of small appliances had been carefully arranged in the bed and strapped down with bungee cords to keep them secure. He glanced uncomprehendingly at Hannah, who smoothed down her wind-battered hair as she exited the vehicle.

"If you think this is bad, you should see what Jim's shed looks like," she said. "I didn't want to leave all this stuff at Fitzgerald Farms in case Jim tried to sneak it back into the house."

"You know, I'm almost glad Laney's not around to see what's become of the place… or Jim."

Hannah glanced at the house, then back at Ray. "Bernard's making dinner?"

"He insisted. I think it's his way of apologizing for our little spat in the field—and, well, a few other things."

She nodded. Despite the fact that he was hardly ever indoors, she had to admit Bernard was a half-decent cook. Plus, after all the work she'd done weeding Laney's garden and decluttering Jim's house, the last thing she wanted to do was cook for a group of hungry cowboys and her daughter.

Ray studied Hannah's face, with its greyish tinge and web of fine lines, and felt dread well up inside him. "How bad is it?" he asked as Jaxon lingered in the passenger seat, staring at his phone.

She met his gaze. "When did looking after Jim become my job? Why am I the only one checking up on him and throwing away the expired food in his refrigerator?" Hannah raised her arms and let them fall back to her sides with audible disappointment. "My mom used to say that women always have to choose, but this doesn't feel like a choice—it feels like an obligation."

"Honey, you know if I had the time to go to Fitzgerald Farms, I would. But I just can't right now."

"I have been asking you to help me clean up the house for months—long before you tore down the old fence. And now, I'm the one who's calling around trying to find a place that will agree to house Jim that won't feel like an institution to him. Again—I didn't decide to take on that role, it was simply expected of me."

"What do you want me to do? Do you want me to make some calls?"

She sighed, flicking her eyes at the ground. "It's not that simple."

"Then tell me what you want me to do." When Hannah didn't speak, or even look at him, Ray's concern for her wellbeing quickly turned to frustration. "I'm trying to communicate with you here, and now you're shutting me out?"

"I'm not shutting you out, Ray, okay? I'm just tired of having the same conversation over and over and getting nowhere." Hannah gestured to the disarray. She felt an odd sense of satisfaction for having used Ray's vehicle to cart around Jim's unwanted belongings: maybe if Ray was forced to do something about the junk himself, he'd develop an appreciation for the burden she'd been forced to carry alone. "Now if you don't mind, I'm going to go take a shower."

"Fine by me." Ray stared at the dust covering his boots as Hannah made her way into the house.

At last, Jaxon opened the passenger door and stepped outside. As his gaze waffled between his dad's stony expression and his mom's back, he asked, "What did I miss?"

"I'm about to teach you a very important lesson about marriage," Ray stated, raising his hand to point at his son. "The fight isn't over until your wife decides it's over, and there's no telling when that moment will be."

"I thought the fight ended when both people apologized."

"When I figure out what your mom wants me to be sorry for, I will." Ray peered at the jigsaw puzzle of boxes. "Seems like you and mom put quite a dent in the mess."

Jaxon shrugged. "I feel like I've been taking one step forward and two steps back all day. Jim yelled at me when I tried to clean out the guest room, since that's where he keeps Laney's old clothes."

"I'm not surprised. Her clothes meant a lot to her."

"I know. I also found something else, when I was going through one of the boxes."

Jaxon reached into his pocket for the article. The truth was, he didn't want his mom to know he was still thinking of Saul and what happened to the mustangs. After today, he could see she had enough to worry about.

"Check this out." Jaxon handed the square of paper to Ray, who unfolded each of the quadrants. "The woman in the picture—her last name is the same as Saul's."

"I see that." Ray furrowed his brows as the wind rippled a corner of the page. "I remember hearing about this. It was a long time ago, but it caused quite a stir in town. A lot of people believed the fire was set intentionally, but nothing was ever proven as far as I'm aware."

"Why would someone burn down a barn on purpose?"

"If I had to guess, I'd say they were trying to collect insurance on the place. Or maybe they were trying to get revenge on Saul." Ray handed back the article, but Jaxon was too distracted to accept it.

"Revenge for what?" he asked.

"I don't know. People don't always have good reasons for doing things."

"But this woman—Yolanda—she must've been his wife, right? And just the other day, Saul showed up and threatened us with legal action if we came onto his property again." Jaxon shook his head. "Something's not adding up here."

"It's definitely a strange case," Ray admitted, "but I don't think it's something we should be worrying about, especially now."

"Dad, think about it: maybe this isn't the first time Saul's been involved in shady business. Maybe he was doing something he knew would get him in a lot of trouble, and he set the fire himself to hide the evidence." Jaxon's eyes darkened. "We have to go back to the stockyard."

"Jax, we can't go around falsely accusing people of committing crimes. That's a crime in itself."

"But he did commit a crime when he killed those mustangs," Jaxon argued. "You're The Bionic Cowboy, for crying out loud. You're supposed to advocate for abused and neglected horses, remember? Or did you stop caring about them when the tour ended and the money stopped coming in?"

"I don't know what's gotten into you lately, but if it makes you feel better, we'll go to the stockyard and talk to Saul." Ray sighed. "It may be the last thing I do, but I'll do it for my son's peace of mind."

He passed the article back to Jaxon and walked up to the house. The lively crescendo of laughter and conversation rose on the warm currents of air as he opened the front door and stepped inside.

Jaxon looked down at the images on the page. As long as a fire had fuel, it would continue to burn. So, too, would his fight for justice, until there were no more wild horses in need of saving.

Twenty

Saul couldn't remember a time when the stockyard hadn't been a part of his life. As a child, his afternoons and weekends had been spent in the company of livestock while his father, Peter Biffman, conducted business with local ranchers. While his friends were off playing games, Saul was mucking out bullpens and wheeling carts of hay down the pitted dirt aisles. Then, when new stock came in, he'd watch the yardmen direct the cattle wherever they needed to go, a cacophony of bellows rolling like thunder above the clanging of gates and shouting of cowboys.

There was an art to getting cows to do what you wanted, and Saul had proven to be a quick learner—so quick, in fact, that he'd been put in charge of running the sale barn at just fourteen, giving his father more time to drink or chat with the auctioneers. Most of the yardmen had treated this changing of the guard as inevitable and carried on without a fuss, but the handful who complained or tried to stir up trouble found themselves out of work in short order.

Now, Peter Biffman was long dead, and Saul, having come of age in this business, knew too well why a job like this drove a man to drink. As the cost of raising cattle climbed higher each year, it was only a matter of time before the family-owned ranches disappeared and factory farming took over. With any luck, Saul thought now, he'd be dead by then, too.

The day was shaping up to be like any other: men and women in cowboy hats and Wranglers trickled into the sale barn to check out the available stock, while Saul's employees moved almost undetectably among the crush of brown and black hides. The tangy fetor of fresh manure was everywhere, and yet Saul hardly noticed the way his office, truck, or clothes smelled anymore. He patrolled the pens like he did every morning, stopping to make small talk with his customers or observe if heifer 523 was lame. He'd have to get the vet out here, have him do a proper assessment. Saul flagged down a yardman in a blue plaid shirt and red ballcap, told him to keep an eye on the cow in question, and headed back to his office to place the call.

As he came around the side of the barn, a familiar pickup truck nosed into a space between two others. Saul turned away, eager to return to his previous task and forget about the bridges smoldering behind him.

"I thought I told you to stay off my property," he said, his voice lacking in both vitriol and conviction.

Ray closed the driver's door. He indicated the parking lot, every inch of gravel choked with trucks and the silver gleam of livestock trailers. "Technically, I'm not trespassing if you're open for business."

"If you're not here to buy anything, I don't have time to deal with you," Saul went on. His eyes flickered over Jaxon, who'd just climbed out of the truck and now stood shoulder to shoulder with Ray. "Young man, I'm afraid you've caused a spot of trouble for your dad here. It's a shame, too, since he's one of my best customers."

"Mr. Biffman, we know about the fire," Jaxon said. He reached into his pocket and handed Saul the article he'd uncovered in the box of chinaware the day before.

Saul's gaze went back to Ray, who nervously adjusted his cowboy hat. "What do you know?" he asked.

"We'll tell you what we know about the fire if you tell us what you know about the mustangs," Ray replied. "Sound fair?"

Saul sighed and motioned for them to follow. "Let's head up to my office."

They climbed a flight of stairs to a small room above the pens, where a large window allowed Saul to observe matters in the barn without leaving the comfort of his swivel chair. A series of metal shelves along the backwall held binders stuffed with paperwork, and bankers boxes so old their labels were no longer legible. In the middle of it all was a desk containing four drawers and a cylindrical waste basket overflowing with disposable coffee cups and brown paper napkins. As Jaxon trailed Ray into the room, his eyes went to the pictures lining the walls. Most of them were in black and white; seeing them, Jaxon was reminded of the images he'd found online of the hundreds of culled mustangs. Before the Internet—and long before social media—this was how people viewed the world: no filters or editing, just the truth in shades of grey.

Saul sank down in his chair and kicked his heels up on the corner of the desk. Seeing as there was nowhere else to sit, Ray and Jaxon stood between the desk and the window, breathing in the dry smell of paper and dust while they waited for Saul to speak.

He joined his hands over his stomach and looked at Ray shrewdly. "Every once in a while, I see your name come up in the news. Very rarely is it for anything good."

"What can I say? I seem to attract trouble like a magnet," Ray confessed.

"Hmm. Well, since we're on the topic of bad press, why don't you tell me what you think you know about the fire?"

Ray took the article from Jaxon and laid it on the desk in front of Saul. "The woman in the picture here," he said, lightly tapping on the page, "was she your wife?"

Saul's gaze dropped to the photo. He picked up the page and held it by the edges. His grief felt like the tightening of a screw, the sight of her face pulling the pain of that tragic night back together in his mind.

After a moment's reminiscence, he set the article down and rubbed the sandpaper edge of his jaw with his other hand.

"Yolanda and I were separated at the time of her death," he explained. "Not that that made it any easier. The rumour around here was that we were headed for divorce. A lot of people believed she set the fire on purpose so she could collect part of the insurance in the settlement."

"Is that what you believe?" Jaxon asked.

"I know who started the fire, and it wasn't Yolanda." Saul levelled his gaze at Jaxon. "It was trespassers. They'd snuck into the barn at night—apparently a woman who was driving by at the time saw a bunch of kids running toward the woods. They were never identified or charged with arson, and since I didn't have security cameras at the time, I'll never be able to bring them to justice." He removed his feet from the desk and leaned toward Jaxon with a hardened expression.

"Yolanda knew how much this place meant to me, and I believe she died trying to put the fire out. I don't need to tell you how fast hay burns," he added with a glance at Ray. "There's a fire extinguisher in the payment office, on the other side of the sale barn. Unfortunately, most of the structure was engulfed in flames before she could reach it."

"What an awful way to go," Ray said quietly. He looked over his shoulder at the maze of pens below them. He could only imagine the horror of finding himself trapped in this giant tinderbox, with the smoke stinging his eyes and burning his throat, knowing his fate now lay in the hands of an insatiable inferno.

Saul told Jaxon, "When I saw you on my security camera a few nights ago, I naturally assumed the worst. But seeing as this place is still standing, perhaps you'd like to tell me what your real intentions were."

"Our neighbour saw mustangs on his property. He called the BLM to round them up, and somehow, they ended up here. I know it was wrong of me to trespass, but I was worried the mustangs were going to get hurt."

"And what did you discover when you entered my property without my consent?"

"One of them was dead. A few others were obviously sick or dehydrated."

"And how do you know they weren't already sick when they were rounded up?"

"Because we found the rest of the herd, and those mustangs looked fine. Look, I'm not saying their injuries were your fault. I'm just wondering why you didn't try and treat them."

"Jaxon's heart was in the right place," Ray said. "You and I have known each other for a long time, Saul, and you've always been concerned with the welfare of your livestock."

"As any cattleman should. If your animals aren't earning you money, then they're costing you money. If it's lame, sick, or dead, I can't sell it."

"What was your plan with the mustangs then, given that at least half of them fell into one of those three categories?"

"I was holding them for a buyer. Blackwell Slaughterhouse."

"So, you did sell them—at a steep discount, I'd imagine."

Saul held Ray's gaze, his eyes flicking back and forth over his face. "Yes."

"Jaxon's done a ton of research on the subject." Ray looked at his son, staring down at the article in his hands. He'd chosen to remain silent during this exchange, and for that, Ray was grateful. "It's standard procedure that any mustang over ten years old, or one that hasn't been adopted out after three attempts, be sent to slaughter. The BLM has a network of middlemen across the country who buy these animals at auction and arrange to have them transported to rendering plants. Even though there are laws against the slaughter of horses on American soil, plenty of places still do it. Now that I know Blackwell is one of them, I plan to terminate my contract immediately."

"I'm not in charge of Blackwell's operations. I just sell livestock."

"I know. You're running a business. But running a business doesn't absolve you of responsibility when there's human or animal life on the line." Ray held Saul's gaze. "From one businessman to another, I'd suggest you reconsider whom you do business with, or someone else may try and burn your barn down in an effort to end these sales."

"Noted. Now, if you don't mind, I have a stockyard to run."

Jaxon lifted his head as Ray placed a hand on his arm to indicate that it was time to leave. As they headed for the stairs, Jaxon stopped and spun back toward Saul's office.

"Mr. Biffman? I'm really sorry about your wife."

Saul met the boy's gaze and saw an innocence he hadn't noticed before. "So am I."

191

Jaxon returned to Ray's side. As father and son disappeared, Saul rose from his chair and approached the window to look out over the sea of cows and cowboy hats. Down in the corner, his scruffy ballcap setting him apart from the regular customers, was the yardman in charge of looking after heifer 523. Turning back to the desk, Saul lifted the phone from its cradle and dialed the vet's number.

Twenty-one

"I didn't think you'd actually survive out here," Jaxon said over breakfast, his voice muffled by the cereal he'd spooned into his mouth only moments before. "Congrats, I guess."

Kyleigh offered him an indulgent smile. Her own bowl of oatmeal, which she'd seasoned with brown sugar and topped with a handful of fresh berries, had grown cold on the table in front of her. "It was definitely an interesting visit, thanks to you."

As she tucked into the semi-congealed cereal, Ray walked through the front door. He removed his hat and hung it on one of the pegs, took off his boots, and made his way into the kitchen for another cup of coffee, even though it was barely seven A.M.

Jaxon turned and looked pointedly at the clock. "Already?"

Ray returned the coffee pot to the hotplate and faced his son. Lifting his mug in toast, the steam dissipating around his face, he replied, "We all have our vices, bud. Yours is your phone, mine's caffeine." Ray brought the mug to his lips and took a deep sip.

"Don't you worry about your health?"

Ray chuckled. There were certain expectations that came with being a cowboy that Ray had treated like a religion. For instance, treat the horse as you wish to be treated, and the animal will reward you with eternal devotion. Honour your father and your mother (but especially his mother). And most importantly: cowboys don't cry. For most of his life he'd worshipped this lifestyle, even when the land or the work caused him great personal suffering. But the thing no one had told him was that the boy in 'cowboy' would one day have to grow up—and that was assuming he survived the hell he put his body through year after year.

Rather than answering Jaxon's question, Ray turned his focus to Kyleigh. "Are you finished packing?"

"Mostly. I mean, I only had a carry-on. Doesn't take long to throw a few socks and shirts in a suitcase."

"You're a lot like Hannah. Well, not really," Ray amended after a moment's reflection. "She used to colour-code her packing lists. It was all very fancy. But she did enjoy travelling."

"Colour-coded packing lists? That sounds borderline OCD."

"I wouldn't know; I didn't go to college. You're going to college, though." Ray met Jaxon's gaze.

"I thought my destiny was to inherit this ranch," Jaxon murmured.

"It is. Imagine how much better you'll be at running it once you get an education." Picking up his coffee, Ray beat a swift retreat back to the front door. "If either of you need me, I'll be in my office."

Having finished his oatmeal, Jaxon slid back his chair and rose to place his dirty dishes in the sink. Through the kitchen window he saw Ray making his way down to the barn, the orange-tinged light of dawn capturing only the edges of his receding figure. Bernard was feeding the horses in the paddock: he usually got up hours before everyone else did, his body set to an entirely different clock. Hannah had once said he was on "mountain man time", which Jaxon found both admirable and impossible to comprehend.

He turned back to Kyleigh, scraping the sweet pulp of a smashed blueberry off the side of her bowl with her spoon. "By the way, I've been meaning to talk to you about something," he began. "It's about the ranch."

"Okay."

"You know how there's this tradition where the ranch gets passed to the oldest son on his eighteenth birthday? Well, I've been thinking about that a lot. I never asked to be born into this family, much less male. And yet, my dad's already talking about the future as if it's set in stone. Basically, I'm his retirement plan."

"A lot of people stake their old age on their kids, which is kind of sad when you think about it. My best friend is a doctor. She says in her

194

culture, multi-generational households are the norm. I guess I was pretty surprised to see it here, of all places."

"Yeah, well, that's just it. Family's really important to us, even if we don't always get along. I guess what I'm trying to say is, if you're thinking of sticking around, maybe you could be co-owner or something."

Kyleigh set down her spoon and picked up her coffee. "What exactly does being a co-owner involve? I want to know what I'm getting into before I agree to anything."

"It means we'd be business partners. If I need advice about something, I'll talk to you, and if you have ideas for how to make things better, you'll talk to me."

"And what about… financial gain?" As Jaxon stared at her, Kyleigh said, "Sorry, but I had to ask. This is a business, right? That means you do it for the money."

"Right. Well, we're not rich, as you've probably noticed. My dad made a lot of money during his tour, but I don't think he's going on another one anytime soon."

Jaxon returned to his seat. He hadn't worked out all the kinks in his plan yet, and Kyleigh's point about finances only proved it. Really, what he wanted was to know he wouldn't be alone in the ranch's successes—or failures—when the time came for Ray to pass the torch.

He toyed with the corner of the table runner, rolling and unrolling the cloth material distractedly as he spoke. "I just don't think it's fair how my parents had you and gave you away," he confessed. Kyleigh was looking straight at him now, her eyes wide and a little glassy. "I know my dad regrets it a lot. And my mom…"

"Doesn't want anything to do with me." Jaxon glanced up, his face registering shock at her words. "Well, it's true. We ran a few errands together, and went on a bunch of walks, but the whole time I've been here, you've been her main priority."

"Yeah, I guess." He cleared his throat.

"I'm not saying she's a bad person," Kyleigh went on, "I guess I'm just disappointed. I had this vision of all of us sitting down and talking about everything, but that's just a fantasy. The truth is, you can't make someone feel the pain they caused you."

She wiped at her tears. Jaxon was trying not to stare, so he traced a knot in the table instead, the dark eye of the wood reminding him that in every tree—even family trees—there were losses and imperfections. And somehow, the tree just kept growing.

"I don't even know why I came here," Kyleigh said. "I can't hide from Derek forever. I can't go back in time and wish for a different outcome."

"No, but you can change what happens next, like I tried to do with the mustangs."

Kyleigh smiled as another tear landed in a shimmering bead on the table. She dabbed it with her sleeve, wiping away the spot of moisture. "You're brave, you know that? It takes balls to stand up for what you believe in, especially nowadays."

Jaxon shrugged. "If you don't stand up for what you believe in, who will?" He glimpsed the window as a singular headlight beamed up the driveway. Rather than parking the Ducati down by the shed like he normally did, Josh circled toward the old maple tree by the house and quieted the engine with a gentle turn of his wrist. The sky was lightening to the east; as the sun crept over the mountains, it reflected off the dome of his helmet in a blinding streak of amber.

Kyleigh rose from the table and emptied her coffee cup into the sink. She pretended not to notice Josh swinging his leg over the bike's seat and looking around the front yard as if searching for something. Ray, perhaps? But of course, Josh knew exactly where to find him.

"Will you consider my offer?" Jaxon asked as he stood up.

"Sure. But I'm not making any promises."

Jaxon steered around her and headed for the front door. Ray would be expecting him to help with morning chores, but all Jaxon really wanted to do was figure out what the future of the ranch looked like.

He'd come from a long line of cattle ranchers, but with how often Ray complained about feed costs and federal regulations, it wasn't hard to see why so many people were leaving the industry. Besides, with livestock agriculture being one of the leading causes of climate change, Jaxon wondered if he was even doing the right thing by following in his father's footsteps. Maybe what their business needed wasn't a changing of the guard, but a total pivot into something brand-new, a direction that would enable them to preserve the natural environment instead of competing for dwindling resources.

He'd just pulled on his boots when a knock came at the front door. Jaxon straightened, reached for the knob, and found Josh standing on the front porch.

Josh lowered his hand and smiled. "Morning."

"Morning. Kyle's right here," Jaxon told him as he slipped outside.

Kyleigh stood on the threshold with her arms crossed. She met Josh's gaze and smiled. "Hi."

"Hi. I'm glad you're still here. Ray mentioned yesterday that you were leaving, and I wanted to come say goodbye one last time."

"Don't worry, it's not goodbye forever."

"I hope not." Josh hesitated a moment. "Look, I know we've only known each other for a few weeks, but I just wanted you to know that you've really helped me."

"How?"

"I've been taking my dad's death pretty hard these past few months. But then I come here and I talk to you and for a little while, I forget that he's gone. So, thank you for that. It's been nice to think about something else, for a change."

Kyleigh's smile widened, and a warm flush filled her cheeks. "You're welcome. And thank you for making sure I didn't accidentally staple myself to a fencepost."

Josh cracked a grin. "Looks like I finally found something useful to add to my résumé." He hooked a thumb at the barn in the distance. "I should get to work. Safe travels, Kyle."

"You too," she told him, even though he hadn't mentioned where he would go next. But the open road was filled with possibilities. "Hey, Josh?" He turned back to her expectantly. "If you think about it, we're practically neighbours, with Montana being on the Canadian border and all."

He nodded. "Maybe I'll see you around the neighbourhood."

"Maybe." She watched him follow the path to the barn as she shut the door, the heat in her face lingering long after he disappeared.

*

Hannah was an expert at goodbyes. She'd said it to Ray countless times in airports, to her mom at the end of every phone call, and to old friends she thought she'd never lose. Yet when it came to her own daughter, goodbye had felt like a foreign language. Instead, they'd shared a hug on the porch while Ray loaded Kyleigh's bags in his truck. As they'd climbed into his Chevy Silverado, Hannah had been surprised by the prickle of jealousy she felt at seeing them together. Though she'd hoped Ray would be able to bond with their daughter, Hannah hadn't expected it to come so easily to him. Besides, if Jaxon hadn't been so wrapped up in saving the mustangs, perhaps Hannah would've had more time to devote to Kyleigh—or at least, that was what she told herself to blunt her guilt.

Later that day, Ray found Hannah in the guest room, stripping the covers and sheets from the bed. He leaned in the doorway as she tossed a pillowcase onto the growing pile, her face set in concentration.

"Kyle just messaged me to say she made it home safely," he began. As Hannah shucked the second pillow, he added, "She said Jaxon talked to her about potentially co-owning the ranch. I told her I'd leave the decision up to them."

Hannah turned to him, her brows furrowed. "What do you mean co-own the ranch?"

"Jax didn't tell you?" Hannah stared blankly, waiting for him to elaborate. "He said when he turns eighteen, he wants to add Kyle's name to the papers. I know that's not how we typically do things around here, but maybe this place is overdue for some serious change."

"Do you really think that's a good idea?"

"I don't know, but I respect Jaxon for considering her."

"She doesn't know the first thing about running a ranch."

"Neither did you, when you first met me." Ray smirked, although Hannah was clearly not amused. "She did pretty well working on the fences. Sure, she still has a lot to learn, but she's a quick study."

Hannah gathered up the linens and carried them down to the laundry room. Some days, she felt as if she spent most of her life in this cramped space, sorting, washing, drying, folding, and mending her family's clothes, while Ray got the whole barn and fields to himself. But this arrangement had worked for them for years, and Hannah knew better than to allow her complicated feelings about Kyleigh's visit to derail their routine.

"I agree she's smart," Hannah said as she stuffed the sheets into the washing machine. "So is Jaxon. I just don't think he really understands what going into business with her would mean. Trying to make plans and decisions with someone who lives in another country…"

"Oh, come on. Who understands that better than us?" Ray asked. "We still have two years before Jaxon turns eighteen. For all we know, maybe Kyleigh will have forgotten about us by then."

Hannah turned around, and that was when it hit her: not jealousy, but a wave of sadness. "I don't want her to forget about us," she whispered.

Ray's expression softened. "Me neither."

"I thought this visit would be different. I had hoped we'd be able to find some common ground, but I just felt like there was too much to catch up on to really get to know each other." Hannah shook a scoop of laundry powder into the machine and closed the lid. "I always swore I'd never turn into my mother, and here I am, judging my daughter for her choices."

"Hey, listen to me: you are *not* your mother." Ray took a couple of steps into the room and placed his hands on Hannah's shoulders. "If you'd been in Kyleigh's position, do you think your mom would've given you the chance that you gave our daughter?"

"Considering Jeanette barely accepted me when I lived with her, I doubt it." Hannah cupped Ray's face, then rose onto the balls of her feet to kiss his lips. "Thank you. I needed that pep talk."

Across the house, they heard the front door open as Jaxon came inside. He'd been helping Bernard in the barn, and his clothes were still covered in bits of hay and pine shavings. He brushed the debris off in the entryway and made a beeline for the laundry room.

"I just got a text from Bodhi," Jaxon announced. "He said a few people from school are having a party tonight. Can I go?"

"Where is it?" Ray asked.

"At a chalet downtown. Sydney's dad owns it." Jaxon caught the look his parents shared and added, "Bodhi said he'd pick me up and drop me off, so you guys don't even have to drive me."

Ray glanced at Hannah again, leaving the final verdict up to her. After everything that had happened with the mustangs, he fully expected her to say no. Instead, she looked at him and asked, "What do you think?"

Ray blinked. "I think it might not be a bad idea for Jaxon to take the night off."

She nodded, telling their son, "You can go. Just try not to stay out too late, okay?"

He cracked a grin. "Cool. Thanks, mom." Spinning on his heel, he climbed the stairs to go get ready for the party.

"I was sure you'd say no," Ray admitted when he heard the bathroom door close.

"I thought about it, but then I realized that even if I'd said no, he would've probably snuck out and gone anyway. Just once, I wanted to be the cool parent."

"Wait, is that what all this is about? You don't think you're a cool parent?"

"I know I'm not. That's why Kyleigh spent almost all her time with you."

He shook his head. He hadn't realized being a parent was a competition—and if the thought had crossed his mind before now, he would've assumed he was the loser. "That's ridiculous, but kind of funny." Ray followed Hannah out of the laundry room. "And Kyleigh hardly spent any time with me. If anything, she spent most of her time talking to Josh."

"Really?"

"Yes. Not that I blame her—he's a nice young man."

Hannah chuckled. "Sounds like he already has your blessings."

Ray sobered. It had only been five months since they'd made the trek up to Montana for Mickey's funeral, where Ray had sat with Hannah and Jaxon in the third pew and watched the son of The Horse God eulogize his idol. When the service was over, Josh had stood near the doors and thanked each and every person for coming, undaunted by the size of the crowd or the weight of his grief.

As Ray had made his way across the church to offer his condolences, a beam of wintery light had passed through one of the stained-glass windows and landed on Josh's suit jacket, painting him in shades of rose and gold. Since then, whenever Ray looked at Josh, he saw a bright spot in a dark and unforgiving world. It was no surprise that Kyleigh had been drawn to the son of a man who'd once been larger than life. Whether they meant to or not, every parent rubbed off on their child in some way.

"You're right, though: he is a nice young man," Hannah agreed. "Speaking of young men, I should probably wash Jaxon's sheets, too."

"You may not think you're a cool parent, but you're a good one," Ray said.

She turned back to him and smiled. "So are you... even if Jaxon doesn't always see it."

"By the time he does realize it, I'll probably be long dead." Ray turned and headed for the door. "I'll wait up for him tonight. After all this, you deserve the night off."

Twenty-Two

Jaxon had never particularly liked Bodhi's girlfriend, Sydney, and it wasn't because of her family's wealth. Like so many people their age, Sydney was chronically online, liking, sharing, and posting content for hours at a time. Over the past couple of years, she'd amassed a considerable following on TikTok: most of her videos revolved around makeup and fashion, although she'd recently started using her platform to help promote her dad's business.

Aspen had always been a popular travel destination among the rich and famous, and those who could afford to splurge typically rented out chalets like the Mountain Jewel, a five-hundred-dollar-a-night mountainside retreat offering breathtaking views and total privacy. Jaxon could understand wanting to be involved in the family business, even if most days it seemed like Sydney was just flaunting her privilege to those less fortunate. What he hated was that the people who could afford to make a difference in the world often preferred to spend money on themselves. If Jaxon had their money, he'd adopt every mustang he could. But he wasn't rich, so he had to settle for raising awareness instead.

The party was in full swing by the time Jaxon and Bodhi pulled into the driveway, a wide swath of gravel that climbed gently toward a two-story log cabin surrounded by conical pine trees. Knowing the company Sydney kept, Jaxon had been expecting to see several expensive cars parked out front. Instead, most of the vehicles were pickup trucks or old, cheap sedans like the kinds he saw in the parking lot of his high school. The only difference was, no one was blasting terrible music or passing around a joint before class.

Bodhi parked his truck. As they both got out, Jaxon glimpsed the living room window and spotted several girls dressed in bikini tops and shorts navigating the crowd. Jaxon had opted to keep his outfit simple tonight: a white t-shirt, branded hoodie, jeans, and the roper boots he wore everywhere. While he liked to party as much as the next teenager, he'd never really considered himself popular. When he wasn't hanging out with Bodhi, he was either doing homework in one of the computer labs, or clinging to the fringes of whatever group he thought he could blend into most easily—in other words, the kids who lived on neighbouring ranches and wore Ariat instead of Birkenstocks.

As they walked through the door, a raucous "Hey!" greeted their arrival—mainly Bodhi's. Jaxon glanced toward the living room to see several guys sprawled on the leather furniture. A gas fireplace with a rustic stone chimney served as the focal point of the room, and the hand-carved, wooden coffee table was littered with beer bottles, shot glasses, and empty plastic cups.

"You made it," one of the guys said as Bodhi crossed the room to them.

"I'd never miss one of Syd's parties," Bodhi replied. He brought Jaxon into the conversation by saying, "This is Jaxon. Jaxon, meet Cash. Jaxon's dad owns the spread about ten miles south of here—the big one with the white sign out front."

Cash raised his brows, impressed. "I know that place. We took one of our horses there last year."

"I think everyone in town knows my dad," Jaxon said sheepishly. Sometimes, attending these parties made him feel like he'd been plucked out of a fishbowl and dumped into the ocean to fend for himself. "Which horse was it?"

"High Caliber. He's my dad's horse technically, but he lets me compete on him."

Jaxon nodded. He remembered High Caliber, the roping horse that had taken to rearing whenever he was in the chute. Ray had managed to cure him of that unwanted behaviour, and Greg Lannister, Caliber's owner, had paid him generously for his time.

"You guys wanna sit down?" Cash asked, gesturing to the sofa behind him. "There's more beer in the kitchen. And food."

"You want anything?" Bodhi asked Jaxon.

Jaxon surveyed the room. Sydney's dad must've put some kind of limit on the number of people she could invite, since there was still plenty of room to sit, dance, or just hang out in the corner and observe the crowd. Almost everyone was drinking, including the group of kids packed into the hot tub outside. Jaxon looked at Bodhi and nodded.

As Bodhi disappeared to procure refreshments, Cash indicated one of the couches and said, "Sit down." Jaxon lowered himself onto the nearest cushion. "So. You ride bulls too?" Cash asked, taking a sip of his beer.

"No, just horses. I've seen you around school. I didn't realize you roped."

"Half the people in this room rope," Cash chuckled. He had short, reddish-blond hair, a slightly doughy face dusted with freckles, and wore his blue and white checkered shirt tucked into his Levi's to show off his belt buckle. Looking at him, Jaxon couldn't help but feel underdressed.

Bodhi returned from the kitchen carrying two Coronas. He passed one to Jaxon, then flopped down on the couch between a couple of his buddies before tipping his beer bottle into his mouth.

"Bodhi, there you are," Sydney called from the patio doorway. Wrapped in a beach towel and wringing the water from her hair with one hand, she padded across the hardwood floor and rounded the end of the sofa. "Come hang with us in the hot tub."

"I will when I'm a little drunker." Bodhi placed his beer on the table, his one hand reaching for Sydney's wrist. She pretended to resist his advances, but ultimately gave in and wedged herself between Bodhi and the guy on his left, who squeezed himself into the corner to give the couple more space.

Bodhi began nuzzling Sydney's neck, brushing aside the wet strands of hair with his fingers. It didn't seem to matter that they weren't alone: virtually everyone else was staring at their phones, with the exception of Cash, who'd moved to sit on the hearth with a girl from school and was laughing hysterically at something she'd said.

Sometimes, Jaxon wished he hadn't grown up on a ranch. It wasn't just because his dad treated him more like an employee than a son: his life, but especially his summers, had always been about work and preparing for his future occupation. Even then, whenever Jaxon got a chance to shed that identity, he took it.

"So, Jaxon, what have you been up to all summer?" Sydney asked.

He shrugged. "You know, just working for my dad." He raised the Corona to his lips and took a sip, the frothy liquid rinsing away the taste of boredom.

Bodhi came up for air long enough to say, "You should quit and come work at the tire shop with me."

"You hate working at the tire shop," Sydney pointed out, picking up Bodhi's beer and taking a sip.

"I wouldn't if my best friend was working with me."

"I can't quit," Jaxon said. "My dad needs me. And my mom too."

"I thought your parents had a hired hand."

"We do, but he's not going to be with us forever. And, besides, my dad said if I take over the ranch, I can run it the way I want."

Jaxon didn't even like beer, really, but it made opening up about things so much easier. He'd only taken a few sips, and already his lips felt looser, his worries about the mustangs floating away like clouds over the mountains.

"My sister and I might be co-owners," he went on, not caring that he only had half of Bodhi's attention. "That's assuming she even wants to be on the papers. I still have two years to figure out how all this is going to work."

Sydney pried her lips off Bodhi's to pull the towel around her shoulders. Glancing at Jaxon, she said, "You have a sister?"

"Her name's Kyle. She's way older than me. My parents had her before they were married."

But Sydney wasn't listening. Bodhi had checked out of the conversation ages ago, too busy trying to get between the towel and

Sydney's browned-to-perfection skin to notice they weren't the only people at the party.

Stung by their lack of interest, Jaxon rose from the couch, saying, "I'm going to get some air."

He crossed the room to the glass door through which Sydney had entered, opened it, and stepped out onto the deck. A large hot tub sat in the corner, and scattered around it were multiple pairs of shoes and piles of discarded clothing. A number of beach towels were draped over the railing, all within easy reach of the six or seven kids who'd chosen to linger in the roiling turquoise water, drinking and talking about nothing.

Jaxon headed toward the firepit and took a seat in one of the Adirondack chairs encircling the inferno. He couldn't tell if the beer actually tasted better out here, or if he had crossed that invisible threshold where alcohol stopped tasting like alcohol and started tasting like water.

"You look lonely," a female voice said from somewhere behind him.

Jaxon twisted around, a rueful smile breaking over his face. "Ironic, right? Sitting by yourself at a party." He gestured toward one of the empty chairs. "Do you want to sit down?"

"Sure."

He turned back to the fire, trying not to look overly interested as the girl sat down on his left. Flickers of light danced on her dark skin; twin flames lit up her eyes. Leaning forward, she set her red Solo cup down by her feet and pinched the corners of her towel over her chest. "By the way, I'm Cassandra."

"Jaxon."

"I know who you are."

"You do?"

She smiled, a flash of white teeth breaking through the shadows. "You're Bodhi Henderson's best friend. He talks about you all the time at the rodeo grounds."

Furrowing his brows, Jaxon asked, "Really? I hope Sydney's not too jealous." Cassandra laughed, the music of it filling his ears. "What do you do at the rodeo grounds?" he asked.

"I compete. Wanna take a guess at what event?"

"Let's see... well, you're a fast thinker, so it must be a speed event. Barrel racing?"

"Good detective work. You must be a huge fan of true crime shows."

Jaxon looked away, not wanting to tell her that he did have some experience in dealing with crime, and it wasn't nearly as exciting as Netflix made it out to be. The memory of the dead mare would haunt him forever, and every time he heard a helicopter, he'd remember those mustangs in the valley running for their lives.

Cassandra picked up her cup, took a sip, and set it down again. "How's your summer so far?"

"Honestly? It's a mess. My older sister, who's basically a stranger, decided to visit, my dad's making me fix fences with him, and to top it all off, I'm third-wheeling with my best friend and his girlfriend tonight."

"I'm sorry."

"It's okay. What about your summer?"

Cassandra wrinkled her nose and shrugged. "It's been kind of boring. I picked up a part-time job at the library, but no one reads anymore, so there's not much to do during the day."

"I read."

"Really? What are you into?"

"Lots of stuff. I'm very into current events at the moment, but I like history too." Jaxon averted his gaze. He felt embarrassed, as if the state of the world, and the United States in particular, could be traced back to his ancestors and the proprietary choices they'd made. "I know I grew up with a lot of privilege. Not this kind of privilege," he said, gesturing to the luxuries only a handful of people could afford, "but the kind that comes with being white and male in a first-world country. It makes me sick when I think about the atrocities that were committed by the colonists."

"You don't have to apologize for the colour of your skin," Cassandra said, "and neither do I. But you're right about the colonists being terrible people."

"Not just toward other humans, but toward animals too. Even now, when we have the choice to be better, so many people choose to look away." Jaxon ran a hand through his hair. He could feel Cassandra's gaze like a burst of sunlight on a winter morning, reminding him that brighter days lay ahead.

She turned toward him, her knees inches from his. "Did you know the song 'America the Beautiful' was inspired by Pike's Peak?" she asked.

"Yeah. I went to Colorado Springs with my mom once. We stopped in a tourist shop and bought a fridge magnet that was shaped like a gold nugget, even though we weren't actually tourists." He added, "Did you know there's evidence of human habitation in Colorado dating back to 13,000 BC? Paleontologists discovered a bison kill site on the eastern plains where it's believed that groups of people gathered to hunt. Some of these gatherings were so big, they managed to kill hundreds of bison in a single day."

"Seems like that trait isn't specific to any one racial group," Cassandra pointed out. "Did you know that Colorado was home to numerous Native American peoples? With so many miners flocking to the area in search of jobs, conflict with local tribes arose. 230 people were killed in the Sand Creek Massacre in November of 1864, when Colonel John Chivington led an unprovoked attack on a village populated by members of the Southern Cheyenne and Arapaho tribes."

"I've always wondered if my family ever played a role in those kinds of conflicts," Jaxon admitted, furrowing his brows as he gazed into the fire's pulsing light. "I asked my dad, but he said he doesn't really know. All he knows is that his great-grandfather left West Virginia and headed toward the Rockies. I think he's afraid of what he'll find if he digs too deep." He flicked his eyes at Cassandra again. He hadn't realized it, but in the course of their conversation, he'd shifted closer to her as well. Only a few inches separated her arm from his, and right now that space was occupied by a thin veil of smoke and the sweet scent of her hair product.

"Did you know," Jaxon said, his heart skipping a beat as the towel slipped off her shoulder to expose the spaghetti noodle of her bikini strap, "that a third of all the land in Colorado is owned by the United States government?"

"That one I did know, but only because my family goes camping on public land every summer."

"Have you ever seen a mustang?"

Cassandra looked taken aback. "Like, on TV? Or in real life?"

"In real life."

"No, I haven't. Have you?"

"Yes. They're beautiful, but since they interfere with local ranching, they're in danger of being culled. I've been... trying to raise awareness of what's going on, but my dad doesn't want me to do anything that might make it harder for us to do business."

"I mean, I get where he's coming from, but I get where you're coming from too. It's hard going against your family's wishes."

Jaxon nodded, his head growing fuzzy from the combination of alcohol and fire smoke. Still, there was a moment of clarity in all this: why was he relying on his dad to speak out about the mustangs when every teenager he knew was ten times better at using social media? Up until now, he'd felt alone in his fight for justice, but with Cassandra in his corner, maybe they could find a way to get their message across to a larger audience.

"So, I guess I'll see you at the library sometime?" Cassandra asked as she stood up, Solo cup in hand.

Jaxon lifted his gaze to hers and smiled. "Wild horses couldn't keep me away."

As Cassandra started toward the hot tub, Jaxon wondered if the flush in his cheeks was the result of the beer hitting his bloodstream, or the fact that he'd finally found someone who understood him. He lingered by the firepit for a while, sipping his drink until there was nothing left, then rose to his feet and went in search of Bodhi.

The music was louder now, the crowd bunching and unraveling as the heat of their bodies raised the temperature of the room. The rodeo guys who'd been gathered around the fireplace had all dispersed: some had been absorbed into the drunken throng, some had gone outside for a smoke, and a handful had retreated to the kitchen to snack on whatever remained of the chips. Jaxon scanned the hubbub for Bodhi and Sydney, but all that remained of the couple was her towel, caught in the creases of the couch.

Jaxon shouldered through the crush. Someone raised their cup and accidentally elbowed him in the back of the head. "Sorry!" the cup-raiser shouted as Jaxon rubbed the sore spot. He turned to see who'd hit him, but only caught glimpses of bare skin and bad lighting.

Jaxon eventually reached the kitchen, where Cash was leaning against the white granite countertops talking to someone Jaxon didn't know. Compared to the living room and patio, the room seemed too bright— or maybe this was just what alcohol did when you drank enough of it. Each tile on the mosaic backsplash reminded Jaxon of the inside of a conch shell as he reached for an empty Solo cup and filled it with water from the sink. He'd never been buzzed before, and unlike so many of his classmates, he wasn't sure he liked it very much. An animal that couldn't control its movements was at risk of becoming another animal's dinner.

Cash crossed his arms, studying Jaxon from across the kitchen. "First time?" he asked, his tone teasing but sympathetic.

Jaxon drained the cup. "Is it obvious?"

"Kind of." Cash shrugged. "You get used to it."

Jaxon looked around the room before asking, "Have you seen Bodhi?"

"Oh, sure."

"Like, recently?"

Cash smirked and hooked his thumb toward the stairs, visible through the doors at the far end of the kitchen.

"He said it was getting crowded in here, so he and Syd disappeared for a while," Cash explained.

"How drunk was he?"

"*Drunk.*"

"Fuck." Jaxon looked around the space, considering his options. He could walk home, but that would take forever. An Uber was too expensive. At this rate, he might as well go back outside and look for Cassandra, see if she knew anything about the BLM's roundups and if she'd be willing to help spread the word. Who was he kidding? There wouldn't be any talking involved, although he knew a way to keep his lips busy.

Cash quirked a brow. "Is everything okay?"

"Yeah, fine. It's just that Bodhi's supposed to be my ride."

"Can you call your parents?"

"They're probably both sleeping by now." But what choice did he have? Besides, he knew his mom would be upset if she knew Bodhi was driving under the influence.

Cash reached into his pocket and pulled out his keys. "Come on. I'll drive you home."

"But haven't you been drinking, too?"

"I just had a couple of sips. The truth is, I don't even like beer or parties that much. I only came because my friends are here."

They forded the crowd, Cash leading the way, and emerged near the front doors just as two other guests were arriving. Cash had parked his truck down the street, far away from the Subarus and barely functional Buicks clogging up the driveway. As the music faded into the background, the only sound Jaxon heard was the alternating tempo of their boots on the pavement. To his right was a steep, grassy ditch and the cloying smell of wildflowers. He tried to stick to the edge of the road, but the road wasn't as straight or as smooth as he remembered it. Cash walked beside him, his tall silhouette briefly eclipsing the lights on the houses they passed, each one surrounded by a small forest of trees that blended with the mountains behind them.

When they finally reached Cash's truck, Jaxon had to hold onto the sidewall of the bed to prevent himself from skidding down the hill.

Jaxon climbed into the passenger seat and fastened his seatbelt. Country music exploded from the speakers as Cash started the ignition.

Switching off the radio, he put the truck in gear and said, "You don't have to give me directions. I've driven past your place a hundred times."

"Cool. I'm kind of losing the ability to talk anyway." Instead, Jaxon rolled down the window and slung his arm outside, letting the fresh air clear the cobwebs from his head.

They drove toward the outskirts of town, the houses turning to homesteads as the night sky brightened overhead. Conversation was scarce, but Jaxon didn't mind. Aside from knowing how to throw a rope, what did he and Cash actually have in common?

Jaxon squinted as the truck rounded a bend. The Hoyts' property lay on the opposite side of the wooden fence that paralleled the road; he recognized the stock tanks, each one resembling an island in the middle of the grassy field. Jaxon had grown up around cows and could spot their square bodies even in the dark, but these creatures lacked the typical bovine shape and size. He told Cash, "Stop the truck."

Cash steered onto the shoulder of the road. Now that they were stationary, it was even easier to see the animals' features. Definitely not cows, and the Hoyts had never kept horses in this pasture.

"You can drop me off here," Jaxon said as Cash leaned across the console to try and see what he saw.

"Are you sure? It's only another half-mile to your driveway."

"Yeah, I'm sure. I think a walk might help me sober up." When Cash continued to stare at him, Jaxon added, "I know a shortcut to get home. I take it all the time."

Cash shrugged. "Suit yourself." He reached over and pushed the button to unlock the doors.

As Jaxon got out, he turned back to the truck and said, "Thanks for the ride."

Cash drove off, a plume of exhaust smoke curling like a pig's tail behind him. As the taillights grew dim, Jaxon eased down into the ditch and up the embankment on the other side, then grasped the top board of the fence and pulled himself over.

Hard clumps of dirt pressed against the underside of his boots. He headed straight for the nearest stock tank, the stink of manure and cattle inescapable. It was after midnight now, but with the moon parked in the centre of the sky, he could see for miles in virtually every direction. Which meant the mustangs could also see him.

Jaxon approached the nearest tank and crouched down, watching the wild horses spread out across the field. One of the mustangs raised its head to sniff at the air, froze for a second, then returned to its grazing, unconcerned by whatever had captured its interest.

Jaxon counted the herd's members. He thought of the mustangs in the valley, the ones they'd tried to save, and allowed himself to hope that at least a few of them had gotten away. Could it be—were these horses the survivors of that awful, unjust day?

When he saw the foal, he knew.

Jaxon stood up slowly, painfully aware of every muscle and joint in his body. He began to walk toward the herd, placing his feet ever so quietly so as not to startle them. The last thing he needed was to trigger a stampede, but the mustangs, despite being downwind, barely acknowledged his arrival. Jaxon wondered what he smelled like to them… if he smelled like beer. Maybe that was the secret, he thought, amused by the irony of his circumstances. Many domestic horses had developed a taste for beer due to its grainy flavour. Jaxon had even seen Ray mix a couple bottles into their water to stave off dehydration during the winter months when their fluid intake was reduced. Or perhaps, having sat by the pond that morning after finding the herd, these wild horses were already accustomed to Jaxon's scent, beer or no beer.

When he was within ten feet of it, the foal raised its head and looked directly at him. Jaxon froze, his hand outstretched, and waited.

The foal extended its neck. Its mother was behind it, nibbling on the grass in a sweeping, side-to-side motion. Wracked with nerves, Jaxon began to shiver. *Just one tiny step*, he begged silently. The foal, having apparently read his mind, dared to advance. It sniffed cautiously at his cupped palm and the tips of his fingers, and Jaxon responded by lightly stroking the side of his muzzle, the warmth of it instantly putting an end to his tremors.

He smiled, so excited he could barely breathe. "You know me," he whispered.

Suddenly, the foal jerked its head away. Jaxon stumbled back, watching the herd assemble. They fled toward the trees, kicking up clods of dirt as they galloped thunderously across the field.

He faced the road again, and that was when he saw the truck. A burly silhouette climbed over the fence, dropped to the other side, and crossed the field to where Jaxon stood. His stomach churned; he was going to be sick. Had Cash called someone? Had Mr. Hoyt seen him creeping around the stock tanks and decided it wasn't worth the hassle of telling his parents, when his brand of discipline was just as effective?

It wasn't until his visitor got closer that Jaxon recognized the walk, the shoes, the jacket. The man raised a hand to his hood and slipped it off his head. Jaxon stared, petrified by Jed's empty eyes and cold, Cheshire cat smile.

"You're not supposed to be here," Jed told him.

Jaxon replied, "Neither are you."

"You found the mustangs. Good boy." Jed reached into his jacket, presumably to retrieve something concealed in an inner pocket. Jaxon's heart hammered in his chest as the metallic taste of panic filled his mouth. "Now, why don't you help me catch them?"

Jaxon didn't think—just turned on his heel and ran like hell.

His muscles clenched, pain ripping through his body. As he hit the ground, he thought for sure he was going to puke. Instead, he rolled onto his side, his knees pulling toward his chest involuntarily, and gritted his teeth through the spasms radiating out from his lower back.

Jed crouched over him and cocked his head. He was still fucking smiling, like this was all a big joke. Jaxon tried to form his mouth around an insult, but the words slid off his tongue like melted butter and dripped to the ground in an agonized moan.

"How do you like them apples?" Jed asked, holding up the taser. "Yup, she's a beauty. Normally these puppies aren't available to the general public, but I've got a few buddies in law enforcement. Having connections comes in handy, don't you agree?"

Jaxon couldn't think. His body no longer belonged to him, but he couldn't just lie here and let Jed do his worst. Rolling onto his stomach, he attempted to slither away, digging his elbows and fingers into the dirt to propel his body forward.

Jed slipped the taser back into his pocket and grasped Jaxon's sweater. The world tilted and blurred as he was yanked upright, the neck of his shirt tightening around his throat. He wrested himself free and swung a fist toward Jed's face, only for Jed to shove him back toward the ground. He drove the toe of his boot into Jaxon's stomach, causing him to expel the hot, bitter contents.

Jed panted. "Come to think of it, you have a lot in common with those mustangs. Thinking that if you can just run away, everything will be fine. Well, I've got some bad news." He reached down and hauled Jaxon up by his clothes again, his mouth inches from Jaxon's ear. "There's nowhere to run that I won't find you."

Jed dragged Jaxon over to the nearest stock tank, lifted his chest above the rim of the trough, and held his head underwater.

From the moment the water touched Jaxon's face, his chest locked up and refused to breathe. His lungs were burning, burning, like the sale barn all those years ago. He felt Jed's hand pushing down on the back of his head, the edges of his fingernails biting into his skin. Still, Jaxon squirmed and kicked at the ground, making himself impossible to hold onto, like a wild horse that would break its own neck just to be free of the rope.

Right as Jaxon was about to breathe in—the water would put out the fire in his lungs—a blinding white light flooded the field.

Jed turned toward its source, squinting at the floodlights mounted to the roof of the pickup truck. Two men got out. Jaxon lifted his head from the stock tank with a rattling gasp for air. Weakened from the attack and the lack of oxygen, he flopped backward and landed in a sodden heap a few feet from where Jed stood, his hand already reaching into his jacket for something else. *Run*, Jaxon wanted to scream, *save yourselves.*

Then he heard Waylon's voice, low and steady in the dark. "I thank you to get the hell off my property."

"He was trespassing," Jed stated as Jaxon scrambled up and made a run for the truck, water sluicing off his hair and clothes.

"So are you."

"I was doing you a favour," Jed went on as Waylon approached him. "That boy's trouble. We caught him trying to stir up a herd of mustangs near the old mines…"

Bellamy rounded the front of the truck and pointed to the passenger side.

"Get in!" he yelled. Jaxon clambered into the cab and closed the door. He tried to catch his breath, but all he could smell was leather, hay, and his own putrid vomit smeared on the front of his clothes. In the glow of the floodlights, he saw Waylon take another step toward Jed, raise his fist, and level him in a single punch to the head.

Mud sprayed from the truck's tires as Bellamy shifted to reverse. After the longest five seconds of Jaxon's life, the tires found traction, but he couldn't tear his eyes from the scene unfolding before him: Jed lying on the ground, and Waylon, his knuckles bloody, bringing his fist down on his face again—not once, but several times, each blow altering the landscape of flesh and bone.

Bellamy drove past the house, followed the path leading to the Fishers' north pasture, and parked at the edge of the trees. He'd long ago turned off both the headlights and the floodlights, and now he turned to Jaxon with wide eyes, his breaths coming short as he spoke.

"Listen," Bellamy said, swallowing, "what you saw back there never happened, okay?"

"I have to tell my parents," Jaxon argued. "I can't just show up like this and not say anything."

"Then lie." Jaxon stared at him, too stunned to form a reply. "We saved your life. You owe us."

It was true. He was in the Hoyts' debt now, probably forever. "I'll think of something," Jaxon promised.

He pushed open the passenger door and got out, his body battered and bruised. *A fight broke out at the party*, he would say when he got inside. *I couldn't just stand there and watch. I had to do something.*

Clutching his ribs, Jaxon shuffled along the old tractor path until he reached the barn. He walked all the way to the house, up the porch steps, and through the front door. A light came on in the living room as he crossed the threshold.

Seeing him, Ray shot up from the armchair. "What happened?" he demanded, taking in Jaxon's soaked clothes, his stricken expression.

Lie, Jaxon ordered himself. "I got in a fight."

"A fight." Ray was walking toward him now, his eyes wide. "With whom?"

Jaxon didn't answer. Instead, he sank to the floor, his body overcome with violent tremors, and wrapped his arms around his stomach. It was difficult to tell which part of him hurt more, and he certainly wasn't about to tell Ray what he'd witnessed in the fields just now—no matter how sick it made him to keep a secret like this.

Ray must've called Hannah, because suddenly there she was, racing down the stairs and over to where Jaxon had curled up on the floor. Pressing his face against the cool planks, he screwed his eyes shut as tears burned across the bridge of his nose. In his mind, all he could see was Mr. Hoyt delivering a series of punches, his knuckles slick with blood, red spatters coating his face and neck. When it was all said and done, Waylon had straightened and looked down at the mutilated face of his opponent before turning, briefly, to gaze at his truck. *You never saw this,* his expression seemed to say. But Jaxon had seen everything, and now he'd have to live with that horrible, gruesome memory for as long as he lived.

"Jaxon, talk to us," Hannah pleaded, smoothing his hair out of his eyes. "Who did this to you?"

He shook his head. He remembered his face breaking the filmy surface of the water, and then, as if to compensate for those terrifying moments when he thought he'd never breathe again, his body exploded into sobs until he was crying so hard he thought he'd be sick again.

He cried until he ran out of oxygen, then gladly let the darkness swallow him whole.

Twenty-three

"We just want to know what happened," Hannah said. Her voice was frayed around the edges, her hair unbrushed. There'd been no time to change, which meant she was still wearing her faded pajamas and a pair of flip-flops.

Jaxon's gaze dropped to his lap. "I can't tell you."

"Well, you're going to have to," Ray, standing at the foot of the bed, said. He gestured to Jaxon's upper body, clothed in a standard blue hospital gown. "You're covered in bruises and have two cracked ribs. Someone was responsible for your injuries, and we need to know who."

"I can't," Jaxon said again, "I'm sorry."

Ray stepped back from the foot of the bed and rubbed a hand over his chin, trying to remain calm in the face of his growing frustration.

"Jaxon," Hannah said softly. She perched on the edge of the bed and took his hand in hers. "I know you want to handle this yourself, but we're your parents. We just... we can't take action against whoever did this to you unless we know the full story."

"I don't want you going to the police. Okay? I know you're my parents and you think you're doing what's best for me, but if you knew what I knew... if you'd seen what I saw... you'd understand why I can't say anything. I made a promise."

"Who? Who did you make a promise to?" Ray pressed as he turned back from the door.

"I can't tell you!"

Jaxon's voice hitched. Yelling hurt. Hell, *breathing* hurt. Too fraught with pain and worry to sleep, he'd lingered in a state of semi-consciousness for most of the night, the memory of Jed's pulverized face splattered on the walls of his mind. If he'd just let Cash drop him off at home, he would've never climbed over the Hoyts' fence to approach the mustangs, and Jed would've never attacked him… again. Jed had obviously known the mustangs would be there—for all Jaxon knew, perhaps he'd planted them himself, like a hunter baiting a trap. Was this payback for that day in the valley? And how was Jaxon supposed to look Waylon in the eyes again knowing what he was truly capable of?

Jaxon composed himself, then said, "I made a promise to the person who saved my life that I wouldn't tell you what happened. Because if I tell you how I got these injuries, I also have to tell you how I got out alive."

"Did you fight back?" Hannah asked.

"I tried, but the guy who attacked me was a lot bigger. And he, well, he came prepared. With the taser, I mean."

He saw her flinch again and look toward the window. At first, she'd thought Jaxon had gotten into a scuffle at the party, which was bad enough. But when the doctors had discovered an identical pair of barbs lodged in his lower back, she'd realized the truth was much, much worse.

Jaxon swallowed. "I'm sorry, mom. Really, I am."

She squeezed his hand and smiled weakly. "I know. It's okay."

Jaxon's gaze flickered to the doorway as a doctor appeared. She had her hair pulled back in a ponytail and was carrying a file of some sort, which she held against her chest in an effort to be discreet.

"Mr. and Mrs. Fisher? May I speak to you both in private?" she asked.

Hannah stood up and followed Ray and the doctor out into the hallway. As they convened a brief meeting, Jaxon rolled onto his side and stared at his reflection in the window. He looked like a ghost, and he felt just as empty inside. Somewhere between one thought and the next, Jaxon closed his eyes and finally allowed sleep to overcome him.

Hannah, Ray, and the doctor walked to a small room at the end of the hall. In it were a pair of couches separated by a rectangular coffee table covered in nothing but a single box of tissues. Watercolour paintings of misty ponds and water lilies adorned the blue walls. Hannah and Ray sat down on the couch nearest the door. He reached for her hand, pulling it onto his lap and linking his fingers with hers as the doctor took a seat across from them.

She began, "Before I get to the reason why I pulled you both aside, how are you holding up?"

The couple looked at each other. Hannah replied, "We're doing as well as can be expected, given the circumstances."

The doctor nodded and looked down at her paperwork again. "I'm very sorry this happened. Jaxon seems like a sweet kid."

"A sweet kid who's keeping secrets," Ray muttered. Hannah squeezed his hand, causing him to fall silent.

"Right. Well, that's just it, you see: during our initial assessment, Jaxon told us he'd gotten into a fight with a friend. We were prepared to believe him until we took a closer look at his injuries…" Her eyes flicked between them. "I'm not trying to pressure anyone into anything. My job is to treat patients, regardless of how they end up in my ER. But if you'd like to file a report, we can arrange to have police come in and talk to your son."

"How can we file a report if we don't even know what happened?" Hannah wondered.

"Is there some way the police can trace the taser? You know, like how they can trace a bullet back to a specific gun?" Ray asked.

"The police have ways of determining that information. Personally, I'd suggest talking to them about what you *do* know. It may not seem like much, but every little piece of the puzzle helps." Sympathy filled the doctor's eyes. "I have a teenager myself. She's fourteen, so naturally, we don't see eye to eye on everything. But she knows she can always talk to me, no matter how bad the problem is."

Hannah wasn't sure where to look. She couldn't look at Ray, who was crushing her hand in an effort to hold himself together. She couldn't look at the doctor, smiling politely as if to hide the fact that she was judging their relationship with their child. She tried looking at the paintings, but their forlorn depictions only heightened her feelings of despair. In the end, Hannah chose to focus on the box of tissues, thankful she wasn't the only thing in this room that felt thin and breakable.

Ray surprised both of them by saying, "Let's hold off on the report for now. When Jaxon's ready, he'll tell us what really happened."

The doctor nodded perfunctorily. "All right. If you change your mind, you can have one of the nurses page me."

She led them out of the room and went on her way. As she disappeared down the hall, Hannah turned to Ray and asked, "Why did you do that?"

He shrugged. "If he won't talk to us, what makes you think he'll talk to the police?"

"You're worried he's done something wrong," Hannah whispered.

"Of course I am. I'm not saying he…" Ray closed his eyes. "I don't know what I'm saying. But Jaxon's a good kid. I will always see the best in him, even if he's covered in bruises." He thought of the baby bird that had fallen out of the nest, the mustangs in the valley, and Jaxon's anger over Yolanda Biffman's tragic death. Ray hoped this was a simple case of being in the wrong place at the wrong time, and that Jaxon hadn't gone further down the path of delinquency.

Hannah pulled her phone out of the pocket of her sweater.

"I should let Kyle know what's going on," she said. "It's only right."

"Even *we* don't know what's going on."

"No, but we will."

She walked toward the waiting room at the end of the hall. At a loss for what came next, Ray retreated back into Jaxon's room to watch over his son while he slept.

*

Kyleigh took a sip of her Grande Americano and tried not to be angry about the fact that Derek was late. Summer was in full swing, meaning the sidewalks were swarmed with pedestrians, beggars, street artists, and hot dog vendors, each one determined to guard their little patch of concrete. Kyleigh couldn't tell what bothered her more: the blaring of sirens and car horns, or the horrendous reek of garbage. How had she lived here her entire life and not noticed how awful Toronto was? Maybe this was just how it felt to come home after a few weeks away: like gazing into a kaleidoscope, even the smallest shift was enough to make her forget whatever pattern had come before.

She pulled her phone out of her purse and texted: *Where are you? I've been waiting for 20 minutes.* As she set the device down again, Kyleigh glanced toward the door. Another customer entered, a gust of hot air sweeping through the shop. They walked up to the counter, placed their order, and tapped their credit card, then stood off to the side with their eyes locked on their phone as the barista blended caffeine and sugar in a plastic cup. No polite chatter, not even a "Hi, how are you?" to start the conversation. Here, everyone was too busy with their lives to see other people as anything but obstacles to dodge on the sidewalk.

Kyleigh's phone buzzed. It was Derek. *Sorry, be there in 5.*

Why the hell was she here? It was a question she'd been struggling to answer since she'd left Sam and Terry's condo almost an hour ago. It wasn't like she wanted to get back together with Derek, and even if she did, it was only a matter of time before he got bored of her and found another playmate. Then what? How many times could she hit the reset button before it broke?

The door opened again, and this time, when Kyleigh looked up, there was Derek, dressed in a pale blue button-down shirt and beige khaki pants, making his way toward her table. The worst part about his arrival (nearly half an hour past their agreed-upon time) was the way her body automatically responded to the sight of him. It was like her heart had totally forgotten what her eyes had witnessed all those weeks ago. For a second, her stomach didn't feel like her stomach at all, but like a warm and fuzzy ball of kittens curled up in a basket of yarn. Why did certain organs have to be so stupid?

He grinned and hung his backpack on the back of the wooden chair before taking a seat across from her. "It's so good to see you," he said. After a brief hesitation, he reached across the table for her hand.

"It's good to see you too," Kyleigh replied. His hand was sweaty, which would've been revolting if she weren't caught up in his eyes, drinking her in as if she were the only source of fresh water on a desert island. "But is it too much to ask that you show up on time?"

"I'm sorry. Really, I am. Our meeting ran late." Derek glanced back at the counter. "Do you mind if I grab a drink before we talk? I need something cold."

"Go for it."

He slid off the chair and walked up to the counter. *Get it together,* she told herself, drying her hands on her jeans the way she'd seen Ray do a hundred times. She wasn't here to proclaim her love to Derek or beg for his spare key back. She'd come here today with one purpose: to tie up any loose ends before she closed the door on this relationship for good.

When Derek returned, Kyleigh wasn't surprised to see that he'd ordered a Venti Iced Matcha Latte. He took a drink of the green elixir and his face melted into an expression of pleasure.

"How can you drink that?" Kyleigh asked, wrinkling her nose. "It's not even coffee."

"You're right, it's tea. I guess I'm high maintenance."

She scoffed.

"How was Colorado?"

"It was fine."

"Really? That's all I get?" Derek smirked, one hand wrapped around the cup. "I know we didn't exactly leave off on a good note, but it's been more than a month, Kyle… I guess I hoped you'd be happy to see me."

"Did I sound happy on the phone the last time we spoke?"

"Not exactly."

"Then why would you think I'd be happy to see you now?"

"I don't know. Maybe because we were together for five years? Most people in serious relationships talk things out like adults. Instead, here you are, treating me like some fling." He sighed, scratching his brow. "I know what I did was wrong. I said I'm sorry about a hundred times. What else do you want me to do, short of branding myself with a scarlet letter?"

"How poetic. You know, I could probably ask my biological father for a brand if you're that committed to martyrdom."

"You know what I mean."

"No, I don't. Derek, when you love someone, you don't act on your stupid, fleeting impulses."

"Says the woman who up and left to go stay with a family she hasn't seen since she was six years old."

Kyleigh glared at him. "Seriously?"

"You're right—that was a step too far."

"More like fifty, but who's counting?" Kyleigh shook her head. "I just want this to be over, okay? I don't want you to hang around for months thinking that we're going to get back together one day."

"Why not? People do it all the time. Kyle—" This time, when he tried to grab her hand, she leaned back, a few inches out of his reach. "Listen to me. I love you. I always have. But if you want to take things slow, then that's okay too."

"You're not hearing me. It's not that I want to take things slow. It's that you either trust someone, or you don't, and right now, I don't."

Kyleigh glanced down at her phone, surprised to see a WhatsApp message from Hannah. *When you have a minute, could you please call me?*

"I know you don't, and I don't blame you," Derek replied. He paused for another sip of his drink.

"Good."

Hannah: *It's about Jaxon. We're at the hospital.*

The hospital? Now she had Kyleigh's attention.

"Can you at least tell me what you did down in the States? I know you said your birth parents own a ranch, but I can't picture you in a cowboy hat." Derek chuckled, hoping to ease the tension between them.

Kyleigh typed back: *Is everything okay?*

Hannah: *He's fine now, but we're worried. I can tell you more over the phone.*

"Kyle? Are we going to talk, or am I just supposed to sit here and watch you play with your phone?"

"Yeah…" she started to say, but stopped. She pictured Jaxon sitting at the kitchen table a few days earlier, his mouth full of oatmeal. This was her little brother they were talking about, her soon-to-be business partner of the aforementioned family ranch. How was she supposed to focus on whatever drivel was coming out of Derek's mouth when something far more important demanded all of her attention?

"I've gotta go," she said as she stood up.

"But I literally just got here."

Kyleigh held his gaze. "My family needs me. And that's something I won't apologize for."

She lifted her purse onto her shoulder. Her phone was halfway to her ear as she picked up her coffee and stepped out from behind the table. Leaving Derek to his Matcha and his excuses, she stepped through the glass door and let it close behind her for the last time.

Twenty-four

Hannah heard the scream and was out of bed in a flash, moving through the darkness toward her son. He'd been having the same dream every night for the past week, so she knew exactly what to expect as she passed from the warmth of her bed through the drafty hallway and into the choking heat of Jaxon's room. He refused to sleep with the window open now, even at the height of summer. Hannah found him sitting on the floor in the corner, a layer of sweat glistening on his bare arms and face.

Crouching in front of him, she smoothed his damp hair off his forehead. His eyes found hers, his lower lip trembling. "I woke you again," he croaked.

Hannah nodded. "It's okay."

Jaxon swallowed. *No, it's not.* Ever since the night of the party, he'd dreamt of his own death a thousand different ways. In one dream, he'd been running through the woods, fleeing from some unknown threat. It was winter, and the ground was covered in a layer of crisp, white snow. As he ran across what he thought was a barren field, the ground beneath him gave way and black water filled his boots, pulling him under the surface. The current swept him downstream; he saw himself gliding beneath the ice, heard the hollow beating of his fists on the frozen glass as he struggled to hold his breath. The moment he gave in to the urge to breathe, he woke up gasping for air, soaked in his own sweat.

In another dream, his circumstances were the opposite: he was in a barn, one several stories high, and every inch of the timber structure was engulfed in flames. That was when he realized it wasn't a barn, but the hoist house of the mines, abandoned and glowing in the night. He started to climb anything he could, trying to get to the opening near the roof, but in the end the smoke filled his lungs like a balloon until both sides of his chest exploded in searing pain.

"What did you see?" Hannah asked now.

Jaxon whispered, "Bodhi." He met her gaze briefly, like he was embarrassed to utter his best friend's name in the middle of the night.

"He was sitting on me, and he had his hands like this—" Jaxon brought both hands to his throat. "Like he was trying to strangle me. It was so real, I swear I could feel his thumbs pressing against my windpipe. So, I started clawing at his hands, and then, well…" He lifted his chin. In the light of the lamp, Hannah noticed the angry red lines of raised flesh on Jaxon's neck. She took one of his hands and examined his fingernails, blood trapped under the edges. "Why would Bodhi try and kill me?" he asked.

Hannah had a few theories, but none of them seemed worth sharing. Instead, she pulled him to his feet until they were standing face to face.

"Let's go downstairs," she suggested. There was no point in going back to bed now that she was wide-awake. A melancholy tune emanated from the old pine floors as they headed into the kitchen, where Hannah switched on the light before opening one of the cupboards to retrieve the coffee and filters. It was just after three A.M.: Ray would be getting up soon anyway, and that was assuming Jaxon's screaming hadn't already woken him.

As she set the coffee to brew, Jaxon lowered himself onto the couch, picked up the remote, and turned on the TV. Its artificial light filled the room with a flickering glow. The waves of panic, which had been strong enough to propel him out of bed, were nothing but small ripples at the edges of his body now. He picked absently at the dried blood as the infomercial host gave a bombastic sales pitch that ended with "Life is short—why not make it easier?"

Hannah handed Jaxon a dampened dish cloth for his hands. "Do you want pancakes?" she asked.

"With blueberries?"

"Of course."

Jaxon thought about his answer for a moment, then nodded. Hannah retreated to the kitchen to rummage around in the drawers and cupboards for the necessary ingredients.

It didn't take long for Ray to show up. To Jaxon's surprise, he was already fully dressed, even though it was still pitch-black outside.

He took one look at Jaxon and asked, "Bad dream?"

"You heard, huh?"

"It's an old house," Ray replied, reaching over the back of the couch to squeeze Jaxon's shoulder. As Jaxon went back to watching TV, Ray continued to the kitchen. There, he found Hannah standing in front of the stove. Three pale circles of pancake batter, each studded with purple jewels of frozen blueberries, bubbled in the cast iron pan. For as long as Ray could remember, pancakes had been their love language: if one of them was sad, stressed, or simply hungover, out came the milk, flour, eggs. Food couldn't solve every problem, but in times of trouble, a little sweetness could go a long way.

Pouring himself a cup of coffee, Ray announced, "I'm thinking of taking the day off."

"You never take a day off," Hannah pointed out, flipping the pancakes.

"Exactly." He flicked his gaze at the living room and lowered his voice. "It's been a long time since Jaxon and I went for a ride just to talk. I'm hoping if we go somewhere quiet, he might finally open up to me."

Hannah plated the first batch of pancakes and poured another three rounds into the sizzling pool of melted butter. "I think that's a good idea. If nothing else, at least it'll get him out of the house."

Ray carried his coffee into the living room and took a seat in the armchair. Glancing from the TV to his son, he asked, "Where did you get those scratches on your neck?"

"They're self-inflicted…" Jaxon trailed off, watching the commercial repeat itself. Half of these products didn't even need to exist: if people would learn to organize their kitchens a little better, they'd see that a five-in-one food processor or a cloth that could clean every surface was a waste of money. Or maybe he was just jealous that their problems were easily solved by calling the number on their screen, while he was locked in a losing battle with his subconscious.

Ray took a sip of his coffee. "I thought maybe we'd go for a ride later, once the sun comes up. I miss our conversations."

Jaxon nodded, saying nothing.

"A little fresh air might help you sleep," Ray added. When Jaxon didn't respond, he put a hand on his son's knee, making him jump. "You need it."

Jaxon blinked at him, his eyes burning. "Where are we going?"

"Just to the river and back."

Beads of sweat sprang up on Jaxon's forehead. He'd never been afraid of water until now, and the last place he wanted to be was standing next to several million gallons of fast-moving snowmelt.

Rising from the armchair, Ray crossed to the front door, where he donned his cowboy hat and boots. He'd just stepped outside when Hannah set Jaxon's breakfast on the kitchen table. "Do you want syrup?" she asked.

"Yeah." Jaxon slid into his seat and picked up his fork to carve off a side of the pancake tower. "I think I know why Bodhi was trying to kill me."

"Why?" Hannah placed her coffee on the table and sat down across from him.

"I mean, what happened to me isn't his fault, but it kind of is. If he'd driven me home like we agreed, maybe I wouldn't have gotten attacked." Jaxon reached for the maple syrup, poured it onto his pancakes. The auburn liquid rolled toward the edges of the flapjacks and dripped down in golden pearls, forming a necklace around the face of the plate.

"The pancakes are good," he said after he'd devoured half of them, his lips sticky with syrup. "Thanks, mom."

"I'm glad you're enjoying them." Hannah watched him eat, sipping her coffee as her mind turned to the conversation she'd had with Ray three nights ago.

"Sack him out," Hannah had repeated incredulously, "you want to do desensitization training on our *son*?"

"I know it sounds crazy, but think about it. What do all these dreams have in common?" When Hannah hadn't replied, he'd answered his own question. "In all his dreams, he's running from something. Like he's prey."

"Like he's a horse," she'd murmured.

Ray had turned his head. "When I lost my leg and was suddenly afraid to be around a horse, what did Bernard do? He took me into the sand ring and made me face my fear once and for all. Jaxon said something about almost drowning... I'm thinking if I take him down to the river, it'll give us a chance to talk. Meanwhile, he'll be able to confront his fears."

Hannah had been anything but confident that Ray's plan would work. For one thing, Jaxon had good reason to be afraid of the river: plenty of ranchers had lost livestock to the powerful current, and he'd been warned a million times not to get too close to the edge. "What if you end up making the situation worse?" she'd asked.

"Then we seek professional help," Ray had said simply, surprising her. "I don't want Jaxon to wind up like my mom, feeling like he has to hide his pain from the world. I don't ever want him to think he has to fight his demons alone."

Jaxon pushed his empty plate away. As he raised his eyes to hers, Hannah smiled.

"I think I'm going to try and get some sleep," he told her, turning his body sideways and rising from the table.

"That's a good idea. You'll need to be well rested for your ride with dad."

"Right." Jaxon nodded dubiously, barely stifling a yawn. It wasn't quite dawn, but far off in the distance, he saw the seam of the sky glowing faintly like an ember. He crossed to the stairs and headed up to his room, leaving Hannah to clean up the dishes and put everything away.

As she closed the cupboard door, she heard the infomercial host say, again, "You can make your life easier with just one phone call. Don't wait... get your *Kitchen Wizard* today!"

She glanced at the TV screen. It was going to take more than some cooking gadget to make her life run smoothly, but for a minute, she almost considered reaching for her credit card. There was a reason why these commercials aired in the middle of the night: people tended to make poor choices when they were sleep deprived.

Hannah picked up the remote and pointed it at the TV. As the screen went black, she refilled her coffee and carried it outside. There, she took a seat on the bench swing and waited for morning to save her from the recurring nightmare of worrying about her family's safety.

*

For most people, a day off meant not thinking about work at all. However, Ray didn't have that luxury. Even as he was saddling a pair of horses in preparation for his ride with Jaxon, his mind kept coming back to the future of the ranch and how they were going to manage its operation with Kyleigh potentially co-owning the business.

But before he could worry about any of that, Ray had to figure out what was truly bothering his son.

"Is there anything in particular you need done this afternoon?" Bernard asked.

Ray tightened his horse's cinch. "Just make sure the horses have plenty of water—it's supposed to be hot." Stepping around his gelding, he proceeded to tack up Jaxon's mount, lifting the saddle off the hitching rail and slinging its forty pounds of leather onto Barbell's back.

As Ray drew up the second cinch, Bernard said, "Not that you asked for my opinion, but I think it's good that you're doing this."

"You're right—I didn't ask." Ray glanced over at his father, and in that moment saw an old man. Bernard's hair was almost fully white, save for two small patches of silver that marked his sideburns. His hands had always been strong, but now they were covered in wrinkles and areas of hyperpigmentation, the latter resembling the pattern of brown spots on an Appaloosa's hindquarters. Ray turned back to his task, troubled by the knowledge of what these changes meant.

Bernard went on, "I've never really believed in talking things out. I realize now that my life would've turned out a lot differently if I had. Maybe I could've saved your mother."

"I used to think that too, but now, I'm not so sure. Once a person sets their mind to something, they tend to stay on that course until they get where they're going." Ray sighed, looking out over the shining green of the foothills and the hazy blue of the sky. "Of course, mom was a grown woman when she made her choice, whereas Jaxon's still a minor. He might think he knows what he wants, but only because he hasn't seen what other paths are out there. As his father, it's my job to show him."

Bernard smiled, reaching out to place a supportive hand on Ray's back.

"In that case... good luck."

Moving with the cautious pace that older age demanded, Bernard started up the laneway toward the shed. Halfway there, he passed Jaxon walking in the opposite direction. He wore a faded pair of Levi's, a plaid shirt the colour of a spring meadow, and a white straw cowboy hat that shielded his eyes from the sun. With his hands tucked in the front pockets of his jeans, Jaxon nodded perfunctorily at his grandfather before approaching the hitching rail and untying Barbell's reins.

"Did you manage to get any sleep?" Ray asked.

"A little." Jaxon adjusted his hat. "You said we're going to the river?"

"Yes."

Jaxon glimpsed the trail in the distance. Every year, Ray promised to clear the dead trees and overgrown grass from the winding forest path. And every year, nature proved it couldn't be contained. One day the trail would cease to exist. Hopefully, the mustangs—wherever they were— would be thriving by then, beholden to no one but themselves and the wild land under their hooves.

Jaxon climbed onto Barbell's back and reined the pinto toward the trail entrance. As Ray rode up beside him, his horse vying for first place on the narrow stretch of dirt, he said, "I'm really glad we're doing this...

I know this summer hasn't turned out the way you hoped. I'm sorry if you feel like I've been unfair, putting Kyleigh's needs ahead of yours."

Jaxon shrugged. "It's okay."

"No, it's not. You're my son. We should be spending time together in a way that doesn't involve fixing fences or running the ranch."

"That's okay," Jaxon said again, "I know you wanted to get to know Kyle."

"Seems like you got to know her, too."

"Yeah. She's cool. I never really thought about what it'd be like to have an older sister until she showed up."

"It's nice to see you two getting along. Compatibility is important when choosing a business partner, although I'm still not sure how this is all going to work if you're here and she's there…"

Jaxon had been around two years old when he'd started asking a million questions per day. Some of them had been predictable—*why is the sky blue?*—while others had seemed downright silly. At the time, Jaxon's insatiable curiosity had driven Ray insane. He'd longed for peace and quiet, telling himself that if he answered just one more question, then that would be the end of it. But now, he would've given anything to have all the answers again.

Eventually, the trail widened into a grassy plateau dotted with clumps of wildflowers. The river was at the highest level it had been all year: the stone perch where Ray had stood the day after finding the mustangs was now several inches closer to the frothing current, and far too dangerous to risk moving in for a closer look. He led them downstream to a spot where the water wasn't quite so apoplectic, then swung down off his horse and walked over to the riverbank. Jaxon followed.

"The level's higher this time," Ray said conversationally, pointing to the partially submerged rocks. "This was where we refilled our water bottles, remember?"

"Yeah," Jaxon replied dryly. Had his dad really dragged him all the way out here for this?

Ray crouched down, dipping his fingers in the chilly current. Confused, Jaxon squatted next to him, thinking this was the start of some lesson on how to manage natural water sources on a working ranch—not that he didn't already know plenty about rivers.

As Ray looked out across the mountain's bounty, he said, "I guess you're probably wondering why I brought you out here."

"Kind of."

"It's true that I wanted to spend time with you—but that's only part of it." As Jaxon raised his gaze, Ray told him, "The other part is, now that we're alone and there's no risk of anyone overhearing us, I was hoping you'd tell me what happened the night we took you to the hospital."

Jaxon looked down at his hands. "I already told you that I can't," he muttered.

"Can't, or won't?" Ray shifted. "I know it's hard to tell the truth, but—"

"If you knew that telling the truth would mean getting someone else in trouble, would you still do it?"

Ray considered his reply. He felt the pull of the river beside him and the shards of broken sunlight glinting on its surface. A warm, steady breeze kept the grass and the trees blowing in the same direction. The answer should've been simple, but he knew it wasn't. Now that he was a father, everything seemed that much harder.

Tired of waiting for Ray to speak, Jaxon sat down on the bank and cradled his knees in his arms.

"I made a promise and I intend to keep it. It's called being loyal," he said, squinting at the current.

"Loyalty is a great quality to have. In fact, I'd say it's more important than just about anything else."

"Then why can't you accept my answer?"

"Because I'm your dad. Your safety is my main priority, and if someone is threatening you, then I need to know about it." Ray watched as Jaxon picked up a twig lying next to him and began skinning its bark with his fingers. "Jaxon, please talk to me."

"We *are* talking."

"But you're not really telling me anything. I want to understand what you went through." Ray lowered himself to a sitting position, trying to get comfortable on the hardpacked dirt. "If you don't want to talk to me, then that's fine. You can talk to a therapist instead."

"And not talking about it isn't an option?"

"Not if you want to stop having nightmares." Ray added, "After I lost my leg, I had a lot of nightmares, too. There was this one dream I kept having where I was in this old house. Every so often I'd think someone was watching me through one of the windows, but then I'd look and there'd be no one there." He glanced at Jaxon, watching him curiously. Turning back to the river, Ray continued, "Eventually, near the end of the dream, I'd fall asleep on the couch, thinking I was safe. But then I'd hear this sound, like a door opening slowly. I'd look around the room, and I'd see this dark, shadowy figure standing in the corner, just watching me. It had no face, just these two slitted eyes and a weapon in its hand."

"What kind of weapon was it?"

"I could never be sure. It might've been an umbrella or a flower vase, for all I knew. When we're in a dream state, even ordinary objects can be terrifying. Sometimes, it's the things you don't know or don't understand that scare you the most." Ray shifted his weight. He hated sitting on the ground, unable to find a comfortable position for his right leg.

"Did you ever figure out what it all meant?" Jaxon asked.

"Yes, but it took a little help from your mom. Her theory was that the house represented my childhood, and the figure was my dad—someone I couldn't see clearly. As for the weapon, whatever it was, that was the pain your grandpa had caused when he left." Ray subconsciously rubbed his leg. "Once I talked about the dream and dealt with the trauma that inspired it, I was able to sleep better."

For a long time, Jaxon was quiet. When the mustangs were in trouble, he'd refused to remain silent—and yet, here he was, in the same kind of danger and unable to speak for himself. But he had to try: even if he couldn't save the wild horses, there was still a chance to save his family.

"You know Jed, from the BLM?" he started. When Ray nodded, Jaxon said, "He was the one who attacked me. He had the taser."

"Where did he attack you?"

"On the Hoyts' property. I ended up leaving the party early that night. Bodhi was too drunk to drive, so this other guy, Cash, offered to drive me home instead. When I saw the mustangs, I decided to climb over the fence for a closer look. And for some reason, Jed was there. I think he knew I'd come back, and he waited for me so he could finish what he started."

"Why didn't you tell me earlier? We could've called the BLM and gotten this straightened out right away."

"Because you threatened him."

"He *tased* you."

"He's dead," Jaxon said quietly. His hands were shaking, his fingers ice-cold. "Waylon killed him because Jed tried to drown me in one of the stock tanks. And I was worried that if they found Jed's body, they'd think you were responsible for his death. After all, you said you'd kill him with your bare hands." He raised his gaze to Ray's. Tears were flowing down Jaxon's face now, the river a low, grating hum in the background. "I was just trying to protect you, okay?"

Ray's entire body had gone numb. "Are you positive that Jed is dead?" he asked carefully.

"I—I don't know. I mean—his face was all bloody, and he wasn't moving." Jaxon wiped his eyes with his sleeve. "Bellamy was driving. He told me to get in the truck and we drove away... I couldn't see anything clearly after that, but my gut says he is. Dead, I mean."

Suddenly, Jaxon stood up and took a few steps toward the river. Hanging over the unbridled torrent was a large rock that had once been part of the mountain, the face of it worn smooth by the endless erosion of the water. Jaxon sized up the boulder, which was wide enough for three people to stand side by side, then stepped up onto it and gazed at the swaying pines and rippling grass in the distance.

Ray rose as well, his heart making itself known as it pounded in his chest. Jaxon was standing several feet above him and had to shout in order to be heard.

"I keep Googling Jed's name to see if anyone's reported him missing. I keep thinking about the fact that he has a kid… I know Jed tried to kill me, but what will his family think if he doesn't come home?" he wondered.

"Jaxon, you're too close to the edge."

"If no one's reported him missing, then that means no one cares about him. How fucked up is that?" Jaxon leaned forward, peering over the lip of rock at the leaves and twigs bobbing downstream. The smaller debris got sucked into the current and disappeared somewhere in the frigid depths. "If I hadn't charged him that day, none of this would've happened."

"Please step back." Ray's hand was trembling as he inched forward to grab the back of Jaxon's jeans.

Jaxon glanced over his shoulder. "You told me not to trespass. I should've listened to you."

Ray adjusted his footing. *Never let a horse know you're scared,* he recalled Bernard telling him once. Not just because animals could sense fear, but because giving in to the urge to panic would only cloud his judgment. He took another tentative step in Jaxon's direction until his fingers grazed the shirt's pattern. "It's okay. I know you stopped listening to me a long time ago."

"I did," Jaxon admitted, his voice practically inaudible.

"We need to go home now. Okay?"

Jaxon nodded, turned away from the river, and slipped.

Forty-five years of working on a ranch had given Ray two things: chronic pain and lightning-fast reflexes. In the blink of an eye, he could throw a rope and have it looped around an animal's neck or hind leg. His hands went out now, their speed and direction as sure as the river's course, and closed on Jaxon's upper arms. Jaxon was flat on his stomach, his boots dangling over the side of the rock. Ray was sprawled flat as well, his fingers locked on his son.

Fear raced along Jaxon's nerves like an electric current. He kept his gaze on Ray's face, too afraid to turn his head and risk being swept away.

Ray swallowed. "I'm going to pull you up now. Just keep your eyes on me, okay?" Jaxon's elbows scraped against the wet sandpaper of the rock as Ray dragged him to safety.

When they were out of harm's way, Ray collapsed back in the grass. Jaxon knelt a few feet away from him, the taste of guilt resting like a penny on the roof of his mouth.

"I'm sorry," he croaked, "I shouldn't have gotten so close to the edge."

Ray breathed, swallowed again. The sky was a thick, unblemished blue. He sat up slowly and rubbed his eyes as if it might help him forget the look of terror he'd just witnessed on Jaxon's face.

"This is my fault," he admitted. "I shouldn't have brought you down here, just as I shouldn't have taken you to the abandoned mine that night." Ray looked at Jaxon. "You've been handling problems no person your age should have to handle. I'm the parent in this situation—I think it's time I started acting like it, even if it means confronting Waylon directly."

Jaxon's eyes widened. "Then he'll know I told you."

"That's okay. Whatever happens next, I'll deal with it."

Ray stood up, grimacing at the tightness in his right leg. *Like father, like son*, he thought as they made their way back to where the horses were grazing. First Bernard had run off, then twenty years later Ray had followed. Now Jaxon was learning from him, picking fights he had no hope of winning and throwing himself into increasingly perilous situations. If he didn't wise up, then Ray had only himself to blame if Jaxon wound up incarcerated or dead.

"Are we going to tell the police?" Jaxon asked.

"I don't know yet. Let me talk to Waylon first. Once I have all the facts, then we'll make a plan."

Twenty-five

Despite the difference in their ages and their opposing philosophies about parenting, Ray had always considered Waylon to be a friend. When Ray had lost his leg and been unable to work for a year, Waylon had taken it upon himself to check on Ray's cattle and arrange any veterinary care they required. When Jaxon was little, and Ray would occasionally drop by to assist the Hoyts with work around their ranch, Waylon would send his two youngest sons down to the basement to show Jaxon their gaming setup and play Super Mario Bros until it was time to go home. And while Waylon had been unable to attend Ray and Hannah's wedding on account of his father passing away the week before, he'd still found time to send the couple a gift: an attachment for their tractor and an envelope stuffed with hundred-dollar bills.

These were the memories Ray focused on as he drove to Waylon's house the following day. In theory, Jaxon couldn't be totally sure of what he'd seen on the night of his encounter with Jed: perhaps Jed's injuries had looked worse than they really were, or the stress of the event had caused Jaxon to misremember certain details. When Ray's sister-in-law had taken her abusive ex-fiancé to court, her ex's lawyer had stated that witness testimonies were notoriously unreliable—especially if the witness was also a victim. At the time, Ray had thought this to be a weak defense. After all, how could a person's own memories betray them, especially when the act of survival required full cooperation of the senses? But now, with Jaxon forced into the role of the victim, Ray was struggling even more to reconcile his son's version of the story with the person he knew Waylon to be: a generous neighbour and friend who loved his kids and believed in letting boys, be boys.

He parked his truck down by the barn. In a nearby chute, Waylon and Cal were doctoring a steer. The animal bawled as Cal gave it an injection of some sort. After a quick inspection of its mouth, Waylon signaled to Roman to open the chute. The steer bolted out, its hooves skidding on the ramp as it retreated to the safety of its herd on the far side of the corral.

Waylon turned and saw Ray approaching them. "Well, howdy, neighbour," he said with a grin.

"Morning, Waylon." Ray nodded to Cal and Roman, who nodded politely back.

As his sons returned to their work, Waylon asked, "So. What brings you over to my side of the tree line?"

"Actually, I was hoping you might have a few minutes to talk."

Waylon observed Ray for a moment, his eyes narrowed against the sun. Soon, he indicated the house behind them, its red brick façade occluded by creeper vines. "Yeah, of course. Do you want a coffee?" Waylon asked.

"Coffee'd be great. Thanks."

He led Ray through the front door and into the kitchen. The rooms were small, but practical, each one filled with a lifetime of family memories. The basement, Waylon had explained once, was the boys' domain: in it were a couple of old couches, a flat-screen TV, a gaming console, and plenty of storage space for toys, books, movies, and gadgets. There was also a small bathroom and kitchenette, which came in handy for those times when one of Waylon's adult sons needed a place to crash but didn't want to pay for a motel room.

"Have a seat," Waylon said. Ray pulled out a chair at the kitchen table and sat down, taking in the white cabinets and wooden countertops around him. A collection of copper cooking pots had been artfully arranged on the wall, right beneath a hanging sign that simply said *Home*.

Waylon poured two cups of coffee and set the first one down in front of his guest.

"Tara bought a cherry pie at the farmer's market the other day," he said as he took a sip of his own coffee. "You want some?"

"No, thanks." As Waylon slid into the seat on his right, Ray couldn't help but notice the knife block on the counter. It seemed absurd to think

Waylon was capable of violence—sure, the man had a touch of a mean streak, but Ray hadn't met a single cowboy who couldn't throw a decent punch or wrangle up a few choice words for an insubordinate ranch hand. Ray picked up his coffee and pulled in a sip, hoping to take the edge off his nerves.

"Hey, how's your boy doing?" Waylon asked suddenly. "Word around town is he spent the night in the hospital."

Ray avoided looking at him as he replied, "He's doing better. Hannah and I are a little concerned that he's keeping secrets from us though."

"Boys do that at his age." Waylon chuckled, picking up his coffee. "Even my boys did shit I didn't know about when they were younger. And they all turned out fine."

How the hell was he supposed to start this conversation? Ray wondered. He had hoped he'd feel comfortable enough around Waylon to be direct with him, but now that Ray was here, he could barely muster more than a few words. In his mind, he could still hear the spirited crescendo of Jaxon and Bellamy playing video games downstairs, and Dwight acting like he was too cool to hang out with his little brother (while secretly enjoying every minute of it).

"Waylon, I need to ask you something," Ray began. "And I need you to answer me honestly."

"Shoot."

"Are you familiar with the name Jed Thompson?"

"In what context?"

"He works for the BLM," Ray explained, praying this was still true. "When I met him, he and his partner were conducting a roundup of a herd of mustangs. Jaxon was with me that day."

"Hmm. Well, I know the BLM, but the name Jed doesn't ring a bell." Waylon shrugged.

"There was an incident where Jaxon became upset because he felt that the BLM's use of helicopters was inhumane, and he… he ended up charging Jed. And Jed reacted by pushing him hard enough to make him fall and cut his face."

"Did you contact the police?"

"No. At the time we were more worried about not incurring the BLM's wrath."

Waylon quirked a brow. "The BLM might think they're God, but they're still beholden to the law like everyone else."

"I know. I guess I was worried that they'd find some way to retaliate if they found out we'd gotten the police involved." Ray didn't like the way his heart was kicking at his ribs, or the clamminess of his fingers as he held his coffee. "I need to ask you something else."

"What?"

"The night we took Jaxon to the hospital, he said he'd climbed over your fence. Supposedly, Jed was waiting for him on your property. Jaxon said he saw you drive up in your truck and assault him. I need to know," Ray said evenly, "that my son wasn't lying to me."

Waylon studied him, the stubble on his chin the same shade of silver as his eyes. The room had become deafeningly quiet; all Ray could hear was the ticking of the clock on the wall behind him. His mouth felt the way it did after a filling, his tongue heavy and his lips numb, the taste of metal all around.

Finally, Waylon spoke. "Your son's telling you the truth."

Ray was relieved—until he wasn't.

Waylon went on, leaning on the table as he spoke. "I heard a disturbance. It was the middle of the night, and the herd was going nuts—I figured something must've spooked them. I thought it might've been a coyote or maybe a bear. So, I woke Bellamy and we got in my truck, drove out into the field there—" He pointed to the kitchen window. The field in question, a wide, slightly rolling expanse of dirt and cow manure with trees rustling in the distance, lay just beyond it.

"It was dark, so I turned on the floodlights on my truck. Normally we save them for calving season, so we can see where the calves are dropping in the middle of the night. But I had an eerie feeling, so I turned them on. And there in the headlight glow, I saw a man and a boy.

"The man was middle-aged or so. Big fellow in the middle, almost bald, and clearly up to no good. No idea where he came from or how he got here, but it didn't matter. What mattered was what he was doing—what he was *trying* to do."

Ray had stopped breathing. Waylon's description matched Jed exactly, but he didn't say this. He just kept listening.

"I didn't know who the boy was in that moment—did it really matter though? He was in trouble, so I got out of my truck and—"

"When did you realize it was Jaxon?"

"When the big guy turned around, and I saw your boy's face. And in that moment, well, something inside of me... it just snapped." Waylon looked down at the table, his expression sober. "Do you recall that I was in a bar fight once?" he asked, taking Ray by surprise.

"Yes."

"Good. Then you understand why I did what I did." When Ray stared at him blankly, Waylon snarled, "The girl at the bar. Do you remember what happened to her?"

Ray struggled to remember anything about Waylon's infamous bar fight story besides the fact that he'd won. And frankly, he didn't care. They were talking about *Jaxon*. He needed to know the full story, even if he had no idea what the hell he was going to do with it yet.

Waylon sighed. "She was the bartender. I was at a bar in Frisco and this son-of-a-bitch came in and started harassing her. Eventually, they tossed him out. That's the end of it, right? Wrong. I hung around until last call—I was on a bit of a bender that night—long story—so I got to talking to the girl. Sweet little thing, college graduate from UC Boulder, very nice to look at and listen to. Two A.M. rolled around and she told me 'we're closing up.' So, I made my way outside. And as I was standing on the sidewalk having a smoke, I heard this sound in the alley behind the bar. I decided to check it out..."

At this point in the story, Waylon's voice trailed off and his eyes appeared to glaze over, like the scene was playing on a screen in front of him.

Ray prompted, "You checked it out."

"And that's when I saw him—the son-of-a-bitch from earlier in the night. He had a knife to this girl's throat, just about to break the skin. Hand on her mouth, crazy in his eyes. The Devil himself, standing right there before me."

"You called the cops?" Ray guessed.

"No. I walked up to him, saying if he didn't let her go, I'd beat the piss out of him. And I did. He stumbled off into the night, and I helped the girl get somewhere safe. I'll never forget the look in her eyes: makeup running, cheeks red as traffic lights, and this tiny, pink mark on her neck from where the knife nearly broke through. She thanked me and I left, blood running down my face. My nose was broken, but the girl, she was alive, and that was all that mattered."

"What does this have to do with Jaxon?" Ray asked impatiently.

"*Everything,*" Waylon replied, "because that girl and your boy had the same look in their eyes. When I drove out to the field that night, and that Jed guy had your boy's head in a stock tank and his full weight on top of him, I knew what I had to do." He leaned back and levelled his gaze at Ray. "I know you would've done the same, if it had been one of my boys."

No, I wouldn't, Ray wanted to say. *I'm not like you.* He took another sip of his coffee, even though he thought he might be sick.

"In life, you have to make choices," Waylon told him. "Either you stand by and watch, or you take action. If I hadn't been there that night, where would you be today? Not here drinking my coffee, that's for damn sure."

"Did you…" Ray couldn't finish his thought.

"Did I what? Kill a man?" Waylon's eyes flicked back and forth over Ray's face. "What do you think?"

Ray pushed back his chair and stood up. "I think I should go home."

"Ray." As he turned back to the table, Waylon said, "If you decide to go to the police, I won't stop you. But we've known each other for a very long time, and I've always had your back. Just think about that before you make your choice."

As Ray made his way out to his truck, he paused for a moment to watch Roman and Cal tending to another steer. Plastered on the young animal's face was a look of primal terror—was that what Jaxon had looked like, what the bartender in Frisco had looked like? Ray didn't want to think about it. *Couldn't* think about it.

He turned back to the driver's door of his truck, and that was when he noticed the shovel resting against the side of the shed. It had a long wooden shaft, a rusty handle, and a square blade. Why would it be out here, he wondered, and not in the shed with the other tools and equipment?

What do you think? Waylon had asked minutes before. Ray understood now that his neighbour had been testing him. Did Ray really believe Waylon was capable of murder? Of beating a man to death and burying him in a shallow grave? Or was that just what Ray wanted to think because it was easier than confronting the scant possibility that Jed was still out there, crossing names off a hitlist of his own?

Waylon turned away from the chute and nodded at Ray. Ray nodded back. All he knew was that Jaxon was alive, and for now, that was enough. Ray climbed into his truck and reversed down the driveway. The vines on the house trembled in the breeze, spreading like rumours, like secrets in the night.

Twenty-six

One excruciatingly long, sweaty bus ride later, Kyleigh stepped into the air-conditioned lobby of the condo where she'd been raised and pressed the elevator button to go up. As she waited for the doors to open, she adjusted her backpack again, trying to keep the weight of it off her shoulders and lower back with limited success.

She was living with her parents again. So, what? Most of her friends had roommates or significant others with whom to share the financial burden of paying rent—it was their generation's curse. But living with family hadn't carried the same stigma on the ranch, where everyone had a role to play and a story to tell; where she'd discovered a strange sense of belonging despite knowing next to nothing about their way of life.

At last, the elevator doors opened, and Kyleigh stepped inside. She pressed the button for the fifteenth floor as the doors glided shut, the cables humming as the car rose.

She turned to the mirrored wall on her right. Dark strands of hair spidered across the rosy flush of her skin. She smoothed down the errant curls as best she could, then hitched her backpack off the patch of moisture on her hips as the elevator sped past the first ten floors before stopping briefly on the eleventh.

When the doors opened again, a lady in a pink blouse and white capri pants scooped up the Pomeranian at her feet and ferried him onto the lift.

"Oh, I'm going up," Kyleigh said.

The lady smiled and turned to face the doors. "So am I." She reached across Kyleigh and pressed the *R* button on the panel.

Kyleigh glanced at the dog. A mane of orange fur haloed its ashen face.

Looking over at her, the lady said, "You look like you've survived a long journey."

"Yes: the TTC," Kyleigh replied, feeling self-conscious about her sweaty clothes and disheveled hair.

"Perhaps I'll see you around the pool then," the lady said as the elevator stopped on the fifteenth floor. "It's a great day to look out at the harbour."

Kyleigh smiled politely. As a kid, she'd spent countless summer days splashing around in the rooftop pool while Sam read a book in one of the loungers or Terry replied to work emails on his laptop. Toronto had seemed so beautiful from thirty stories up, like most things did when viewed from a distance.

Kyleigh stepped out as the doors opened again. The Pomeranian gave a little yip as she rounded the corner and headed down the hall toward Sam and Terry's unit.

Unlocking the door, Kyleigh slipped into the foyer, where she was greeted by the citrusy scent of kitchen cleaner. The granite counter was bare save for a glass bowl overflowing with apples and clementines. She plucked a Granny Smith out of the pile and retrieved a bottle of water from the fridge. With Derek, *home* had meant curling up on the couch to watch movies and eat whatever mouth-watering dish he'd been inspired to cook that night. It had meant furniture that didn't match and bedrooms that doubled as offices, since that was all they could afford. It had meant feeling hopeful about the years ahead, about the places they'd go and the people they'd become, but now *home* meant starting over and letting go of these dreams. It meant accepting that some things were not meant to be, after all.

As Kyleigh lingered in the cool air spilling out of the fridge, Samantha entered the kitchen and set her mug of tea on the counter. "Welcome home."

"Thanks. And before you ask, yes, it is hot out there."

Kyleigh shut the door and turned back to the counter. Samantha stood at the far end of it, her expression vaguely troubled. "What's wrong?" Kyleigh asked.

"I was going to text you while you were at work," Samantha began, picking up her mug to put it in the sink. "Derek came by."

Kyleigh folded her arms, her voice turning instantly frigid at this news. "What did he want?"

"He said you left some things at his apartment, and that he figured you'd want them back. They're in your room." Samantha hesitated, then moved in for a hug. The warm squeeze of her embrace, the soft kiss of flannel on Kyleigh's cheek—that was home too, although in this moment she was too angry to take comfort in the gesture.

"He said he was sorry," Samantha added as she pulled away.

"And did you tell him he could stuff it?"

Samantha laughed. "I should have."

Sighing, Kyleigh picked up her apple and water bottle and announced, "Well, I guess I should go see which articles of clothing I'm missing. He better have given me back my Niagara Falls sweater."

"I didn't open it, so I have no idea."

Kyleigh headed for her room at the end of the hall. The décor hadn't changed since she'd moved out: there was still the twin-size bed and her maple dresser, a collection of souvenirs from her travels arranged on top of it. In the corner was a closet hidden behind a pair of bifold doors and a laundry hamper she'd decorated with stickers when she was little. A purple shag rug covered the floor in front of the standing mirror.

Kyleigh set her refreshments down on the nightstand and turned toward the bed. In the middle of it was a black garbage bag with red handles, the top loosely tied.

"A garbage bag. Very classy, Derek." She lifted the bag up, as if she could judge its contents by how much it weighed. "At least I know what you think of me now."

Kyleigh untied the bag and reached in for the first item: a t-shirt she'd purchased at a sidewalk sale that said *Oh, whale* accompanied by an image of an orca shrugging. (She'd made Derek Google whether whales had shoulders. They did.) Next came a pair of jeans she'd never gotten around to returning. And some tennis shoes. And another t-shirt, this one all black. Kyleigh had been planning to pick up the rest of her belongings eventually—or send Anvi over, since that was what best friends were for. For three weeks, Kyleigh had lived out of a carry-on and a backpack: turns out, most of what she'd needed to survive on a working ranch had nothing to do with her wardrobe. Ultimately, home wasn't stuff. It was people.

She pulled out the pink sweater she'd purchased on their trip to Niagara Falls a few years back and set it in the pile of clothes to be washed. Wrapped up in towels were her collector's mugs—two of them were cracked, the third missing its handle. Furious at Derek's carelessness, Kyleigh rummaged around in the bag until she located the horseshoe of broken ceramic. Part of her wondered if he'd done it on purpose after how she'd left things at the coffee shop. She'd bruised his ego, so he'd wrecked her cups. Petty bastard.

The next item was soft. Furrowing her brows, Kyleigh pulled it out of the bag.

It was a teddy bear. Over the years its white fur had become thin and rough, and one of its beady glass eyes was tarnished. Sewn onto the bear's chest was the Colorado state flag, the red *C* superimposed on bands of blue and white. Throughout Kyleigh's childhood, the bear, which she'd named Snowy, had lived in the hammock in the corner of her ceiling along with all her other stuffed animals. When she was younger, she used to pretend that Snowy had been to the highest mountains in the world and come back to share his discoveries with his friends. She'd had no idea at the time where Colorado even was, much less the significance of the bear's insignia. When she'd gotten a little older, Terry had told her about how, on the day they'd picked her up at the hospital in Kamloops, Ray had pulled the bear out of his backpack and given it to his daughter's new parents as a keepsake. "So she'll have something to remember me by," he'd said.

Kyleigh lifted her head as Samantha appeared in the doorway, her hand wrapped around a flat, blue object.

"I wondered where Snowy was," Samantha said as she took a seat next to Kyleigh on the bed. She reached around to look in the bag, wondering what other treasures she might find.

"Derek made fun of me for having a toy in the apartment. I'm just glad he didn't throw him out." Kyleigh glimpsed the item in Samantha's hand: a folder of some sort with a neatly organized sheaf of pages tucked inside. "What's that?"

As if suddenly remembering why she'd come in here, Samantha said, "This? Oh, it's just some research I've been doing."

"Planning my next trip already, eh? Where am I going? Edinburgh? Cape Town? Madrid?"

Samantha smoothed her hand over the folder's cover without looking at her. "Not exactly."

She opened the folder and laid it on Kyleigh's lap. Setting Snowy aside, Kyleigh began sifting through the contents, her curiosity dissolving into confusion as she skimmed the pages. Words like *immigration* and *sponsorship* jumped out at her, so she turned an inquiring look on Samantha instead.

"I know it's a little complicated, but there's a lot of information out there. Plus, we can always talk to a lawyer, if it comes to that."

"If what comes to that?"

Samantha raised her gaze to Kyleigh's. "If you want to go, I won't try and stop you."

"Mom, I don't understand."

"This is everything I could find on how to become a US citizen. Of course, you'd need a green card first, then after a few years you can apply for citizenship through family or an employer. Ray would have to sponsor you if you went the family route—as your biological father, he can file all the paperwork. I know he did it for Hannah when they got married. I'm sure he would be more than willing to do it for you, too."

"Mom, you've never wanted me to move to the US," Kyleigh reminded her. "You always said my home was here. And it is. I mean,

I'm happy to visit the ranch from time to time, but I can't just… leave everything behind, especially now that I finally got it all back." She indicated the bag behind her.

"I know. But if you ever decided you wanted to live there, you could. I've always told you that the world is your oyster, haven't I? After all," Samantha laughed, "your dad and I didn't travel to all these different countries just for you to feel trapped in Canada." She reached over, picking up the bear and holding it in her hands. "Remember all those adventures Snowy used to go on? He'd climb to the summit of Mount Everest one day, then dive to the bottom of the Mariana Trench the next."

Kyleigh nodded, a wave of nostalgia breaking over her. "Snowy could do it all."

"And so can you… Kyle, I just want you to be happy. If that means staying in Toronto, then that's great. But if home is somewhere else for you, then you should go there."

"What about you and dad?" Kyleigh could feel her voice starting to crack. She curled her fingers around the folder, the wad of pages bending in her grasp.

Samantha put a hand to Kyleigh's cheek.

"You are my daughter. No matter where you go, I will always love you."

"I love you, too," Kyleigh whispered.

She leaned in for a hug, Snowy trapped between their bodies. Things may have been over with Derek, but that only meant Kyleigh had more time for people like Hannah, Ray, and Jaxon. Time to learn everything she could about co-running a commercial ranch.

As Samantha pulled away, she looked at the items scattered across the bed and said, "I should let you get back to work."

"Actually, I have a better idea," Kyleigh replied, setting the folder on her nightstand as she stood up. "Let's head up to the roof. On a day as hot as today, I could use a little time in the pool."

Twenty-seven

Bodhi could have taken a page from Kyleigh's book about how to travel light. Instead, he'd managed to fill the bed of his truck with what appeared to be an entire store's worth of clothes. He had a whole suitcase dedicated to his jeans alone, and another filled exclusively with snap shirts in every colour. There was a third, smaller suitcase for his crash vest and helmet. A separate box for his cowboy hat. Another for his boots. All of this did not include the socks and chaps he'd received from his sponsors and would be expected to endorse on TikTok and Instagram. And finally, there was a grocery bag filled with just food, because what was a road trip without snacks?

"Just to be clear, we're going away for a weekend, not a month," Jaxon said as he trotted down the porch steps. He opened the rear passenger door and tossed his backpack inside as Bodhi came around the front of the truck, dressed in jeans and a plain grey t-shirt.

"Yes, but this weekend could make or break my career. I need to be prepared."

They were headed to Salt Lake City, where Bodhi would be competing against professional bull riders in his first televised show. In addition to the branded apparel and safety gear, Bodhi also needed someone to pass him the ice packs after his ride and talk his name up behind the chutes. So, Jaxon had agreed to tag along, figuring this might've been Bodhi's way of apologizing for bailing on him after the party.

"Whatever you say," Jaxon said at last.

"I'm surprised your dad is even letting you go. Aren't you supposed to be building something right now?"

"A second bunkhouse," Jaxon clarified, glancing in the direction of the existing one. "Yeah, we are. But dad's got other people who can help him. And like I said: it's just one weekend. I'll make it up to him when we get back."

"Still, you'd think after everything that happened…"

Bodhi didn't get a chance to finish his thought when Hannah came out of the house and walked over to the truck. Ray, as usual, had been down at the barn since dawn, but Jaxon was certain his dad wouldn't let them leave without giving them a lecture about safety.

Hannah passed Jaxon an insulated lunch bag. "I know you have food already, but since I can't be sure of its nutritional value, I made you some sandwiches for the road."

"Thanks, mom."

"Yeah, thanks Mrs. Fisher. Don't worry—we have lots of fruit," Bodhi assured her.

Hannah nodded, a disbelieving smile stretching across her face. "I'm sure you do."

Ray walked toward them, the crunching of his boots drowning out the buzzing of flies and the low drone of bees. He looked at Jaxon, his hair short and gleaming in the sun, then glimpsed the thermal bag in his hands. "Do you have everything?" he asked.

"Yup," Jaxon replied, eager to be on their way.

"How are your tires? Do you want to borrow the gauge?" Ray asked, looking at Bodhi with what Jaxon thought was a slightly wolfish look. "The altitude change is going to wreak havoc on your tire pressure."

"That's okay. My dad gave me his pressure gauge already."

"Yeah, but ours is better. I just bought it last year, so I know it works."

"Dad, it's fine. If we get low on pressure, we can just top up the tires at a gas station somewhere."

Ray didn't look convinced. Instead, he circled around the truck, inspecting anything he thought might slow them down or leave them stranded by the side of the road. As he called Bodhi over to ask about the last time he'd changed the oil, Jaxon turned an exasperated look on Hannah. "Mom, can you tell dad not to worry so much?"

She reached out to place her hands on his upper arms, and smiled. "He can't help it. You're his only son and this is the first time you've been away from him for more than a day."

"So, what's he going to do when I leave for college next year? I don't want him to have a complete mental breakdown."

"He won't. Bernard and I will still be here to help him."

Jaxon nodded. By this time next year, the ranch would officially be his. As long as Kyleigh was still on board with the idea of co-ownership, then the only thing Ray would have to worry about was enjoying an early retirement. But even Jaxon doubted that would happen: like his grandpa said, a cowboy never stopped being a cowboy.

Hannah pulled Jaxon into a hug. "See you in a few days. I love you," she whispered, kissing his cheek.

"Love you, too," he murmured back.

Ray had finally completed his inspection of the truck. He turned to Bodhi, who broke out a grin to hide his annoyance.

"See?" Bodhi said. "Everything's up to snuff."

Ray jabbed a finger at him. "You better drive safely. Because if you don't, I'll hunt you down and hurt you."

Hannah reached for his arm to pull him back. "That's enough."

Jaxon flicked his eyes between his parents again, then said, "Well, I guess we should get on the road."

"If you need money for food or gas, we're only a phone call away," Ray told him.

"And even if you don't need anything, you can still call us anytime," Hannah added.

Jaxon turned to the passenger door and climbed into the truck as Bodhi fired up the engine. Placing the sandwich cooler on the floor,

Jaxon rolled down his window and smiled, excitement sizzling in his gut. He met Ray's gaze, which was stony and suntanned with just a hint of sadness lurking in his eyes. "Don't worry, dad. I'll be home soon."

Bodhi put the truck in gear. As they drove away from the house, Jaxon stole one last glance at the sideview mirror, watching the clouds of dust obliterate his parents' reflection.

"Next stop: Salt Lake City." Bodhi leaned forward and cranked on the radio.

As music pulsed from the speakers, Jaxon turned to look out the window again. Even though it was still summer, many of the trees were already changing colour in pops of russet and gold. And somewhere out there, in a valley that would soon be covered in snow, a herd of mustangs grazed in peace beneath a spotless blue sky.

If there was one thing Jaxon knew, it was that nothing tasted as sweet as freedom.

Other books by Jessica Ingold:

Fate Unwritten (Moving Mountains, book 1)
Roads Untraveled (Moving Mountains, book 2)
Words Unspoken (Moving Mountains, book 3)
Faith Unbroken (Moving Mountains, book 4)
Hearts Unbound (Moving Mountains, book 5)

—

The Spirit Catchers
Captured

—

The Absentees

—

Our Infinite Depths

—

Quiet: Poems about love, loss & healing
Listen: Poems for a noisy planet

www.ingramcontent.com/pod-product-compliance
Lightning Source LLC
Chambersburg PA
CBHW031310170626
46807CB00001B/360